PROLOGUE

Mid-afternoon on a wet busy. There was plenty alone, so Edward Horbri irritated when the scruffy man wearing a hoody pulled up over his head and upper face joined the train in Macclesfield and chose to sit next to him. He glared, but to no effect; the intruder was too busy sorting his luggage, a medium-sized black rucksack which he manoeuvred under the table and to the right of his feet.

Edward, a man in his seventies with a permanently displeased air, shuffled abruptly in his seat to further indicate his censure for the incursion. It availed him nothing, the student-like figure stretching his feet out into the aisle and producing a book from inside his khaki parka, then settling down to read for the remainder of his journey. Edward couldn't see his face, but assumed from his clothing that he was a teenage idiot.

The train sped on through the suburbs, heading towards London, returning from Edward's attendance of the AGM of one of the companies whose stock he held. He had been unhappy with the dividend he'd received the previous year, and he liked to share his unhappiness in full technicolour. He had prepared a brief but blistering speech, the contents of which even a trainee solicitor would have blanched to read or hear. His stock holdings were not significant; at the AGM he had been the smallest shareholder, but that never diminished his sense of self.

He had an impressive total of investments, but all in small amounts. If questioned, he would have cited the spreading of risk, but this would have been untrue. The more companies that he could critique, in his wide-ranging and vicious enthusiasm, the closer he approached what happiness meant for him. Any shortfall in his achievements versus ambitions were always placed firmly at the door of 'Them'.

'Them' varied in definition. Some were faceless, 'bloody idiots' who peopled the corridors of power in central and local government, utilities companies and national retail chains, to name but a few of his targets. Others were less anonymous, from the bank teller who shrank inwardly each time she saw Edward approach her guichet, the GP who internally considered euthanasia each time he berated her, through to the new neighbour who had unwittingly dropped a rubbish bag in the wrong kerbside bin. And who was also an unacceptable colour for 'his' neighbourhood.

Edward considered himself to be a plain speaker, which he believed conferred upon him the right, nay duty, to announce his disapproval. In reality he was bluntly rude, often to the point of reducing others to tears. This afforded him satisfaction; not solely because of his innate sadism but because he believed the tears or distress were clear admissions of guilt. He often proclaimed this in public disputes, attempting to draw appalled bystanders into sharing his delight in what he saw as the crumbling of his opponent's defences. He never once, in his long and fractious life, saw an issue from any other perspective.

One thing only protected his unwanted travel companion from Edward's immediate and fluent ire. Mr Horbridge, Esquire, as he liked to describe himself, was a very poor traveller. On trains, as long as he maintained a rigorous focus out of the window and ahead, he could tolerate the journey. He would not cope with the necessary loss of this focus were he to turn his attention to his left, even briefly. So he enthusiastically occupied himself with preparing his diatribe for the moment the train next drew to a station halt, on the swift journey from Manchester Piccadilly to Euston.

His pleasure was to be thwarted within minutes. The train slowed as it coasted into the Stoke on Trent station. The man next to him waited until the train was almost at a standstill, the platform and waiting travellers visible through the window. He then stood, pulled up his bag and stepped out into the aisle and away in one fluid movement, before Edward could utter even his customary opening of 'I think you need to reconsider your attitude...'

Even more incensing, as the rucksack was whisked out of his vicinity, it bumped his arm, quite hard, and he was startled enough to turn his nascent sentence into a yelp. He stood slightly, fleetingly considering pursuing the miscreant to the platform, but the one combatant that consistently defeated him these days prevailed again. Age had slowed his more physical displays of temper and he knew he would not succeed in cornering the idiot man.

Hindered too by the absence of an audience at the four seater table he inhabited, he restricted himself to an 'Hrrumph' that would have pleased a 1920's political cartoon character. He settled back, fixed his gaze ahead out of the window and slowly subsided into a light doze as they completed the miles to London.

An hour and a half later the train reached its destination and the middling number of passengers alighted, leaving Edward Horbridge in his seat, dead to the world. Literally.

Since the train was due to return northwards within a matter of minutes, the Train Manager tended to walk briskly through the train to the First Class car, before admitting the next round of travellers. Since this was the carriage that afforded the most complaints he concentrated his very few minutes here - the rest of the train was too long to merit the time it would take to run even a cursory check. The cleaning team would alert him to any major issues. Edward Horbridge was in the last car before the prestige one and Joe Sothwell sighed as he went to shake the chap awake. It took less than a moment to recognise what might have been unconsciousness and Joe quickly used his mobile to dial 999.

ONE

Dear Diary

I haven't ever writed this diary before. It might be dangerus if he finds it. Or if she finds it, becus she'll show it to him. She does everything he wants. I don't know why they have me. They don't like children. Or anyway, they don't like me. Bout three years ago, when I was five, she said I was a naccident. I didn't know about that. But I do now. So they did never want me.

Granny gave me this diary. He didn't see it because he was outside to do something to the car. So I came up here and hid it. There's a gap under the wardrobe, but you can't see it.

Today he locked me in the hall cupburd again. He says I'm asking for it. He didn't hit me though. Just left me there till bedtime. I was hungry, but he wanted to smack me, so I looked at the carpet when he yelled at me and I went to bed when he stopped. I've been trying to add up how many times I've been in the cupburd. In this house I'm thinking it's nine now, but I can't rember how many times in the old house. We've been here bout three months.

I do try really really hard not to ask for it. Today it was becus of my socks. The other children at school all have white socks. Mine are dark grey becus thats what my old uniform was. The other children tease me. I knew there was no point in asking for white socks. But my teacher spoke to Mum at the end of school and then after she told him. I knew he wanted to hit me, but I've worked out sometimes he won't in case anyone sees. He says I'm getting new socks at the weekend, when Mum goes to Woolworths. So he'll hit me on Friday after school, but on my back. And he'll give me a note to miss PE next week.

In my dreams I'm adopted. Or sometimes I'm at a lovely bording school, like the Chalet School.

TWO

The Transport Police were on the scene within a couple of minutes, dispatched from their office situated by the Melton Street exit. At this stage there was no indication of cause of death, though his age certainly influenced the professionals. The two officers checked with the Train Manager that an ambulance had been summoned and, wearing nitrile gloves, carefully extracted the wallet from Edward Horbridge's inside pocket. Following protocol, the younger officer then reported the matter to their Greater London Control Centre, who in turn informed the Metropolitan Police; in both centres it was entered onto the HOLMES 2 system, although at this stage as information only. To all intents and purposes this was the natural demise of an elderly man.

The Station Manager, alerted to the situation, made the swift decision to cancel the train, informing both his own staff and the rail operator. Whilst he was fully aware that there would be uproar from the waiting passengers, currently grouped in irritable subsets at the closed barrier, he also knew that traffic congestion could and probably would delay an ambulance way past the planned departure time, now only three minutes away.

Nobody wanted a photo of a dead body being taken off a train by anyone other than officially sanctioned agents. What the Station Manager didn't do was seal the train to allow for further official inspection, since neither he nor the police noted any unusual circumstances. Once Edward Horbridge made his final exit from the carriage, in the careful custody of the paramedics, a duty cleaning team was deployed to descend upon the train, with particular stress that they ensure there was no indication to be found of where the body had been discovered. Within the hour the train had been reassigned to another timeslot and within two hours it was making its way northward once more.

It wasn't until mid-afternoon on the following day that both the British Transport and the Metropolitan Police were alerted to a potentially sinister discovery by the Forensic Pathology Team at Chelsea and Westminster Hospital.

Detective Constable Aiden Cervantes, dispatched by his Guvnor, Detective Inspector Fleur Cooper, regarded the hospital department with some interest. It wasn't his first visit to such a facility, but the hospital was new to him. Since his inclusion in the broader Major Incidents team under Superintendent Steve Reith a few months earlier, he'd learned a lot. And one of those things was the huge value to be found in making good contacts, with strong mutual respect. So he viewed the opportunity to widen his 'little black book' with enthusiasm. But, in common with most of his colleagues, he was apprehensive as to what he'd see. Peaceful dead bodies were one thing, but over and above that, some horrors were best avoided. As a new member of the team he'd brought as much as he'd learned. Nicknamed 'Don', a link from his surname to the author of Don Quixote, he was a bright, open-minded youngster. He'd learned when to stay quiet and when to fight the good fight, so he was a largely popular officer in the broader populace of his assigned nick. The case that had brought him into the fold had been an exceptional one, with a clever, twisted protagonist. He'd learned a great deal from his Superintendent, Steve Reith and from Fleur Cooper, as well as from his fellow team mates. Not afraid to demonstrate his intelligence when needed, he saw no value in dumbing down his vocabulary but, as a naturally shy bloke, never got in their face with those who might have taken offence.

Fortunately for Cervantes, on this occasion he wasn't to be subjected to any such scenes. Once he reported to Reception, he was asked to wait in a small room, quite obviously furnished as a relatives' facility – two boxes of tissues, privacy blinds and dusty silk flowers. After five or six minutes he was collected by a very short man in a white coat who introduced himself as Ashok Khan, Chief Forensic Pathologist. Khan held out his hand and as they shook, said 'Thanks for coming. I've taken over this case because it may prove a little problematic.' As he spoke he led the police officer back out to the corridor, Cervantes starting to enquire 'How so?' but Khan turned slightly away from him - standing a little distance from them was a man of roughly the same age as Cervantes. Khan continued 'This is Constable Murthi, from the Transport Police.' The two police officers shook hands and smiled in mutual recognition of being dispatched on an errand that might prove to be important enough for their senior officers, but needed to be assessed first.

'One of our technicians was working on the body and discovered something – I'll show you.' As he ushered the police officers into a large and brightly lit room, equipped with a plethora of medical apparatus, but with only a few personnel, he said, 'I should explain. Like every facility now, we're stretched. Not just lack of funding; now it's got even harder to recruit with Brexit. So our technicians do a lot of the core work and we, sorry, I mean the pathologists, get involved to declare cause of death or if something's a bit off.' Ashok Khan had a rather lovely West of England brogue; Cervantes, with a much loved Aunt Peggy now living in Bath, would have pinned the accent somewhere in that region.

He continued, 'I'm not embarrassed to say it was initially assumed that this fellow popped off as a result of natural causes – at his age any number of things would do it. But Nick,' he gestured across the room at a middle-aged man, not much taller than Khan but substantially more rotund, 'Nick spotted this'. Khan and Nick moved towards a covered body on a high metal table and, standing opposite to each other, pulled back the covering. Both officers observed, without outwardly sharing their amusement, the rolling gait adopted by the pathology technician, like a Womble in a hurry. Nick, with the careful respect Cervantes had come to expect from most professionals working in post-mortem services, lifted Edward Horbridge's left arm slightly and indicated a mark just above the elbow. A small bruise was centred around what looked like a puncture mark. Nick picked up the thread. 'I didn't like the look of this mark. To me, it looks like a larger bore needle, like an EpiPen. But you wouldn't inject it there. A very difficult place if you were self-administering and just illogical if you were a medical bod injecting something.'

Ashok Khan continued. 'So Nick and I reckoned we needed a full blood check – what the darned TV progs call a tox screen. It came back first thing this afternoon, which is when we called round. Mr Horbridge was given a substantial shot of acepromazine.' 'Do what?' queried Cervantes.

'It's a tranquiliser, though it started out as an anti-psychotic, back in the 60's, I think' said Khan. 'Now, I think vets use it, and I've a feeling it's generally used on horses. Similar to ketamine. Like any tranquiliser, the human body will shut down if it gets too much. This is clever though, in a twisted way. Injecting it gets it right into the blood stream, with virtually no time to counteract it. If he'd ingested it at this dosage, chances are he'd have vomited it back up. Took some confidence though, to administer it. It must have been done on the train – it's fast when injected, like any other sedative used in surgical work.'

Murthi cut in. 'But why are we both here? Transport and Met? He was on a train.'

'Well, exactly,' responded Khan. 'Because this is the *second* case we've had here this week. The day before yesterday we had virtually the same presentation, albeit on a much younger female. That happened in the street, literally just down the Fulham Road from here. A woman was found, reeling along the road; she collapsed and by the time the ambulance got to her, she was dead.' Cervantes noted to himself that Khan maintained the approach that he'd noticed before in Pathology staff. The victim was dead. Not gone, or passed over.

Outwardly Cervantes was calm. 'Thank you. You can guess I'm going back to my station to let the powers that be know.' Inwardly, he was already processing to himself. 'Blast and bollocks. I bet there are no witness statements or list of travellers or anything useful.' To the forensic pair he just said, 'I'm guessing you'll be able to keep a hold on the body for now? Can't release him for a funeral or whatever. Do you know if he's been formally identified?' Murthi nodded in general acquiescence to Cervantes taking some sort of lead; both officers knew the first case would take precedence, so the onus would be on the Metropolitan Police.

Khan replied. 'Actually, his wife is coming in now,' he glanced at his watch, 'ten minutes or so. So we need to move him to the viewing room.' Cervantes recalculated his next moves. It made sense to talk with Mrs Horbridge, at least in broad terms, before he went back to his team. But he also had a strong sense of professional nous, and thought it would be wise to stay with Murthi for now. He tuned towards him and said 'D'you think it's a good idea to interview her together, if we can? We don't know what the powers that be are going to want to do.'

Murthi nodded again, 'Makes sense.' If he'd achieved nothing else, Cervantes had kept the Transport man on side. In these days when the majority of police work is actually mental health care, the investigatory side for both police forces was the interesting stuff. Shutting Murthi out at the personal level would have implied a hierarchy that Cervantes assessed as iffy at best.

THREE

Mrs Horbridge was to be found in the relatives' room. She was alone, and this obviously worried Khan. He asked her if she had a friend or family member she'd like to be called in, to support her. She responded with a nervous twittering. 'Oh no, Edward wouldn't, I mean, it's fine, I can do it. There's no-one...I mean....' She trailed off hopelessly. Cervantes and Murthi looked at each other and the Transport officer jerked his head from Cervantes to the new widow. He recognised that she'd be instinctively more comfortable with someone from, apparently, the same cultural background. Cervantes spoke. 'If you'd like, Mrs Horbridge, I can come with you while you make the formal identification. Would that help?'

She looked up at him in a mute mix of fear and hope. 'Is that all right? Is it allowed? Edward likes, liked....oh dear....' Cervantes smiled down at her and said 'Of course it's allowed. And it would please me to help you, if I can.' She looked sincerely shocked at this but nodded gratefully.

The viewing took very little time. Mrs Horbridge confirmed her husband's identity and was then taken back to the relatives' room, where Murthi sat waiting. He rose at their appearance. Cervantes guided Mrs Horbridge to a chair into which she subsided, rather than making a conscious decision to sit. Murthi asked 'Can I get you a drink? A tea, or some water?' She looked at him, seemingly stricken. 'Oh no, surely not. I should get...Edward...but I don't know where anything is...' Again, her speech petered out.

By now both men without having asked a single exploratory question had a fair grip on the character of the deceased Edward Horbridge. Murthi departed to find a vending machine and Cervantes passed Mrs Horbridge a box of tissues. She took one and began to twist it in her hands. Cervantes didn't want to start any sort of interview without his colleague, but he did say, gently, 'Mrs Horbridge, we do need to ask you a few questions about your husband. When Constable Murthi gets back, will that be OK with you?'

She looked at him with nervous eyes, the tissue now disintegrating in her hands. 'I don't know what Edward would say.'

Cervantes had a practical streak strong in his character. He recognised the terrors this woman was suffering, but he also knew that letting her wallow wasn't going to help her or the investigation.

'Mrs Horbridge. I'm so sorry for your loss but Mr Horbridge, Edward, is gone now. *You* can decide what you want to do.' She looked even more troubled, but this time Cervantes sensed a glimmer of realisation.

'Of course. You're right. I'm just not sure…' Cervantes was conscious of time and was about to push to reach a decision, when Murthi reappeared with a paper cup of tea and some sugar sachets. Without asking her, he tipped two of these into the tea and stirred it with a wooden stick he extracted from his breast pocket. She took the cup and smiled shyly at Murthi. 'Thank you. That's so kind'. Then she straightened in her seat.

'Of course I can talk to you. But there's nothing I can really say to help. But, I suppose I must learn to, to…' she hesitated, '…to think for myself.' This seemed to be a shattering concept and she fell silent.

After exchanging glances at their respective notebooks, Murthi sat in the corner seat, as far behind Mrs Horbridge as he could and set his notebook open on his knee. Cervantes thanked him with a tilt of his head and sat down a seat away from Mrs Horbridge, but leaning towards her, unthreatening and supportive.

'Well done Mrs Horbridge. Now, just some easy questions for you'.'

In short order Cervantes ascertained that her name was Caroline Horbridge. She'd been Edward's wife for thirty two years. Before her marriage everyone had called her Caro, but Edward hadn't liked that so now she was Caroline. He'd been a fair bit older than her. They had one child, a daughter called Rose, after Edward's mother. She didn't know where her daughter was. 'Edward, he said

17

she, they, they couldn't see, it was just impossible…I tried, but he…they never…so she left when she started college. And she didn't come back. Not ever. I tried writing to her but there was never an answer. And Edward wouldn't let me…he said it was good riddance…I couldn't afford to go to see her. And that was thirteen years ago.…...nothing.' Her gentle blue eyes blinked as she tried to control the tears for her daughter that had not been evident for her husband.

Cervantes let this go for now. It shouldn't be hard to find the daughter if they needed to do so.

'So, can we talk about Edward's trip to Manchester? Had he been away long?' She replied quickly, 'Oh no. Just for the day. He went up on the first train, went to his meeting and then back to the house again.' Murthi, writing notes, thought to himself, 'a house, not a home'. The Horbridge house was in Wimbledon.

'And what was the meeting about?' 'It was an Annual General Meeting for one of the companies where Edward had some shares. He liked to go to all of the AGMs. He said you had to keep them on their toes. He was always very angry and disappointed with them. But..,' she stopped, then blinked in recognition of something, 'but it always felt like he enjoyed being disappointed with them all. He spent a lot of time writing speeches.' She looked taken aback by her own bravery and shrank back a little in her seat.

'Did he travel with anybody?' 'Oh no, just on his own. He rang me at home when he got to Euston. And again when he was at the station in Manchester, and afterwards just before the meeting. And he called me when he was back at Manchester Station. No, no, it's Piccadilly isn't it? But then he never rang again, and I knew something was wrong. I didn't know what to do. If I rang the police or hospitals he would be so angry. So I just waited, and then a policeman came halfway through the evening and told me what had happened. And now I just don't know what to do next.'

The two police officers responded to her distress in the way that practical people always will, and made a list for her, on a sheet torn from the back of Murthi's notebook. The things that needed to be done, who she'd need to talk with. She clutched the list as if holding on to a life raft. Cervantes tried again. 'Is there no-one who you can call for support? A neighbour? Any friends? A sister or brother?'

She gazed at him, weariness evident in every particle of her. 'Edward doesn't like other people to get involved. The neighbours, he thinks they're…..' she subsided again, unwilling to use the language employed by her husband. 'My sister….Edward told her…she was a….I can't say it…but we haven't spoken for over thirty years…she won't want to hear from me now…'

Murthi cut in. 'Families can all be different, Mrs Horbridge. Your sister might be delighted to hear from you. And you can look for your daughter now.'

This truly floored her. 'I can...I could? But what if she doesn't want to see me? I don't know where she is.'

Cervantes left this for now; if they needed to talk to the daughter, they could let her know that her mother wanted to see her, but they couldn't share contact details.

Both officers, again communicating without words, judged the interview to have yielded all that it could. Maybe later Mrs Horbridge would be in a more robust frame of mind. It was clear to each of the men that this was a woman who had endured many years of verbal and emotional abuse, at the very least. It would be a slow process, recognising that she was free of that tyranny.

Cervantes offered to arrange transport for Caroline Horbridge, but she declined. Somewhere in the last few minutes of their discussions she'd begun the long, slow journey she needed to take to achieve some level of independence. She said, 'I walked here from Fulham Broadway tube and there's a pretty park on the way. I think, I think I'm going to sit there for a while. It'll be....it will be nice, peaceful.'

After they'd escorted her to the door of the Forensic suite, the two officers briefly conferred on next steps. They exchanged mobile numbers and then headed back to their own bases, Murthi to share the news of the previous, probably associated, body and Cervantes to alert his DI and, without doubt, to be tasked with getting more information on the earlier fatality.

FOUR

The garden centre in Chelsea was a delight to the eye, for novices through to experienced horticulturists. Its wares, though substantially priced, attracted a broad range of visitors each day. From Monday to Friday the commuters shopped, braced to take home their spoils at the end of the working day, on tube, train or bus. For them, the shopping expedition was a welcome lunchtime oasis in the pressure of their professional lives. At weekends, Chelsea residents and their neighbours flocked to the local facility, to purchase, to discuss landscaping with the on-site experts or just to browse and people watch in the beautiful orangery coffee shop.

Early on this damp and chilly Friday, it was here that Calum Grant now sat. In his russet-coloured elephant cord jeans, Burberry shirt and Beehive sweater he belonged here, though perhaps not so early on a week day. He sipped at the macchiato he'd just purchased, slightly to his irritation. The cost to his pocket was irrelevant, but he was piqued that he'd been invited here and would have expected his host to attend in good time and cover refreshments. Ten minutes of waiting and he was now more than peeved. His colour heightened and he glared around the attractive space, seeking any new arrivals.

Just at that moment a distraction occurred, as he was clapped hard on the shoulder, a man behind him booming, 'Mark! How the devil are you?' As he swivelled to remonstrate with this unwarranted assailant, he glimpsed a tall man wearing a leather brimmed hat and a soft leather coat, zipped high, despite the comfortable indoor temperature. At this point, the intruder pulled back, saying, 'Oh Lord! You're not Mark – my apologies.' In an instant he'd gone, swerving around the potted tree behind Calum's table and disappearing from view. Unconsciously mirroring Edward Horbridge's manoeuvre from two days previously, Calum Grant stood, considering a pursuit, but then sank down again, his demeanour yet more displeased. He rubbed his shoulder and leant back in his chair, suddenly conscious of real fatigue.

Calum Grant's demise did not go as unremarked as Horbridge's. As he passed into unconsciousness, he slid from his seat, taking with him the figured iron chair and most of the tableware, the basin holding packets of sugar, the salt and pepper pots and his unfinished coffee. Although the nearby tables were empty, a waitress heard the commotion and moved swiftly to help with what she thought would be a spillage. A local girl, working in the garden centre's coffee shop for just one more week before returning to her studies at Heriot Watt in Edinburgh, she reacted as she'd been taught to do in St John's Ambulance training. She placed Calum Grant in the recovery position and then ran to the kitchen to raise the alarm and get an ambulance called. That done, she returned to the fallen man and chair and knelt on the floor next to him, hearing only too clearly how his breathing was slowing and becoming more laboured. For once, London traffic was kind, and the emergency service vehicle and paramedics were on site within ten minutes. It was still too late; as the medics began their examination, Grant stopped breathing. Although they tried resuscitation and CPR, nothing availed. The paramedics could not call cause of death themselves, but he would later be declared as dead at scene.

Sue and Derek, the paramedics concerned, checked with Control and were told to deliver the body to Chelsea and Westminster. They were unable to tightly identify possible cause of death, but they'd attended a fatality earlier in the week when they'd been dispatched to a woman who'd collapsed on the Fulham Road. Both Sue and Derek had substantial years in their trade; when they pulled into the receiving bay at the hospital's Forensic Unit they both quit the ambulance, assisted in moving Calum Grant onto the waiting trolley and locked the vehicle's doors. They then followed the porter and the trolley into the building, asking if it was possible to speak to Ashok Khan.

Khan appeared in quick order and Derek greeted him as only a fellow-footie fan could. 'Up the Gunners, Ash. You OK?' Khan grinned, whilst also watching the trolley being wheeled out of the public area. 'Fine Derek. Up the Glaziers though…what can I do for you?' Derek shook his

24

head slightly. 'We just thought we'd better mention that we're a bit bothered by this one; seems too much like the woman on the Fulham road, earlier this week. Might be wrong, but we did pick up on the grapevine that there was something off about that one. This feels a bit the same.'

FIVE

Dear Diary

I'm in big trouble and I don't know what to do. I know what they'll say and everything, but if I don't tell them then school might do it, so that would be worse, because of the shame thing.

School says we have to take money in tomorrow because we all have to buy a puppy. We can't have a puppy.

I'll have to work out the best thing to do. I have to tell them.

SIX

The next morning Reith regarded the core leadership in this team, head to one side, coins a-jingle in his pocket. A Saturday morning and here they all were, geared up for action, no matter how tired. The only sour spot was Sergeant Fletcher's face, but as that never radiated goodwill or bonhomie, everyone ignored him. Only a three line whip had got him in at a weekend. Reith had worked with some strong people over the years but this lot, mismatched as they might be, took the prize, though they were down in numbers at the moment. Fleur Cooper, his Detective Inspector, was now firmly in place within the unit; they were still a Chief Inspector down so Cooper largely fulfilled that role too, as well as doing her best to suck up a workload that had increased because her fellow Inspector was off on long-term sick. Cooper had never actually met him, only knowing him by poor reputation. Fleur was an attractive woman, her mixed Caribbean and Malaysian heritage giving her skin a warm colour. Even when tired, as now, she looked healthy and alert. Dressed as ever in a low key navy tailored suit and cream blouse, her abundant ringlets held under strict control, she exuded calm. Her female colleagues teased her good-naturedly on this front, for no matter what the provocation, she always looked fresh and smart, and the feminine cohort were always curious as to how she managed this. A keen sportswoman, she was currently feeling the lack of exercise. A heavy workload coupled with a shedload of administration with court deadlines attached had kept her pinned to her desk. She stretched her neck, attempting to untie some knots that she would've preferred to lose on a good run.

Reith was also tired, as ever. He managed a Command Unit, which consisted of four Major Incidents teams, each usually managed by a Chief Inspector, though at the moment he only had one of those actually in situ across his four squads.

Seated next to Cooper was Mick Brent, a sergeant technically new to the team but not to the work. He shuffled three slim folders on the table in front of him. A sturdy man who looked shorter than his actual height because of his rugby player's build; he glanced round the table and said, 'We need bloody Miss Marple. Three different victims, same MO, no immediate connections. Gawd knows.' Brent was a man of the people, able to tune in to almost any wavelength. With non-hostile witnesses he was superb; with hostile ones he was even better, quickly identifying their triggers and using them to extract information.

Fletcher, a sergeant of quite a different mindset, glared at the tabletop, his fingers itching to get Brent to stop fidgeting with the files so that he could tidy the clutter before him. Christened as Simon, his fellow police officers took delight in calling him 'Norman Stanley', after the Ronnie Barker character in the vintage sitcom 'Porridge'. Unlike many police soubriquets, awarded with wit and affection, this one was used simply because Fletcher couldn't stand it and visibly twitched when he heard it. He was an irritating, nit-picking little man, not above grassing on his colleagues if he felt they'd offended his strict sense of procedure. Reith and Cooper kept him because of his attention to detail and his natural ability to seek the problems in any situation, thereby averting many of them. These two leaders of people tolerated much else about him that was infuriating, downright rude or just background annoying because of this ability.

One key member of the team, Kurt Groehling, was absent, off for three days teaching at Hendon Police College. In their most recent serious case he'd been instrumental in navigating digital data under pressure and the powers that be had recognised that Reith's use of Groehling, sometimes body swerving procedural mores, had value. So now Kurt spent up to 30 days a year out of the office. Reith, pulling up a chair to join the other three at the table, said, 'Shame Kurt's not here. Really proud that he's getting a good message out across the force; really pissed off that he's not with us.'

Fleur Cooper responded with 'He's back on Monday. The course he's running finishes today. I'll text him a heads-up if there's anything he can do after COP at the College this afternoon.'

Just as Reith was about to formally start a meeting that would be logged onto Holmes 2 and officially launch a co-ordinated investigation, his mobile rang; he glanced at the caller ID and, nodding apologetically to his team, stepped away from the table and into the corridor to take the call. Fleur regarded him with casual interest through the door glass. A tall man, well built, obviously also a rugby player, though she'd a feeling there were two types of rugby and that Brent and Reith were of opposing loyalties. In his early forties, Cooper knew that he'd been married but thought it had ended some years ago, though she wasn't certain of that. As far as she knew, he had no significant other. Their team had half expected that he'd strike up a relationship with a woman they'd encountered in their last case, but that seemed to have come to nothing.

Brent was just beginning to recount a titbit of station gossip when Reith pocketed his phone and returned to the stuffy meeting room.

'Sorry about that. Do you all remember Harry Wilson, from last summer?' Brent and Cooper both nodded. Fletcher provided a crisp and sarcasm laden 'Of course.'

'Well, he just wanted to tell me that David Jerman's memorial service is on Monday. Some of us need to go, I think. I'll sort that later.' Fleur reflected that this was a testament to Reith's respect for Harry Wilson; he'd clearly given the man his mobile number. Reith held out his hand for the files and Brent passed them over. Cooper used her laptop to take the meeting record; she'd be able to copy and paste into the system later, rather than having to transcribe. She too missed Groehling; this was usually his job and always his forte.

Reith began. 'Mick, take us through what we know so far. Three victims, yes?'

Brent was reluctant to agree with this. 'Well, three from the Chelsea and Westminster hospital pathology unit. I've got a query out to all forensics' facilities now; I'm worried that we've just got a local team who've noticed. Dead bodies are usually routed by turn, so that they can minimise pressure on the pathologists, so we can't even say that it's a Chelsea or City issue alone.'

'Fair point,' said Reith. 'O.K. Take us through the three we know about.'

'The first one was Lauren Greenwood. Thirty six, lived in Kensington, near to the Finborough. She was a solicitor specialising in property law. Married – I'm looking for details on that, next of kin and so on. She collapsed on the Fulham Road last Tuesday, dead at the scene, though the paramedics gave it their best shot, I'm told. Sent to Chelsea and Westminster for the autopsy. They found this suspicious bruise, puncture mark on the top of her right arm.

'The second was Edward Horbridge, on the train from Manchester to Euston, Thursday morning. Found dead on the train when the train manager did a quick run through before it departed on its return trip. Retired, but still did some work as a locum dentist. Don went over to the Chelwest yesterday afternoon because the Chief Pathologist sent for us and the Transport Police. They'd found a similar bruise and injection mark just above his elbow.'

Brent soldiered on.

'Don and the chap from British Transport,' he glanced down at his notes, 'name of Murthi, got to interview the widow at Chelwest. I got the distinct impression from Don that Mr Horbridge couldn't have been a popular man. The train was taken out of commission by the Euston Station Manager, but really only so they could get the body off in a seemly fashion. By which I mean so that any ruddy selfies could only have showed ambulance staff. Once that was done, they sent in the cleaners and the train chugged off up north again. I've got Cervantes liaising with his new chum at Transport to see if the booking system can give us any information on who else might have been in that carriage.' Brent looked across at the files now sitting in front of Reith.

'Finally, we've got Calum Grant. Forty two, died this morning at the Blooming Wonderful place in Chelsea, you know, the garden centre. We know about him this quickly because it was the same two paramedics as dealt with Lauren Greenwood. They reckoned there was something hinkey about Grant's popping his clogs and mentioned it to the Pathology people at Chelwest. They checked visually, and there's the same bruise as with the others, on the back of the shoulder this time. They're waiting for the toxicology report now, but they seem pretty convinced. But I haven't got any other info at all on Grant yet – that's my next job.' Brent sat back and the three team members looked towards their boss. Reith dipped his head to one side and again jiggled the coins in his pocket. For a man gifted in internal politics, motivation and meeting management he surprisingly hated them all, but knew they were a necessary evil. The noisy agitation of the coins was both a subconscious protest and an energy filter. He looked at Fleur Cooper.

'Fleur, I think we'd better get interviewing key people around each of these three, while we wait to hear if anyone else has slipped through the net at other hospitals. What do you think about allocation? Divide or conquer?'

Fleur considered. 'If we get one team to interview them all in turn, we might get a better overview, but it'll be slow.' She looked towards the window as she thought. 'No, I think we need to get pairs out soon, on each victim. Because if there are more, then there'll have to be more people up to speed on the case. So having two to a team now means we can split to individual, better-informed bodies later.'

Reith's mobile rang again. Checking it, he stood and moved towards the door. 'I'm afraid I'm off. Six o'clock suit you for a quick review later?' All three nodded, Fletcher quite clearly grudgingly, and Reith disappeared from view. Brent initially felt a surge of alarm on hearing of the 6pm meeting, which quickly subsided. His wife was seriously disabled and until recently his working hours had been curtailed because of her overnight care. Their most recent major case, a bombing and subsequent trail of murders and attempted homicides had produced many results, from negative to positive. For Brent, the publicity that had been afforded to him and his wife, however excruciatingly embarrassing it had been at the time, had resulted in more comprehensive medical support. So yes, he was fine for a later meeting.

SEVEN

Fleur looked at her duty list. She believed that if the general public had any idea of just how tight police resources were, they'd be even more critical of the service. Though perhaps the brighter ones knew where the real problems lay….in those corridors of power that required endless, excruciatingly detailed monitoring and data. Every nick, every officer, every specialist unit lived in daily dread of analysis paralysis dealing them a death blow. More admin staff than uniforms. More mental health care cover than investigation. Even the ever diminishing CID officers assigned to actual detection were frequently pulled into that arena. She shook her head to clear her thoughts. Who to send where?

Logically, she'd leave Cervantes with the Horbridge case. That thought jogged her memory. As she'd worked on her laptop during the leadership meeting she'd noted an incoming email from the British Transport Police. She checked this now and found a request for Murthi to be temporarily assigned to the Met, for this case. The Inspector who'd penned the email explained that Murthi had been in the investigations' unit for a while now and could do with another view on how investigations could be run. Trying to read between the lines, Fleur Cooper speculated on three possibilities. Murthi was good and they wanted to stretch his experience. Or he was inclined to be rigid in his thinking and the Transport Inspector thought he could do with a different perspective. Or he was just a pain in the neck, and they fancied a break from him, even if that left them even more short-handed. It was good practice though; the Metropolitan Police also occasionally sent staff the other way to develop a more rounded view of what the Transport Police did. The clincher was that, if he was halfway decent, she'd get a bonus, a freebie officer. She quickly responded to the email and asked if it was possible for Murthi to attend at 8am the next morning. She then called Cervantes in to tell him of his temporary new colleague and their assignment. 'And while you're waiting, this afternoon you can start looking for the Horbridge daughter, and draw up a list of other people you want to interview in relation to him.'

Fleur watched Cervantes leave her office and smiled inwardly. Don was one of those rare people able to enjoy virtually every aspect of their job. Added to which, his delight in his official transfer to CID was still very evident, despite the heavy-duty training he was now undergoing.

Cooper returned to her staff allocations. She didn't really want a senior officer out yet, but she also knew there was no-one better than Mick Brent at getting the dirt and detail. So she allocated him an experienced PC, Daisy Jones, though she'd have to check whether she was on shift this weekend. Any further allocations she'd leave for now; she wanted to discuss it later with Reith and prior to that she thought she'd try to speak to Groehling, in the hope that he might have some ideas. In theory she could use Fletcher, but he was such a grumpy sod that she knew she'd regret it in the inevitable aftermath of complaints. Sadly, these would be both internal and external.

At the back of her mind was another email she'd glimpsed at the same time as the one from the British Transport Police, from her relatively new partner, Peter. She grimaced to herself. Partner, boyfriend, significant other. The names were all ridiculous. She sensed that he wanted to move on far more quickly than she did, though she did acknowledge to herself that moving forward was something she would want, at some point…. She parked the thought and bent over her staffing list. Until this relationship, she'd enjoyed more fleeting, casual ones, lasting a few months at best, usually brought to a halt by the pressure of her work. Peter Howard worked for MI5 and understood her work demands only too well. A calm, good-natured chap, he'd just quietly refused to be brushed off, until Fleur had reached her current state of mind, certainly keen to develop further but definitely afraid of the commitment.

Brent sat at his desk, aware of the buzz around him, different cases and projects being pursued by his colleagues. Mick Brent wasn't a fan of admin work, but he'd started on the task of researching Calum Grant and that was investigation, not admin. So his demeanour was upbeat; he loved a good dig around to see what could be found.

It didn't take him long to get an overview. Grant lived in Kensington, just like the first victim, Lauren Greenwood. He was employed by a large public relations company in the West End. There were a lot of social media links which came up in the search engine. He was married to a Chloé

Antoine and he had three cars registered in his name, all very up-market.

Brent headed for Fleur Cooper's office, leaning on the door frame as he spoke.

'Wotcher Gov. I've got as much as I think I can from a digital trawl on Calum Grant. What do you want next?'

'Well, I've assigned you Daisy – I've checked – she's in. And from tomorrow Cervantes is going to stick with Murthi, from the Transport Police – they've asked for an on-case secondment. I'm just aware that we might need to spread a bit thinner if your worry about the actual number of cases is real, so we can split up later if necessary. But for now, let's work in pairs. I'm not going to be able to get out in the field with you today at least – too many deadlines on too much paperwork, especially the stuff that's going to trial in the next few days. The Chief Super might want to roll his sleeves up – you know what he's like – he does love to get in the middle of it and see what's what, but I can't allocate him a specific task list because Them Upstairs can pull him away whenever.'

Specialist prosecution file administrators worked within most police forces, tasked with ensuring that all necessary evidence was both present and correct, checking evidence chains, interview records and procedural adherence. All good, but a senior officer was still needed to sign off on their summative reports. Cooper was only too aware of the deadlines for each of the files resting on her desk, the bright yellow post-its declaring the dreaded dates. It would be midnight oil for her tonight at least. Her efficiency would be vital since she knew, even on what they already had, that this case was going to be substantial; worse if the search turned up more potential victims. She needed to clear some space by getting a big chunk of her admin tasks to bed before everything kicked off. Certainly before she next went to bed herself. Brent nodded in comprehension, then pushed himself off the door frame.

He headed from the smaller inner office that housed most of the sergeants and their associated admin staff and on into the much larger open plan office that housed the majority of the constables assigned to CID, trainees and fully fledged alike. Quieter at the weekend, there were still some staff present, as well as a small number of uniforms who had been assigned to the department. In most cases these were allocated for a specific case, but a couple of them had been kept on past their first project and by dint of fancy footwork from Fleur Cooper and her sergeants remained as a sort of general pool working on CID tasks. No-one discussed this, as CID were only too grateful for additional help and if the uniformed managers formally noticed there'd be a magic disappearing act; by unspoken agreement these officers wore civilian clothes. Less chance of triggering a uniformed sergeant's memory. Brent looked around and spotted just such an officer at a desk in a window bay.

Daisy Jones was a jolly looking woman, with a healthy Scandinavian air, which belied her actual Irish roots, now a couple of generations removed. She was very good with distressed witnesses and Brent was keen to get over to Calum Grant's address and talk to his widow. Daisy would be helpful in that situation – not because of her gender but because she had a genuinely warm manner which hid her driving need to get answers. Brent brought Daisy up to speed and sent her to one of the small glass boxes which served as internal meeting rooms. He then headed to the other side of the room and corralled Cervantes, dispatching him to the same place. He headed back to his desk, picked up the files and joined them. Interrupting their general chit-chat, Brent laid the files in the middle of the table. He began by letting them know of Murthi's expected arrival on the morrow.

'Don. I don't know if DI Cooper has told you that you're paired with Constable Murthi for a while? You know we want you to stick with the Horbridge case – so who have you come up with to see?'

Cervantes referred to the A4 note pad he was holding.

'Well, I think the daughter might be good for a real character review, though it doesn't seem likely that she's involved at the moment, because we can't see any links to the other bodies. Well, not yet anyway. I thought I should talk to a couple of colleagues and perhaps some neighbours, and perhaps someone from the AGM he was at in Manchester – what do you think?'

Brent considered this. 'Possibly, but the Manchester angle would have to be a 'phone chat first; I'm not authorising that sort of travel unless it's got legs.'

Cervantes continued. 'After that, I'm stuck. First, I think it's a good idea to go back to Mrs Horbridge. She should be calmer now and she should know what his circle of contacts is.'

Brent approved this. 'Yep, good. That said…..you and Murthi met her together yesterday, but I don't want to wait until he joins us tomorrow. Go and see her on your own and get that contact list. Daisy,' he turned to the female officer, 'you and I are going to see Calum Grant's wife, see if she can shed any light.'

EIGHT

Dear Diary

It was bad. I knew it would be. He went mad. He shook me and shouted at me and told me not to tell lies. I just had to keep telling him I wasn't making it up.

So they didn't give me the money. Mum came to school instead and talked to the teacher. It was bad, but Mum doesn't shout in public. So it wasn't a puppy. It was something called a poppy.

When he found out he went mad again. I didn't get any tea.

I don't mind. I was really worried about what would happen with a puppy. It's funny, because I think Mum would like one really.

NINE

Brent and Daisy were preparing to visit Calum Grant's wife, briefly detouring to Brent's desk so he could check emails. He clicked his tongue in annoyance and waved the constable into the chair in front of his desk. Brent scrolled through the eighty or so emails he'd received in the last few hours, selecting two and printing them. He held one out to Daisy Jones and read the other in more detail himself. In silence they then swapped and read the other message.

'So, two more bodies with the same MO. Shit and double shit.' Daisy grimaced in response.

Mick Brent headed back to Fleur Cooper. 'I'm really sorry Gov, I know you're up to your ears. But I've got two more cases. Is there anyone else I can call on to do the backgrounds? I really want to get over to Calum Grant's address.'

Fleur Cooper regarded him mournfully. 'Sod it all to high heaven. It's going to be a nightmare if...when...the media get on to it.' She bellowed towards the outer office, 'Fletcher!' She looked back at Brent and said, 'Give me those and bugger off.' Brent complied then turned away, side-stepping a clearly disgruntled Fletcher. As he signalled Jones to join him in his exit, he heard Fletcher saying, 'I prefer not to be bawled at, Inspector'. He just caught a tired Fleur's response before the outer office door closed. 'Yeah, yeah, and these people preferred not to be murdered. We don't all get what we want.' He smiled to himself. Fleur Cooper, despite the cool image, cared a lot about her work and had developed a dry line with Fletcher that was just what Brent thought the annoying little git needed. At least, in the absence of an empty lift shaft….

Brent and Jones made good time across to Kensington, largely down to Jones' impressive rat-run credentials. They pulled up outside a very attractive block of flats, albeit not contemporary ones. Brent estimated that these had been purpose-built, as apartments, in the late Victorian period. Referring to his notes he then pressed the top button on the intercom setup to the side of the substantial portico. Three sets of two, then one button only at the top of the board, with Grant/Antoine beautifully handwritten on the label. He lifted his warrant card to the camera when he heard a female voice respond to his ring. 'Sergeant Brent, Metropolitan Police. May we come up Ms Antoine?' The intercom went dead, and the door was buzzed open, and Brent and Jones scaled the wide stairs set in the middle of the property. Clearly two apartments on each of the bottom three floors, all with substantial beautifully panelled doors. On each landing fresh flowers stood on side tables. At the top the stairs took a last return on themselves and ran out on a landing facing towards the back of the building. The police pair both reckoned that at some point two apartments had become one.

The apartment door opened, and a tall, voluptuous brunette woman invited them to come in. She introduced herself as Chloé Antoine and listened carefully to their names. Her French accent was charming, but she was certainly proficient in English. She ushered them into a large kitchen diner, to the right of the hall and which faced to the back of the block, overlooking gardens, trees and chimneys. In the substantial window bay at the far end of the room were two sofas arranged opposite each other, with a coffee table between. She gestured to them to sit and then headed towards a large machine on the worktop, saying as she went,

'I need a coffee. Can I get you two one? Or tea if you prefer?' She pronounced tea in the French way. Times of stress, thought Brent, whose French was actually rather good, though with probably more rugby vocabulary than usually encountered.

Brent had rightly identified the machine as a bean to cup of significant provenance, and hell was going to freeze over before he declined such an offer.

'That's very kind. A double espresso, if that's at all possible?' He and Chloé Antoine both looked towards Daisy, who said 'Oh yes please, just an ordinary coffee with milk.' Brent and Antoine both shuddered slightly, but the drinks were soon sitting in front of them. Chloé sat opposite the officers, holding her small coffee cup in both hands. She smiled slightly at them and then looked out of the window.

'I only found out a couple of hours ago. I flew back from Bordeaux this morning and my mobile was off.' She turned back to them, waiting.

'We really are so sorry for your loss.' said Daisy Jones. 'Have you got family or friends who can come to be with you for a while?'

'But yes, my very best friend Harriet is on her way from Manchester.' She pronounced the name 'Arriette.' 'We met at university in Paris and often we have lived in the same areas. She will be here this evening.' She paused, glanced at her hands then looked directly at the officers in turn. 'But I will not be dishonest. I am sad that Calum is dead and that it looks like, as you say, foul play. But I would not have been his wife for much longer. I was divorcing him. He didn't know yet. I was waiting until I had been to Bordeaux. It was for a job interview, you understand. If I got it I would have a safe new destination. He would have been very, very angry.' She smiled again, wistfully. 'When I first met him he was so charming. But later, after we were married I thought he changed. But then I understood he had not changed but that he had hidden his true self at the beginning.'

Brent nodded, keeping her on side, as yet no need to challenge.

'So do you mind if I ask you to describe him? What did he do, what kind of a person was he? Who do you think we should speak with?' He was aware that he was asking multiple questions, but that was a technique. Interviewees usually opted to answer all of the easy ones. The ones they didn't answer were just as useful. When they'd run through the least dangerous topics they were already braced for the hard ones, no pressure needed from Brent. Interestingly, heightened tension tended to provide more clues than not, but it had to be internally produced. The days were long gone when police officers bawled and harangued. Though that didn't make for good telly, so the impression persisted in the wider populace.

Chloé regarded him thoughtfully and then bombed his attempt. 'In turn. He was a Director at Clarion, the PR Agency. He managed most of their biggest corporate clients. Most people don't understand PR, Calum would always say. But in essence, he helped them design their public image and rescued them, as much as he could, from unexpected disasters. What kind of person? Well, he was not kind. He was good-looking and could be most charming, when he wanted. But he was cruel and controlling. At the beginning he tried hard to shape me into the French provincial housewife he thought I should be. I am,' she grimaced a little, 'not that type of woman. I need to work, to have opinions. When bullying didn't work and he sensed me becoming, ah, how would one say, cool, he began something else. The thing from the old film, you know. The emotional bullying?'

Daisy nodded. 'You mean gaslighting?'

'Oh yes, that's the expression. He was very clever, making me doubt myself, things he would say I had forgotten, or not done. It worked for a while. I even went to my doctor, but when I tried to explain to him how I was feeling, it was almost impossible, and I came away. But in my car I thought and thought. And I admitted to myself what I had really known anyway, why I couldn't describe it to the doctor. This was just Calum's latest control tactic. So I began looking for jobs back in France. I love it here, except for your weather! But I knew that it would be easier to start again at such a distance.' For a moment she looked forlorn. 'Do you know, our second wedding anniversary is this week, on Wednesday. I wanted to have my escape plan before then. I could not celebrate his lie of a marriage anymore.'

She continued. 'And who should you speak with? Well, I will tell you anything I can, but it was not me, you know. I was not here, and I could not have afforded an assassin.' In her accent the word sounded almost charming. The accompanying, slightly mischievous smile gave them the clue as to the lively, charming woman beneath the present turmoil and her recent emotional restraint. She carried on, 'I'll give you his laptop – it's here, in his study. And I'll give you a list of the people at his company who I think you should talk with.'

Daisy leant forward slightly. 'I'm really sorry to ask – I hope you understand we need to explore all the possibilities – do you have any reason to believe that Calum was seeing someone else?'

Daisy considered her answer. 'No reason, no. But I knew Calum. The power of the chase, you know. That's why he's, sorry, he was, so good in sales. He liked the hunt and then the thrill. So my guess is that he probably was. I was never able to pin it down, because his working hours were legitimately random, events, receptions, all sorts of meetings. But one thing I did think about. Every few months he changed his PA. He always said that it was impossible to find someone who could keep up with him. And the new ones were always brand new, you know? New to the company, every time. So I wondered.'

Brent couldn't help himself. 'Ms Antoine, your English is exceptional!'

She laughed. 'Chloé, please. Well, it's much easier than French – you have far less participles, you know? The hardest thing for me has always been the pronunciation.'

Brent responded. 'Well, if my French is ever half as good as your English, I'd be delighted.' She smiled in reply, clearly pleased.

Daisy picked up the thread again, her kind and open face taking much of the sting from her question. 'Now I need to ask you another difficult question – I seem to be the bad cop today.' She smiled. 'And are you, or were you, seeing anyone else?'

Chloé shook her head and said, firmly. 'Absolutely not. I'm a very loyal person at heart. Even though I stopped loving Calum some time ago, I would not even think of another relationship until I got myself back. You understand?' She looked enquiringly at the two of them in turn, seeking some sort of affirmation.' Both officers nodded but didn't give a verbal response.

At this stage Brent judged there was only one more area to explore. He was beginning to form the opinion that Chloé Antoine had not engineered her husband's death, but she might have information that could help. This time it was he who leant forward.

'What you haven't been told yet is that there seem to be four other people who have died in the same circumstances, over the past week.' She looked at him, obviously shocked.

'If I tell you their names I need two things from you. First, I'd ask you not to share this part of our conversation with anyone. It's really important that this doesn't get out. The only strength we have at this early stage is that the person or persons concerned aren't yet aware that we know.' Chloé bowed her head in acquiescence. 'You have my word.'
Brent continued. 'So, Lauren Greenwood. Lived here in Kensington, a solicitor, mostly with property.' Chloé sat upright.

'Oof! She is the solicitor Calum used for this apartment!' For the first time, her accent became more apparent, with some of her words pronounced in the French way. 'She was quite a horrible woman. She tried to get the house in Calum's name only, but I also invested my money, so I brought my solicitor in to make sure it was fair. I think Calum must have asked her to do it, but he always said not. She had a habit of standing above me whenever we met. So I talked to her waist. I would not give her the satisfaction of looking up.' She looked perturbed. 'But how can this be? This is two people I know. And the other names? Now I am afraid.'

Mick Brent, pleased at least to have made a connection, said, 'Edward Horbridge. He was a retired dentist. Does that ring a bell?' She looked thoroughly relieved.

'No, thank the good God. *My* dentist is in Manchester, from when I lived there, before I met Calum. He's so good that I go up there twice a year.' She waited expectantly. Brent carried on.

'The last two I have very little information about. Gordon Szabo, from Guildford, and a Mr Kendell Bell, from Basingstoke.' Again, she shook her head.

'No, definitely not.' Brent felt that it was time to call a halt. But it might be necessary to return here at some point and he both liked Chloé Antoine enough to be sympathetic and understood the need to end the interview with good grace. Under pressure it was often necessary to ask questions and get out pronto to act on the information without delay, but it could leave witnesses and interviewees feeling nonplussed and of little worth. So he touched gently on the future, to ease her away from the officialese thus far.

'So, Chloé. Do you know what you're going to do now? Will you go to Bordeaux?'

She raised her chin a little. 'No. I shall decline the job offer. I like it here and it was Calum I wanted to leave, not my job and my friends. Even this apartment I love. Calum wasn't here so much that it feels like I have to leave. And' she paused, clearly debating with herself, 'well, there's also my friend, Harriet. You know, she is coming here today. She has cancer and it's not going so well. I want to be nearer to her, to help.' She leaned back on her sofa, clearly emotional at having said this aloud.

'I'm so sorry to hear that.' said Daisy. 'But there's so much that can be done these days.' Chloé nodded, but was clearly unconvinced.

The interview lasted only a short time after this. Chloé unearthed Calum Grant's laptop, as well as a Blackberry that she said he used to track his expenses and four old address books.

'I'm not sure what use they'll be, but maybe…'

They bid her farewell and walked back down to the spacious lobby. Letting themselves out of the grand old front door, Brent said, 'Interesting. What did you make of her?'

'I really think she was telling us the truth. Either that or she's a better actress than I'm giving her credit for.' Brent nodded, and came back with his view.

'Mm. And it's apparently harder to lie well in a second language. Then again, her English really is very good.'

TEN

Cervantes stood outside the Horbridge semi in Wimbledon. He'd rung ahead and Mrs Horbridge had seemed pleased to confirm that he could call in.

The house was red brick but had a pleasant front door and windows with arched tops, replicated on the upper floor. But in general it was ugly, unsoftened by greenery or colour. Unlike its neighbours, the garden was laid to a meticulously square piece of lawn and a flower bed around this filled with winter pansies. Cervantes thought it looked like a municipal park. He rang the bell and almost immediately the door was opened by Caroline Horbridge. She ushered him in, just as twittery as the previous day but at least now with a home turf purpose. She took him into the sitting room and asked if he'd like tea. Knowing that giving her a practical task would help to calm her, he accepted the offer.

While she bustled about in the kitchen, he examined the room in which he sat. It reminded him of his great-aunt's house. Floral carpet. No television. Upholstered furniture with a patterned fabric that didn't sit well with the floor covering. Heavy lace curtains. No photographs, but a set of pictures of sheep and country scenes that Cervantes recognised as an artist called Farquharson. He thought they were truly dreadful examples of Victoriana.

Caroline Horbridge came into the room bearing a tray with teapot, milk, sugar and two kinds of biscuit. Cervantes stepped forward to take the tray from her and placed it on an incongruously modern coffee table. As on the previous day, this small kindness made her blink with pleasure. She sat down in the chair nearest to the tray and, checking his preferences, provided him with the promised drink.

He smiled at her. 'It's lovely to see a real tea tray!' She gave him a reserved smile.

'It was Edward. He said it was important to set standards. And I do think it's pretty. But this morning', she paused, clearly about to divulge something, 'this morning I made my tea in a mug.' This was obviously a big thing for her, and Cervantes was pleased to recognise that she'd already begun to question the bonds of the dictatorship imposed on her.

He started. 'Mrs Horbridge.' She interrupted him. 'Caroline please...no, no, Caro. Oh my!' It was like watching a butterfly emerging. Already he saw a younger woman than he'd met on the previous day.

'Caro then. It's a beautiful name. Thank you for talking to me again. The thing is, I need your help.' The face that she turned towards him made the young constable think that this was what an eager dormouse would look like.

'When we met yesterday I didn't tell you that there are four other victims who seem to have been killed in the same way as Mr Horbridge. Partly because we didn't know about all of them and partly because you had enough to take in down at the hospital.' She looked quite horrified and covered her mouth with her hand.

He continued, giving much the same warning about confidentiality as Brent had provided to Chloé Antoine.

The very thought of newspapers contacting her made Caro Horbridge pale even further.

'So, let's start with Lauren Greenwood?'

'No, I don't think so.'

'She was a property lawyer.'

'No, I'm sure not. But Edward dealt with all that sort of business. But he owned this house when we met, so he didn't need a solicitor.'

Cervantes provided the other names in turn, with the same negative response. It was evident that Edward Horbridge had kept a very tight rein on his wife. He reflected that Steve Reith's view didn't work for him in this case. Reith liked the investigating team to develop some level of affinity with their victims, using either their first name or their title. Cervantes couldn't provide that internal courtesy to Edward Horbridge. He knew that he'd have detested the man and he wasn't going to award anything other than professional respect to him now.

And because he was a man who had chosen to be a police officer because he liked to know things, relevant, interesting, possibly pointless but always worthy of at least listening, he now asked Caro Horbridge if she was going to be all right.

'Oh yes. When I got home yesterday I saw my neighbour in the garden and I told her what had happened. She was so kind. They invited me to eat with them last night, and even though I said no, they insisted. They've got children and the meal was *so* interesting. They all talked about their day and they were funny and nice to me. Then we watched a comedy programme on their television. I haven't often watched a television, because Edward said they were for idiots, but it was lovely.' She added thoughtfully, 'Edward would have hated it. He never even spoke to them because they, well because they're from Jamaica. I always said hello, but only when Edward wasn't here. And Susannah – that's the wife – she came home with me last night to check all the windows and locks with me. And this morning she brought in some shopping, so I don't have to go out for a couple of days if I don't want to. The eldest boy, Nathan, he's going to teach me how to use a computer.' She said this as if she'd been offered a moon landing, bemused and unsure that it was even possible.

That brought Cervantes back to the task in hand. 'I'm afraid I'm going to ask you to let me look at Mr Horbridge's paperwork and computer. I might even need to take some things away. Is that all right with you or do you want me to get a warrant?'

She recoiled at this. 'A warrant? Of course not. You must take whatever you need. I'll show you his study. I'm not really allowed in there, but I used to clean it every week, with Edward watching.' Cervantes swallowed his facetious retort. His own father worked on some quite confidential material in his small back bedroom, so the family was largely banned from interfering with his ramshackle organisation. But he cleaned the room himself, after intermittent nagging from Cervantes' mother.

Caro continued. 'But he didn't have a computer. He said they were pointless wastes of time. There is something in a box that he won at a dentistry conference just before Christmas. I think it's called a laptop. But it's never been opened.'

She and Cervantes headed to the back of the house. What would have been a rather lovely dining room had been turned into a meticulously neat office. Cervantes couldn't think of it as a study; it had no character, just cold functionality, like the back garden he could dimly see through the window. Even here the net curtains were apparently necessary. She was right, the laptop was still in its sealed and cellophaned box. A very ancient typewriter took the centre position on the large desk. On a shelf above the desk were diaries dating back at least thirty years. The filing cabinets seemed to be full of copies of letters of complaint from Horbridge to an astonishingly broad range of targets, as well as all of the expected household administration. Cervantes would have imagined that Horbridge would like things to be locked away, but he was beginning to understand how rigid was the totalitarianism that Caro Horbridge had endured. She wouldn't have dared. There was no way he could take all of this with him, but it was going to be necessary to check it all. He told Caro Horbridge this and said he'd arrange for it to be collected, if that was OK with her? She replied in the affirmative and he put a memo on his phone to sort the collection.

Ever helpful, he suggested that Caro get the laptop out of the box and charge it up, ready for her first lesson with Nathan. Seeing her nervous reaction to this, he helped her to open it and showed her how to charge it. He also said, 'when you see Nathan say I suggest you start with a mouse. You'll find it easier at the beginning than the touchpad'. This seemed like gobbledegook to her, but she carefully stored it to be repeated to Nathan.

When Caro Horbridge let her police visitor out of the door he was aware that she was sorry to see him go, but also conscious that she was beginning to see that life without her deceased husband was going to be considerably warmer and more fulfilling.

His last words to her were, 'if you want to see if you can trace your daughter, ask Nathan about Facebook. That might help.'

ELEVEN

Dear Diary

Today I got my swimming proficiency badge. Nearly my whole class did it, but only six of us passed the test. There was a ceremony at the end, and we got medals. Everyone else's parents were there, and they took pictures. One of the mums noticed I didn't have anyone, and she took my picture and she said she'd give me a copy. I've worried about that all evening. I've already hidden the medal, but I'm afraid Mum will see the photo if the other Mum gives it to me outside school. My whole class has to go swimming, but the medal was volentery. You had to pay £2.80. Granny gave me the money, but he doesn't know. I don't want to get Granny into trouble.

At school we've been learning about DNA and jeans. I think jeans isn't the right spelling, but I haven't seen it written down yet. Mostly it was about peas in a pod. But it's interesting. And it gave me a big idea. Because the teacher said we inherit some stuff from our families, like the colour of our hair and some people think we inherit the kind of person we are. My Granny and Grandad are lovely. But he isn't. So it isn't definate. But I think I can't have a family when I'm all grown up, because what if one of them got his jeans?

TWELVE

Fletcher glared at his desk. For the third time someone had dropped a file onto its surface instead of into the in-tray. He almost grasped that it was deliberate, that his colleagues had little respect for him and that it amused them to wind him up. Almost, but not quite. Despite his highly analytical brain, emotions and empathy, and certainly introspection, were uncharted territory. He'd made some advances on a previous case and had detected some actual warmth from his workmates, which both pleased and puzzled him. But much of his progress had been accidental and, without comprehension, couldn't easily be repeated.

He shuffled the paperwork back into a tidy pile and resumed his digital search. His first two targets, Gorden Szabo and Kendell Bell, hadn't been hard to find, and he had a general, practical picture of them. The third, Lauren Greenwood, was at this stage more interesting. He needed to call the Solicitors' Regulation Authority, but he felt he needed Inspector Cooper to do it, because of her rank. At no time had it ever occurred to him that people were reluctant to help him because of his approach; he'd never grasped that sugar is more palatable than vinegar.

At that point there was a small flurry of activity at the door to the sergeants' anteroom and Fletcher glanced at the clock. A minute or two to six, so he gathered his files and notepad and joined Reith, Brent and Jones as they headed towards one of the larger meeting rooms. Before they'd had time to settle into their seats, Cooper and Cervantes arrived, with Don carrying a tray laden with a percolator jug full of coffee, paper cups, milk and sugar.

Reith laughed. 'Shame Groehling's not here, he's always got biscuits.'

From the doorway a tall, gangly man echoed the laughter. 'Well, never say I let you down. Don't you lot eat when I'm not here?'

Cooper smiled in welcome. 'I didn't expect you here this evening.'

'We wrapped up at three-ish this afternoon, to let the farthest-away folk get home in reasonable time. We had a couple of Police Scotland there, from Dundee. Apparently not a great journey from the borders upward. And I wanted to get up to speed.' He sat down and tipped a leftover Christmas pack of biscuits onto the tray.

Kurt Groehling, an absolute mainstay to Cooper and the rest of the team, was an odd looking man, very tall and angular. His clothes were often slightly too large if they were the right length, or too short in the sleeve and leg if they fitted his body. Brent could have told people that Kurt generally wore uniform trousers, purloined over the years, because there was a better chance of finding the right waist and length combination. Don, though he'd never have dared day it, always thought that Groehling had a sort of alien air, a bit like Matt Smith playing Doctor Who, otherworldly. His IT abilities only served to enhance this impression.

Reith called the meeting to order, and Fleur Cooper gladly handed the task of detailing information and meeting conclusions to Groehling, whose fingers danced over his tablet like long, thin ballet dancers. Steve Reith reflected that Groehling, impressive as he was in most areas of his work, never seemed totally complete unless he had an interface to the digital world, unaware that this impression was shared by the others and, in Cervantes case, only served to increase his perception of an incomer from Gallifrey. Reith kicked off with,'

'Right. Roundups please. Who's got what?'

Fleur Cooper started. 'Well, first we now have a better timeline, order of deaths, whatever you want to call it. Lauren Greenwood and a Kendell Bell, both on Monday this week. Her first, it looks like. Then a Gordon Szabo on Wednesday, Edward Horbridge on Thursday and Calum Grant on Friday. We'll pick up on them later on.'

Cervantes spoke before he thought. 'No-one on Tuesday? What happened?' For his pains he received the cold stare that Reith reserved for idiot behaviour. Brent chipped in, 'But he's right sir, it does look like there's a list someone's working through.'

Fleur nodded to Brent to continue, and he took the group through the meeting with Chloé Antoine.
Reith queried, 'What was your view? A viable suspect? She knows at least one of the other victims.'

'I doubt it Guv, she wasn't here for her husband's killing and she even said herself that she couldn't afford an assassin.' Brent gave the word Chloé Antoine's French accent, which amused most of the room.

'Fine, but check her alibi, Mick. Don, what about you? I know you've got a new playmate, but that's not until tomorrow, I think?'

'Sir. He's coming in the morning. I spent the later part of the afternoon at Mrs Horbridge's. I've asked SOCO to collect a lot of stuff from his home office – too much to carry. I've never seen so many complaint letters in one place, so other than increasing my view of Mr Horbridge as a proper bastard, not much new from his widow. Beautiful house, obviously decked out to his taste. Like, no taste at all. My Gran would hate it and she likes crimplene.' Even Fletcher gave a small smile to this one.

Reith nodded. 'Fleur?'

'Well, obviously what you didn't know until now is that we've got those two extra victims – Norman's been looking into their backgrounds, but we've not had time to get people out yet.' Fletcher glared ferociously at this use of his soubriquet, but to no avail. Fleur had used it deliberately; she'd observed that if she used it a couple of times a day, Fletcher maintained an attitude of 'I'll show you how good I am', as opposed to his more usual sullen meeting of everyone else's lowest common denominator. On the other hand, if he valued a task or wanted to prove a point, his performance level often far exceeded either expectation or need. Reith turned to Fletcher, raising an eyebrow.

'Do you want me to talk you through what I've found?' No 'sir' was forthcoming from Fletcher. Even for Reith, whom he almost respected. Reith raised his eyebrow even higher.

'Right. Gordon Szabo.' Fletcher pronounced this name as an affront. He wasn't inherently racist, just averse to anything different. 'He lived in Guildford. Thirty six. Something in IT until a few years ago. Big company. He was a director. But he set up his own business – I haven't had time to look into that yet. Married, two children, boy, two, girl eleven. I've alerted the local station that we'll be coming down and will want access.'

The rest of the group inwardly winced at the task now faced by whoever got sent down to Guildford, having to overcome the resistance so neatly shovelled up by Fletcher's undoubted lack of tact. 'Want access' would have been far better phrased as 'would be grateful for access'.

Fletcher continued. 'Kendell Bell. Not called Kendell Bell at all. Birth certificate said Kenneth Balls. He changed it sometime in his twenties. Fifty one. Lived in Basingstoke, big house, if the council tax band is anything to go by. In a place called Old Basing,. Used to work at some tech company in Basingstoke. Married once, to a solicitor.' He paused. 'She's one of our other victims, Lauren Greenwood.' He smirked at the interest now apparent in his audience. A connection. As Reith would no doubt be thinking, 'a thread to pull at.' Fletcher picked up his notepad.

'She lived here in London; she never appeared on the council tax returns for the Hampshire place. No children, to either of them. And she had a very poor reputation professionally. I tried to talk to her current employers, but they said to make an appointment. They said that there'd been quite a lot of complaints and they thought it would be useful if they pulled those together for us. But then I thought we should also contact the professional body, the Solicitors' Regulation Authority. Can you do that Inspector?' No please was offered.

Again, the room's occupants heard a different message. Fletcher thought he'd be palmed off because he wasn't senior enough. Everyone else knew he'd be palmed off because of the high-handed approach he'd take. Cooper resolved to set Brent on the task, but she'd save face for Fletcher by sorting that outside this meeting.

Reith looked around the room. 'Look, lads and lassies, I think this is going to be even worse than our last case with the madwoman. This is true serial killer territory, and we haven't a clue as to motive or connection or how many were, or still are, on the list. The media are going to whip themselves up into a proper frenzy. I've warned the Assistant CC and he's gone further up the chain, but at that point I only knew about three of them, so I'd better update him. I don't know how we've got away with it so far, but someone's going to notice soon. First thing we need is to start plotting tables to look for connections. Some of Fletcher's and Maisie's questions from the Rain Callan case might be useful too. On which note, Mick, what do you think?'

'You thinking about cadging a dinner Gov?' responded Brent. Maisie Brent was a much respected forensic psychologist who'd been instrumental in solving their previous case, though it had nearly cost her dearly. The team had developed the routine of ending the day at the Brent's bungalow in Tooting Bec. The habit had ceased with the resolution of the case, but Reith hadn't forgotten how useful the more informal setting, the wider range of discussion and Maisie's clarity of human understanding had been. Reith nodded. 'Is it too late to rustle something up – we can order pizza? And I know it's Saturday, and you've maybe all got plans?'

Although Fletcher said nothing, the others all shook their heads. Brent said,

'None of us can afford to do anything in January Gov! Let me ring Maisie. If it's too late to cook, she'll order something in.'

After allocating tasks for the following day, everyone departed to their various duties. One and all were keen to participate in the visit to the Brents. Fletcher hated to miss anything, Cervantes still felt like he'd been invited to the grown ups' party and Fleur was just keen to see Maisie again. Daisy Jones had only been included once before and wasn't going to miss any opportunity that might help her secure a permanent placement in CID. Groehling however voiced reservation. 'I've been away for three nights, so I really need to go home first and test the water. Sandy's had the kids on her own and I might be for the high jump if I take it for granted.' The Groehlings had twins, currently in what Sandy called the Fearsome Fours, after the Terrible Twos and the Thuggery Threes.

THIRTEEN

Dear Diary

It's Sunday and we were going to Granny's for tea. Mum wanted to put my hair in plaits. She likes playing with hair. Sometimes, if we're quiet at home she lets me brush her hair.

But today my hair was all tangled and he was getting cross with her, so he took the comb off her and did it. He really, really hurt. There was lots of my hair in the comb and I tried really really hard but it did make me cry. He says I've got to get used to worse things than that.

FOURTEEN

Irfan Patel closed the car door with satisfaction. It didn't slam, but had that reassuringly solid yet muted *thwump* of the luxury car. His first truly beautiful vehicle, but he was certain it wouldn't be his last.

He was wrong. As he stepped into the stairwell of the multi-storey car park he was pushed roughly from behind, stumbling face first into the wall. He slid forward onto his knees, the side of his face scraping the bare brick. He started to struggle back to his feet but was pushed down again, and slightly sidewards by a strong blow to the side of his neck. He subsided to the floor and heard his assailant leave, footsteps running down the concrete stairs. He groped in his pocket for his phone and pressed 999. He was conscious long enough to ask for the police, but not to provide his whereabouts, though his number did appear on the display at the call centre. Hearing only scrabbling sounds, then nothing, the emergency services operator triggered a short voice clip, asking the caller to press 55 if they weren't able to speak but needed the police. With no response to this Silent Solutions option the operator had only an open line and no audio clues. A judgement now needed to be made; whether to forward the call to the police or to hang up after the procedurally required 45 seconds.

The operator chose to end the call. Nothing had been heard that suggested violence or physical distress.

It was only ten minutes later that another call was placed, alerting the services to an unwell man in the stairwell of the Bloomsbury car park. Ambulance and also police were dispatched after the caller described the side of the man's face being scraped.

As with his predecessors in this macabre pattern, the emergency services were unable to revive or save Irfan Patel. They checked with Dispatch and were told to take the body to University College Hospital. This they undertook and delivered their passenger less than an hour from the time of his attack.

Since the earlier alert and query re a bruise and injection mark combo, the technician was awake to the possibility and spotted the tell-tale signs as the corpse was undressed. A call was made to the mobile phone number provided in the email from Mick Brent and he answered, standing in his kitchen chopping onions. He took the details and hung up, gazing into space for a moment.

FIFTEEN

Maisie watched Mick process the information he'd just been given. She waited and smiled slightly as he turned towards her. He'd given her a fairly comprehensive overview of the situation so far. She'd already printed and signed a Non-Disclosure Agreement in preparation for the evening's gathering. She didn't expect to be paid, but it allowed the team to use her skills without worrying about confidentiality. If Steve Reith considered that there were any vulnerabilities to this he could later recruit her formally as a consultant.

'Another one. I've only got the bare minimum at the moment, from his driving licence. I'll need to call it in and get someone to dig out more info.' Brent rang into the station admin number and relayed his request. Probably Fletcher or Groehling would do a more detailed job in the morning, but for now Brent wanted it logged into HOLMES and to be informed if any special circumstances were discovered in relation to the victim. He turned back to his wife.

'So, here we are again. Try not to annoy this one, if you can help it.' Maisie took no offence. The last case on which she'd assisted had culminated in their perpetrator attempting to include Maisie in her deadly roll call.

Maisie ran her keen eye over the kitchen. It was a stylish but practical room, at the moment the large windows black with the night. On the table, cutlery in a large beer tankard, paper napkins in a pile. Mick was currently frying chicken pieces in a very large wok, to which he'd shortly add garlic, onion, green pepper and rice. Thinly sliced chorizo, stock and peas would complete what the two of them called a 'sort-of paella dish', to be augmented by home-made garlic bread. Maisie had already made the batter for her pineapple upside-down cake. No time or inclination to make custard, but she had plenty of cream and crème fraiche. She recalled that Simon Fletcher had loved the pudding and she knew better than anyone just how little he ever felt appreciated. She also knew that it was totally his own fault.

Just after eight thirty the doorbell started to ring, heralding the arrival of everyone except Groehling. Some had shared Fleur's car, others followed. Brent ushered them in, and Maisie distributed drinks, from wine to sparkling water. No-one would over-indulge. As they began settling around the table Kurt Groehling arrived, his colleagues roundly accusing him of abandoning his wife to 'the enemy,' He laughed.

'The ma-in-law is there, so Sandy told me to bugger off. And anyway, I've had police canteen food for days now, and Mick and Maisie run a bloody great restaurant!' Groehling, despite his non-existent body fat, was in fact an Olympic eater. He was rarely to be found without provisions in hand or nearby.

Brent interrupted proceedings at this point, to add Irfan Patel to their worryingly long list. This derailed the social air for a moment but then the team settled and spent a few minutes catching up. Steve Reith shared the details of

David Jerman's memorial service on the Monday. Fleur Cooper and Brent both asked if they could attend, along with Reith. Maisie too expressed her intention to come along, practicalities permitting. David Jerman had been the last casualty of their previous case.

Daisy wanted an update on Fleur's relationship with Peter Howard, the MI5 agent they'd also encountered on their last case. Reith, observing this interrogation, noted both Fleur's reluctance to talk or admit that it might be serious but also the sparkle in her eyes when she spoke of Peter. Reith, cynical after his own marriage battles, nevertheless still believed people could love and like each other for longer than the three years he'd managed. You only had to watch Mick and Maisie Brent if you doubted it.

The garlic bread demolished and everyone happily devouring the paella, Reith asked the team to run through their days, with the detail they needed but also adding any impressions, for Maisie's benefit. Apart from the married couple now included in their victim list, and the property purchase connection between Calum Grant and Lauren Greenwood, they hadn't a clue as to motive or perpetrator. Reith was keen to see if Maisie could help with this.

Once they'd performed as requested, Reith leant back in his chair.

'Not helping is it? Let's try a party game.' With the exception of Fletcher, who simply scowled, they all looked taken aback.' 'Do what?' queried Cervantes, before his brain and mouth connected.

'I want a sentence from each of you that tells me what you feel about you've seen or heard so far. It can be about one person, or the whole situation, one question or an observation. But write it down, so you don't infect first thoughts when you hear each other. We'll leave Maisie to last.'

'Huh,' came the response from Maisie. ' I suppose you want a rabbit out of a hat? No guarantees my friend, and you know it.'

Reith looked around the table. 'Don, you started us off, so you can do the same here. One sentence.'

Cervantes looked slightly hunted, but waded in. 'Edward Horbridge was a horrible man. Were they all unpleasant? And I know it's two sentences.' Reith nodded. 'Fleur?'

She grinned and said, 'Not a lot to say. I've been on admin virtually non-stop, to clear some space, so my sentence is short. None of them seemed short of money.'

Reith continued. 'Mick?'

'Calum Grant didn't do a nine to five job and his contact book is immense.' Reith looked momentarily at the ceiling. 'Daisy. I know you were with Mick, but what's your contribution?'

'From what people around the table are saying, Chloé Antoine and Caroline Horbridge are nice people in rotten marriages.' Reith turned to Groehling, who shrugged and said,

'I need to do a dumpster dive tomorrow because there's not enough detail on any of them yet, especially Irfan Patel, as well as the ones where we haven't even begun to interview.'

'Fair enough,' was Reith's response. 'Simon.' Reith had struggled manfully with this. He preferred Norman, but understood perfectly well why it was best not to use it tonight. It didn't seem to appease Fletcher though; from his expression he clearly though that employing his forename was too familiar.

'I don't think this is a game.' Reith said nothing, raised his eyebrow and gazed steadily at Fletcher

'Oh, all right. Apart from the dentist, and *they're* not usually poor, these all have money, nice cars, live in up-market areas and houses.'

To a man, everyone now turned towards Maisie, who made a joke of gulping nervously. They laughed, and a little of the tension left the air.

'Am I right in thinking that you want a direction?' Everyone nodded in agreement.

'Well, it's not so easy. We've got a bunch of potentially unpleasant people who've been bumped off, that's Possibility Number One. Possibility Number Two, they've all been involved in something, perhaps some sort of crime, that we don't know about yet. Number Three, they all knew something they shouldn't. It's endless. I've even found myself thinking about that old film, where two people meet on a train and kill each other's wives, to give themselves alibis.' Mick interrupted. 'Strangers on a Train.' Maisie carried on.

'But I think it's too early to even think about motive, reasons or whatever. It's connections you need. So I'm going to pick up on what a couple of you have said and sum it up in three words. Follow the money.'

Reith felt a moment of relief. He'd been edging that way, and it did need to be done. He trusted Maisie's instincts.

'OK. Agreed – happy with that Fleur?' 'Yes sir'.

The next few minutes were spent allocating interview schedules and digital dumpster diving for the next day, until Mick pulled the magnificently huge pudding from the oven. Maisie asked Fletcher to serve it up and the last twenty minutes of the long evening were spent discussing the best meals they'd ever had, Fletcher astonishing the meeting by saying, 'My partner does a very good upside-down cake now.' Groehling, astonished, said. 'Didn't know you were married mate.' 'Neither did I,' retorted

Fletcher. 'I'm not. He's my partner. I told him how good Mrs Brent's upside-down cake was and he tried it until he got it right.'

Brent had known Fletcher the longest and he'd never had a clue that there was a partner, or that Simon Fletcher was gay. Which, frankly, seemed like the very last word you'd use to describe Norman Stanley.

SIXTEEN

Dear Diary

I'm nine now. I didn't have a birthday party. My teacher got everyone to sing happy birthday. It was nice, sort of, but then the boys gave me the bumps and wanted to come to my party. And the girls just teased me when I said I wasn't having a party. I pretended I didn't care.

I do care. When I was littler I thought it was like this. But now I read books alot. And there are lots of different families. Some of them love their children. He says the library is all right. He likes books. He doesn't ever damage books, so they're safe. The library is my favourite place. When I started I had three cards, like tiny pockets, so I could only get three books. But that meant I had to go four or five times every week on the way home from school. Last month I asked if I could choose grown-up books because I'd read all the children's ones. So they said yes. But the library lady said she'd help me choose my first books. So she showed me Agatha Christie and Dorothy M Sayers. I love them. Lord Peter Wimsey cares about his family. Hercules Poirot doesn't have a family I don't think, but he still seems like he would care about people. Miss Marple is funny, like a rich version of my Granny. She notices things.

I've noticed a thing. If Granny and Grandad are coming to tea, or if we're going there, he doesn't shout at me or anything before. Once, Granny dropped in when we didn't know she was coming and he sent me upstairs. He told Granny I'd been bad, but I hadn't. But I did wonder if it was because he'd cut the head off my second-best cuddle toy. I usually hide them away but Buzzer got missed. I put both bits into my bed later but Mum threw him away. I cried alot that night. I need to keep Freddie really safe now.

This week was kind of great because the library lady said I could have eight tickets, to save me coming every day. Well, it's mostly great because I never have to worry that I've run out of books. But the library is nicer than our house. I've worked out if I go every three days and only change four books I always have at least four books ready.

I've got a baby brother now. They definitely love him. I don't think he'll be asking for it.

SEVENTEEN

By 7 am the next morning the core team had reassembled, with the exception of Fletcher. Simon Fletcher regarded office hours as the required norm and participated in overtime and extended hours only under direct instruction or if his curiosity was piqued. With the current murder hunt, even he didn't bother debating the issue, but he wouldn't appear until an hour he considered appropriate.

Reith, on a wet Sunday certain of at least an hour before any of the offices he still thought of as the 'High Heid Yins' were occupied, beckoned to his investigative colleagues and headed towards one of the glassed box meeting rooms. This area had all been part of the site refurbishment the previous year and there was still a residual smell of plastic, adhesive and something else which Groehling insisted was crushed custard creams. The upside was that the antiquated heating system had been replaced by more modern means and the initially cool meeting space was quickly at a workable temperature. The lighting was slightly more irritating, as it operated on movement sensors that seemed to have a very high threshold of detection. Every few minutes someone had to stand and wave their arms about to turn the lights back on.

Reith smiled wryly at them. 'I doubt we'll make it through today without the big wide world cottoning on. So we need to get ahead, somehow. Fleur – how do you want to tackle it?'

Fleur offered up a wry smile in recognition of the point. 'I've got digital dives requested on all the known victims, especially the newer ones – I've drafted the requirements for those and identified half a dozen people to get on with it – Daisy – that includes you, but I also want you to make a start on the paperwork that's come over from Edward Horbridge's house, so your to-do list is a bit shorter than the others. Get an admin person to help with that – I think you're going to need to inventory it, to get it to make sense. You're looking for connections, of course, but also a timeline, because that might give us a point of physical connection. Mick – can you do a few things? Get search warrants sorted for every home and every work address for all the victims. We might not need them – I'd like to start by asking if we can search with the owners' permissions, but let's be ready. And Mick – can you talk to Bordeaux about Chloé Antoine's alibi? I might be lying, but I've got an inkling that you've got some French? And also get on to the Solicitors' Regulation wotsit – Fletcher's right, they might know something. Course, it's Sunday, so we might be whistling down the wind.'

No-one mentioned that Fletcher could and should have done this himself.

Fleur took a breath and then continued. 'Kurt, can you start on the finances? We'll probably need warrants for those too, so put that in motion please. I think we've all got the feeling that Maze is right about money being an issue, somewhere in this mess. And can one of you start a hunt for Rose Horbridge, the daughter, please?

She turned to her left. 'Don. You've got Murthi arriving in a minute. Can you sort out the practical stuff first, get him the nick's welcome booklet to start with and make sure we all meet him. I'm still thinking that it's a good idea to pair you for the moment, get him up to speed?'

The welcome booklet was something that Fleur Cooper had quietly introduced the previous year, early in her posting to the station. She'd come across the same problem at every nick she'd ever visited, as well as virtually every office, shop and bar she'd worked in as a student. Newbies were treated kindly on day one and then ignored, to sink or swim. Sometimes they were offered a staff handbook, but as these were generally arse-covering documents, with every policy ever written, they were beyond useless to anyone except Fletcher. So she'd produced a three page leaflet, with irreverent cartoons as illustration, covering things like parking, loos, refreshment arrangements, staff events and how not to offend by nicking someone's treasured mug. Reith noted this, just as quietly, but had reported upstairs only recently that he thought it was the single best improvement they'd made to their induction practices.

Cervantes nodded. 'Apart from looking for Rose Horbridge, what do you want us doing Gov?'

'We've got a list of people we urgently need to speak with now. 'She counted off on her fingers as she named them. 'Family, friends and colleagues of…..Lauren Greenwood, and Ken Bell, Calum Grant, particularly colleagues – and his latest PA might be worth some time, if Chloé Antoine is right about that. Irfan Patel – we don't know anything about him yet, or this Gordon Szabo. I told Fletcher to start on Szabo and Bell yesterday, so Don, if you and Murthi kick off with Guildford and Basingstoke, because they're reasonably close to each other? You'll need to contact Surrey and Hampshire Police for permission, but you've liaised with other forces a few times now – you know the sensitivities. I'll get Fletcher to email you what he's got, so you'll have it well before you get there.' She considered. 'Up to you how you get there. Train might be better, but Sunday is when they prat about with the services. Traffic won't be so bad today, getting back in.'

Fleur stopped for another moment and looked down at her pad. 'I'm thinking that I want to get out and about today and start to get a feel for it all.' She looked at Reith and raised an eyebrow in query. He grinned at her.

'Too right Inspector. I need some fresh air too. So why don't you and I tackle Lauren Greenwood's office and then head for this Irfan Patel's premises, assuming we can get hold of anyone? I've told the switchboard to reroute any vital calls, but other than that they're to leave me alone.

Like me, everyone up there is waiting for the other shoe to drop and for the meeja to catch on. Being able to say they've got me out in the mix is, apparently, good PR.'

At that moment, a member of the overnight admin team tapped on the door and put her head into the room. 'Sorry all. There's a chap at Reception, name of Murthi. Says he's been told to report to you, Inspector.' Fleur Cooper looked at her watch and applauded Murthi's punctuality. A good start, at least.

'Don, off you go and get him started. I didn't think to tell his inspector yesterday to get him to wear civvies, so you might have to beg steal or borrow a jumper, or jacket or something.'

The meeting broke up, most heading off to their tasks, but with Groehling destined for the canteen, to chase up a couple of bacon rolls with his name on.

In Reception, Cervantes found Constable Murthi, in full uniform, reading the disparate array of posters on the board.

'Morning, Mate. You found us all right then?' Murthi smiled at the informal greeting and said, 'Couldn't sleep for excitement, so just got up and got on with it.' Although this was said with any nick's required level of irony, Cervantes recognised a like soul and responded to the enthusiasm. 'Well, I don't think you'll be disappointed. Mind, we're all a bit odd, but it works. And, course, we've got Reith and Cooper, the Dynamic Duo.' Murthi responded with another grin. 'Done my homework, me. You've got Mick Brent too, and the King of Computers, Kurt Groehling.' Like most people, Kurt's name was mangled in its pronunciation.

'True. And we've got Norman Fletcher, but I'll let you work that one out for yourself. Look, my Guvnor's sorry, but she forgot to tell yours that you'd be best in civvies. We'll need to find you a change of clothes.'

Murthi swung a backpack from behind his shoulder and said, 'I wasn't sure, so I've come prepared. I can change if there's somewhere half private.'

'I can do better than that. There's a locker for you and some paperwork for you to play with, including the Idiots' Guide to the Nick. Read that first, it's well helpful.' The two left the reception area and headed deeper into the station.

EIGHTEEN

Brent instigated the request for warrants and then made a to-do list. The 'phone call to the Solicitors' Regulation Authority was a priority, but there was no way he'd be able to sort that on a Sunday, so he made a note to get on to it first thing on Monday. He recognised that there'd likely be a need to make an appointment, so the sooner he got that sorted the better, and he had a feeling that they were based outside London, he thought Leeds or Birmingham.

He looked at his desk 'phone and hoped that his next would be a speedy and successful call; he wanted to get on to Bordeaux and he was aware that, at an hour ahead, he had an 11 am deadline. The chances of talking to the necessary folk over the French lunch hour weren't high, particularly on a Sunday.

He paused and leant back in his chair, marshalling his thoughts. It'd been a few months since he'd last used his French, and he also had to consider his approach. Was it better to talk direct to the company who'd interviewed Chloé Antoine, or to go through local official routes? Mick Brent was broadly aware of the differences between the French and the English police systems, so concluded that he'd better take the formal route, in case anything needed official follow-up, further down the line. He thought a little longer, reviewing vocabulary, then began what he knew could be a tortuous journey of explanation and call transfers.

Brent reckoned he needed to speak to a prosecutor – the name given to members of the French judiciary who led on criminal investigation. So, once he was in friendly conversation with a switchboard operator pleased to be brightening her day by denying that she understood anything Brent was saying, he calmly repeated, four or five times, his need to talk to a prosecutor with experience in leading murder hunts. Once she'd enjoyed her minor victory, the telephonist then settled in to discuss – perfectly understanding him - the weather, both French and English, the last time Brent had visited France and where, and whether he had any favourite French meals. They confirmed the general idiocy of politicians, whatever their nationality and then rounded up the debate on the endlessly delicious topic of whether it should be brandy or whisky. This resolved, she then happily connected him with Monsieur Le Procurateur, JP Marchand, stressing how lucky Brent was to find him available and how she was sure that the English police were not so meticulous.

Brent steeled himself to explain the whole tale and, after the appropriate renditions of 'Bonjour' and associated enquiries after health and busy-ness at work, made a passable fist of it. He knew his ability to use the correct participles was limited, but his vocabulary was surprisingly broad, and Monsieur Marchand had little difficulty in grasping the request. He told Brent that everyone called him JP and, unusually for a Frenchman, insisted that Mick do so too. Without being asked, JP offered to visit the company himself and then the hotel where Chloé had stayed overnight, and thereafter to report back. Both men understood that ruling her out of enquiries was important and relatively urgent.

As is the way of all sensible professionals, the two men also checked each other's career credentials, found two colleagues that they both knew and then moved into the recreation arena, with each delighted to discover a mutual love of rugby. This occupied a few minutes, and they then ended the call, Mick Brent being reasonably sure that he'd made a good contact and not offended his foreign counterpart. In Bordeaux, JP was happily recounting the bits of inaccurate French he'd been offered and telling his colleagues that Brent was a man he'd like to meet. Job done.

Mick Brent checked his list and decided that a trip to the Blooming Wonderful Garden Centre would be in order. Although there were no strict protocols in place within the team, it was generally recognised that it worked well if someone followed a trail as far as they could. Brent had spoken with Calum Grant's widow on the day before. Now he wanted to see the location of his demise. He wouldn't take Daisy on this errand; he was conscious of her needing to get into the papers from Edward Horbridge.

As he headed down the back stairs to the rear car park, he was stopped by Cervantes and his new partner-in-crime.

'Sarge, this is Ajay Murthi, from the Transport Police. Ajay, this is Sergeant Mick Brent.' Murthi smiled in genuine pleasure.

'I've heard a lot about you Sarge. It's a privilege to meet you.'

Brent looked at him, taken aback, and Murthi explained. 'I thought I'd got lumbered with a bloody stupid inter-agency thing, health, us, you, schools and that. But it turned out you'd been on it and got them sorted into something dead useful. Games of Groans they call it, but it's actually doing some really good work at grass roots. We've all got ourselves into teams, so if I need something from the education lot, I ring Tahira, who's a Deputy Head in a big high school. She uses her nous to find what I need and get back to me, and so on, round the group. They said you'd suggested it, and it really cuts out the bureaucracy. Saves time and we're all beginning to realise that we're not as frustrated as we used to be, because now we're dealing with people we know, not just another bloody office.

Mick Brent smiled in genuine pleasure and said 'I'm glad it's working out. Just brace yourself - they'll try and formalise it all next and screw it up. Now, look, I've got to get over to Chelsea, so excuse me if I cut and run.'

Don and Ajay continued up to the CID floor and Don sorted desk room for their temporary colleague. As they worked their way through the large outer room their progress across the space, courtesy of the weekend, was slightly less hindered by bags, coats and endless boxes of paperwork than normal. Don introduced Ajay to Kurt Groehling – kindly and teasing, Daisy Jones – warm and offering help if needed, and Simon Fletcher, now at his desk, who managed a curt greeting tied to a warning never to touch anything in his work space. 'If you've got something to give me, put it in *this* tray, nowhere else. Do you understand?' With a straight face, Ajay acknowledged the instruction, careful not to meet Don's eye.

Once Ajay had deposited his meagre selection of stationery items on his new desk, Don took him through the sergeants' area and into Fleur Cooper's office. Her door stood open, and she was obviously making preparations to leave. She shook hands with the Transport officer and then took him through his paces – previous projects, cases, on-the-job training. She'd trust Cervantes to report back if there were any problems, but she wanted to test whether he was a reject from his team or a star in waiting, being given some additional experience by his managers. She, like Cervantes, recognised all the signs of genuine engagement and hoped this would prove to be supported by intelligence.

As the two were turning to leave, their exit was blocked by the arrival of Steve Reith, coming to collect Cooper for their external tasks. Fleur smiled to herself as the politician in Reith took over. He greeted Murthi with warmth, commented positively on a couple of his workmates and then complimented him on his work in the 'Game of Groans.' Murthi, astonished by this evidence of omniscience, stuttered a grateful response. Fleur knew that Reith's ability to recall virtually every word of the briefing documents he read bordered on the eidetic. It often served him well, and here he was, winning another bloody 'Reith Recruit.'

NINETEEN

Dear Diary

We went on a class trip today, to a castle. It was amazing. We didn't have to pay or anything and there were picnic bags from school, with sandwiches and an apple and a Wagon Wheel! There was a teacher who showed us round. Our class teacher said her proper name was Guide, but she wasn't wearing a uniform, like the Girl Guides and the Brownies. I think this must be something different. Anyway, it was amazing. This Guide lady took us through all the rooms and told us stories. Even the boys were good, it was like a book coming to life. I loved the dining room. It was really pretty. There were two tables set up. The Guide said it was like they would have been then. One was from something called the Middle Ages. I haven't worked out what that means yet. But the table was very big and thick, and there were metal glasses and big round metal plates. The Guide said that the most important people sat at the top of the table and the pheasants sat at the bottom and got leftovers.

The other table was my favourite. The Guide lady said it was from the Regency period, when the castle got a lot of new building going on. She said a new word that I want to look up in the dictionary in my classroom. Renovation. I'm guessing the spelling. But the table was lovely. There were pretty china plates and lots of different glasses and beautiful silver cutlery. There were flowers down the middle and big things full of candles. This was because they hadn't invented electricity yet. I really liked them, that was a new word too. It's a candelabrah, I think. That's another guess.

TWENTY

Cooper smiled happily as she got into the driver's seat of the unmarked police car and put the address of Lauren Greenwood's employers into the satnav. She was an able and motivated investigator but, like every police officer in the land, and particularly those of rank, she was almost drowned by the deluge of paper and administration. Getting out and about, particularly with her impressive boss, was a real pleasure. She'd been nervous around him to begin with, but after their first, very tense investigation together, and then during the subsequent months, she'd been delighted to realise that they were not only becoming mutually respectful colleagues, but also friends. A private person by nature, Reith's broader enthusiasm for the world had simply ignored this and railroaded her into becoming more open and conversational with him.

Reith was just as pleased. He didn't regret his seniority; indeed he planned to advance further because he liked being able to improve the system, up and down the food chain. But he did resent the externally imposed endless counting and reporting and thoroughly despised the politics, internal and external. His people skills actually made him rather good at this and his ability to calmly manipulate if he deemed it necessary made him a dangerous foe. He didn't bear grudges and he didn't mind mistakes, as long as lessons were learned. But he never forgot treachery or back-stabbing and a small number of theoretically promising careers had been curtailed when he recognised those traits in his junior officers. Of course, he couldn't do anything long-term about the officers above him who displayed the same tendencies...

So, all in all, they were both glad to be 'out to play', as Reith called it. Cooper reversed neatly out of the cramped space and they set forth for Kensington. Reith recounted all that he'd remembered from the briefing, Cooper filling in any missing detail. They were both keen to start putting characters to names and so they were in buoyant mood as they walked up the broad, shallow steps of the large Georgian building that housed the law practice. Cooper had pulled a blinder, identifying the law practice's Managing Partner and tracking him down. The man had shown significant willingness to forsake his hearth and home on a wet and cold weekend and invited them to 'Come on over to the offices' as soon as they could make it.

As they entered the reception area they were greeted by a young woman in casual clothes and then ushered into a functional but beautifully proportioned meeting room. Coffee and biscuits sat on a wooden tray on the table.

The presumed receptionist said, 'I'm Nathalie. I'll let Mr Griffiths know you're here – he'll be right through'. She turned back to them. 'Jim rang and asked me to come in as a favour, in case you need anything copied or, or whatever….' Reith and Cooper nodded in unison, acknowledging the kindness, with Reith quickly turning his attention to the refreshments tray.

'I love a good law firm. These are either M and S or Waitrose biscuits.' He demolished three in quick order and then desisted as a man they assumed was Griffiths appeared in the doorway. He greeted both of them with 'Jim Griffiths, Managing Partner', poured himself a coffee and sat opposite them at the other side of the meeting table. He'd appeared with a large folder tucked under his arm and this he now placed in front of him. He looked enquiringly at the two officers, who introduced themselves, starting with their ranks. This obviously struck a chord with Griffiths.

'Good, that's a relief. I didn't really want to talk about this with junior officers, because it's all sub judice. We hadn't even alerted Lauren to our concerns.' His pronunciation of the name seemed forced, and he continued. 'Greenwood. Lauren Greenwood.' To Reith and Cooper it was apparent that Griffiths had already made a journey with regard to Lauren Greenwood. She was no longer a colleague, but rather a case to be handled.

Reith nodded at Fleur Cooper and she took up the thread.

'Mr Griffiths, we're really grateful to you for finding the time to meet with us. We couldn't say a lot on the 'phone and I'm going to ask you to consider what we're going to tell you as highly confidential. It's vital that we keep a grip on this as long as possible.

He looked surprised and slightly alarmed, but nodded his acquiescence. Fleur continued.

'Over the past few days, six people have died in both suspicious and similar circumstances. Lauren Greenwood was one of them. At the moment we have little to connect the victims and we're hoping you can help us with that.'

Jim Griffiths, consummate solicitor that he was, presented a stoic expression, but there was no doubt that he'd been shocked.

'Six? Good God! And you think I, we, will know them?'

'Honestly, we've no idea. And again, I'd ask you to consider these names as confidential.' She referred to her notebook. 'The first one we think is likely to be familiar – Kendell Bell?'

Griffiths tipped his head in acknowledgement and said, 'Her husband.' He looked at them both in turn. 'I think I need to loosen up a bit in this discussion. It's not going to help you if I think and behave like a solicitor. Though,' he added, with a wry smile, 'My missus would say you can take the man out of the law, but you'll never get the law out of the man. I suppose that's true.' He paused again, obviously considering his approach. 'No, I think I need to talk to you man to man, so to speak.' He smiled apologetically at Cooper and took a breath. 'Kendell Bell was a total knob. Unpleasant, bullying, full of himself. He used us for a while for his company work, but after he'd reduced seven different staff here to either tears or utter fury, I advised him to use a company closer to his business premises – that'd be about six years ago. Does that help?'

Reith responded. 'It certainly does. A professional perspective, eloquently and honestly expressed is a marvellous, unusual thing for us.' Jim Griffiths clearly valued the comment.

'OK then. So I'd have to be equally honest and say that I've, we've, come to realise that Lauren was far worse than her husband. Different methods, but just as poisonous. So what do you want to do first? Hear about Lauren Greenwood or go through your names?'

Reith let Cooper call it. She said, 'I think the names, because then if any of them are involved in what you have to say about Ms Greenwood, it'll save time and explanation.' She looked at Griffiths for agreement and then proceeded, 'Gordon Szabo.' She spelled the last name.

Griffiths thought for a moment and then said 'Do you mind if we move into my office? I can access the system then, and check. It'll save me having to talk to key staff to find out, and it'll be quicker for you. Grab your coffees and follow me. He scooped up his file and cup and headed out of the room, the officers following, Reith casting a regretful parting glance at the lemon and sultana shortbread biscuits.

In Griffiths' office, a large room equipped with both upright and more relaxed seating, the legal man shepherded them to a small round table in the corner of the room. He moved a couple of box files away from the table, then collected a laptop from his desk.

'I'm already connected to our intranet on here, so let's start looking. The name Szabo did sound a bit familiar, but he's not one of mine.' He tapped at the keys for a moment. 'Yes, he's here. He first bought a property through us in Guildford, three years ago. We, Lauren, handled the purchase. That's odd, to be honest. We're far more expensive than a Guildford practice would be. Since then we seem to have acted on four, no five, further properties, all around London….interesting…they're all two way – purchase, and then later sales, except for the Guildford one. So there should be some paperwork and notes, and maybe one of the paralegals will be able to help. Sticking with my honesty policy, I'd have to tell you, our paralegals took it in turn to work with Lauren, on sufferance. It's part of what I want to tell you about, so let's park that for now. So, next name?'

'Well, Kendell Bell? Did your company still act for him?' Griffiths started to shake his head, but clearly in sorrow, rather than denial.

'We could have done, perfectly acceptably, as long as Lauren wasn't involved. But that's one of the things that I want to talk about. We've discovered that she handled over a dozen properties for him, after he'd theoretically moved to another practice. She seems to have done all the work herself, but never billed for it. We picked it up when our administrator was reconciling deed and registry searches, which Lauren Greenwood couldn't do herself. We didn't twig on until very recently. We certainly knew him and, as I said, kicked the nasty little sod into touch, but none of us realised he was married to Lauren. But more on that later. Next?'

Fleur Cooper glanced at her list. 'Edward Horbridge?'

Griffiths bent over his laptop once more. He ran his eye down the screen, obviously counting. 'Twenty two properties, all bar one purchased and sold.' He looked enquiringly at Fleur Cooper, expecting the next name. Earliest one, just over four years ago, latest, about six weeks ago, a sale.' He looked up at them. 'Lauren Greenwood.'

'Calum Grant? We know she handled the purchase of his apartment.' Having Googled the area's property prices, Cooper was unable to think of Calum Grant and Chloé Antoine's home as a flat. Griffiths returned to his laptop. 'Same story…..eight, ten, twelve….fifteen properties, over the past five years. All sold except three – one in Fulham, and two in Islington. Also four NDAs – sorry, Non-Disclosure Orders. I'll have to look at those. Obviously they're confidential, and I'll need a warrant to let you see them.' He considered. 'If it's any help, I'll have a quick look and tell you if I think it's germane to the enquiry, if you promise not to drop me in it?'

Reith was warming to the man behind the solicitor's façade. He appreciated the obvious willingness to be as open as possible. Fleur picked up her list and continued.

'Irfan Patel. I'm afraid we know very little about him at the moment – we're still researching.'

After a pause during which he tapped and scrolled, Griffiths nodded. 'I'm horrified to tell you that's a yes as well. More recent, just in the last eight months, but already five property purchases, four sales and the last one pending. They're all in Newham. Oh, dear Lord, what has she got us into?' He regarded the two police officers with a level but concerned gaze. 'You have to know what I'm thinking?'

There was a moment of silence as each of them considered their individual and corporate perspectives.

TWENTY ONE

Reith and Cooper both nodded and replied in chorus. 'Money laundering.' He bowed his head in sorrowful acquiescence. 'Shit, shit and double shit. How on earth did we miss it?' Reith, only too conscious of the quagmire the law firm now faced said, 'The thing is, when someone is determined to do wrong, they only have to work out how to get round the difficulties. It's usually a short journey. The good guys, on the other hand, have to work out what the bad guys *might* do, and install barriers. That's complicated and requires so many "what ifs" that it's inevitable the safeguards can be circumvented.'

Jim Griffiths acknowledged the point, but it clearly did nothing to relieve his ever-increasing anxiety. 'Right, let's get the pain over with. You said six people, so is that all of them?'

Reith responded this time. 'Yes. So I think that's it from us. But you've got a file there that I think you wanted to discuss?'

Jim Griffiths bent his head in assent. 'I do. I've been trying to work out how to handle this for the past week, and attempting to put it into words. I've got an appointment at our Regulation Body, later this week, so I knew it had to come to a head. But everything that you've just told me and that we've discovered together now, puts it into even starker focus. So here goes….I think Lauren Greenwood was operating an illegal deposit account. I say illegal, because we think she's been putting client deposits in there, instead of into our properly sanctioned one. There's a lot of work to do, and it's going to need to be a financial specialist, because we don't have access to this account, so we can't join the dots.' He sighed. 'If they, the Regulators and, I suppose, even you chaps, think we were in any way complicit with this, all of our work over the past thirty years will go up in smoke. To say nothing of the number of claims of malpractice we'll get if people get wind of the affair.

'Earlier, I said I'd come back to some personnel issues, HR matters. Ever since she started here, the admin staff have hated working with Lauren, but none of them ever wanted to make a formal complaint, so we just worked out a sort of rota, so that no-one had to put up with it full-time. I did try to talk to Lauren about it, but she just said she'd wait to hear the evidence in a formal complaint. God knows, now I wish I'd just booted her – an unfair dismissal case would have been a lot cheaper than what we're facing now.

'Then there's Ken Bell. This was just a fluke. We obviously knew that they knew each other, because she'd acted for the sales and purchases when he was legitimately a client and, as I've said, the additional ones we've now discovered after we thought we'd sent him elsewhere. But on Monday last week my wife went to some house investment event, somewhere near Russell Square. Our twins have been at university for a term now, and she's got an idea about property renovation to get herself busy again. Anyway, this event was being fronted by Ken Bell. My wife, Kim, didn't know him, but over coffee, someone asked Ken Bell about his wife, and her name came out in the general chit chat. Kim knew I'd be interested, though she'd no idea what a can of worms we were already in.

'And add to this something else that I only found out on Wednesday. I announced Lauren Greenwood's death to the team and one of our paralegals came to see me later in the day. To cut a long story short, she says Lauren Greenwood was blackmailing her. And she thought that she could identify some others here who were being extorted too. You've met her – Nathalie – I asked her to come in today, partly for admin support, but mostly because I thought it might save you time, if you want to talk with her. She's keen to do it – I haven't encouraged her, or anything.' He stopped, and leaned back on his chair, tipping the front legs off the floor.

'So. The die is cast, as they say.'

The two police officer looked at each other and then at Jim Griffiths. Reith spoke first. 'I'll tell you this, people in your situation can end up feeling grubby, because of what trusted colleagues did. Steel yourself to ignore that because you have two key jobs now.' Griffiths raised an enquiring face.

'First, you need to give us as much assistance as you possibly can. Not only will that really help us, which might speed us to a quicker result, but it'll also stand you in good stead in all of the fallout. I'm sorry I can't do anything about that. And the other thing,' he paused, 'well, you'll say it's none of my business, but whatever. Learn from this. Change things.'

Jim Griffiths straightened in his chair. I've got a good mate who works in this area, I'll get on to him so that we can get ahead of the mess. Meanwhile, do you want a word with Nathalie?'

Fleur Cooper responded. 'Yes please, if you don't mind. We'll be careful – she might feel she needs a solicitor in case she incriminates herself. It's not our job to help her do that.'

Within a couple of minutes they were back in the meeting room, with Nathalie closing the door before coming to sit quietly across the table from them. She looked nervous but resolute, and spoke before either of them had the chance to greet her or lighten the atmosphere.

'I don't want a solicitor. I haven't done anything criminal. I've just been thinking about it all for so long.' She stopped, obviously unsure how to proceed.

Fleur chipped in. 'Look, we know it can be difficult to sum things up, so two things. Try telling it like a story, how it started, what happened next, and so on. And the other thing is, we're not really here to judge you, unless you've robbed a bank! This is going to be upsetting enough so don't add feeling ashamed to the mix – I guarantee you – we've heard it all before.'

Nathalie clearly appreciated this and just said 'Thank you.' She paused for a few more seconds during which moments both Reith and Cooper were able to note both her attractiveness and her current reticence.

She said, 'Right. From the beginning....it was just before Christmas two years ago. I'd got engaged, to Chris; he's a solicitor, works at a big practice in Leeds. It's hard, we're both busy, and we have to really try to get together at weekends and holidays and things, you know. One of the reasons I'm busy is I'm doing a course to move from paralegal to qualified solicitor. It's all part-time, and there are plenty of weekend sessions.' She took a deep breath.

'Anyway, Chris and I had a bit of a row, about not seeing each other properly and we got really mad at each other, you know. It's a pig, having an argument on the phone, and he hung up on me. I was so angry. And the next day, the weekend, I was at a course in Basingstoke – that was part of the row, you know, me and the course. Even though Chris absolutely gets it. But that weekend, I didn't really feel that, and I was still so furious, you know. And there was this guy on my course, Ben, he'd been flirting for months, but it was all just a joke, you know? But that weekend, I had too much to drink after the sessions were finished and well, I know it shouldn't have been inevitable, but it sort of was, you know.

'But then, on the Monday, Lauren sent for me. All the other solicitors come and find someone if they need to, but not Lauren. She'd either bellow if she thought you were nearby, or she'd ring Reception to find us and send us in to her. I didn't for one minute see what was coming, you know. She told me to sit down. She gave me a box of tissues and then she said we needed to talk about Chris. I didn't even think it through, I thought she was telling me something had happened to him, you know. But she just said that nothing had happened to him. Yet. And when I looked at her, she asked me if I'd enjoyed my weekend. So of course, I knew she knew. And she explained that I could save Chris from being hurt if I helped her a bit. I was so panicked that all I said was 'How?''

Reith, grinding his teeth, first at the frequency of 'you knows', but mostly at the wickedness of Lauren Greenwood and the idiocy of Nathalie, just said, 'What did she want?'

Nathalie took a tissue from her pocket and blew her nose. She didn't look quite as pretty at the moment, with a pinched, pale face. 'Admin work, in my own time. Mostly property stuff. I checked a couple of times on the system, and it was always for clients, so I couldn't think why she wanted me to work on them – any of the property paralegals could do it in normal hours.'

Fleur interrupted. 'Those clients were probably never billed.' Nathalie looked relieved, but then the possible implications began to dawn. 'Oh, but that means...oh God.'

Reith asked, 'Did you never think of telling anyone? Getting out of the mess? You said you were already busy before this, so all the extra work couldn't have helped?'

Nathalie sniffed loudly. 'No, it didn't. To start with I only thought about keeping it from Chris. I knew he'd break it off if he found out, so I just carried on, somehow, you know. But then, ten days ago I got the results and found out that I'd failed one of my law modules and it all came to a head with Chris. He couldn't understand how I'd failed, and it turned into, not a fight exactly, but a heated discussion about me letting us down, that all the time apart was only worth it if it gave us a chance up ahead, you know. And I'd had enough, so I just told him. I said if I hadn't felt so unhappy that night, it would never have happened. And he said I obviously didn't trust him enough if I felt it was OK to shag someone else, just because we'd had an argument. But I didn't tell him about Lauren, you know? I knew he'd want to take it further and I needed to think about that. We didn't see each other last weekend, and then on Wednesday, we found out here about Lauren. So I told Jim. Not the details, just that it had happened. He was lovely, asked if I needed a good solicitor, if I'd done something illegal. I didn't think I had, though now...I don't know. I'll have to talk about it with Jim, in detail now. But then this morning Jim rang to tell me that you were coming here, and suggesting that I might want to come and talk to you. So, there it is. Classic stupid. You know.'

Reith, policeman that he was, couldn't disagree. 'You should have told someone, got help.' She nodded.

'I know. I rang Chris as I was on my way here, and told him everything I hadn't before. He's on his way down from Leeds now.' She smiled, wryly, 'Now he's so cross at someone else that he's put my mistake in another box. Who knows what'll happen next...' She trailed off. Fleur picked up the thread.

'Mr Griffiths thought that you knew of other people here, where Lauren was doing some iffy stuff?'

'Yes. Once you're in a shitty place, you sort of notice other people doing similar things, you know? Working later than usual, being given stuff by Lauren at the end of the day, edginess, stuff like that.'

Fleur queried. 'Did you talk to any of them?'

'No. I wanted to be wrong, and I certainly didn't want to be embarrassed any more than I already was.'

Fleur carried on. 'The thing is, we need to know now. It might have bearing on our investigation.'

Nathalie nodded. 'I know. But is it OK if I speak to them myself tomorrow, get them to talk to you? I've only got suspicions and I sort of feel it'd be wrong to act for them, you know?

Reith nodded, but said. 'We do get that, so OK, but you need to understand that we're going to be interviewing everyone here who had anything to do with Lauren Greenwood. So you're going to have to be very clear with your colleagues that it will come out, one way or another. Better if they volunteer.'

Fleur explained to Nathalie that it would now be necessary to take an official statement and that an officer would be in touch. Clearly relieved to have unburdened herself, she agreed to this and offered to let them know how she got on the following morning. Fleur gave her a business card and thanked her in advance.

As they headed towards the exit, they were slightly startled to hear Jim Griffiths calling them from another door on the ground floor. He stepped just outside the room and said,

'OK. I said I'd look at those Non-Disclosure Agreements for Calum Ross. I can't give you any details, but if I said four secretaries who left the company, would that give you any clues?'

Reith and Copper looked at each other and then back at Jim Griffiths. Reith responded.

'It certainly would – that's immensely helpful.' He hesitated. 'Am I right in thinking that an NDA effectively dies with the people concerned?'

Griffiths smiled slightly. 'In principle, yes. NDA's are personal documents. In certain cases I think you'll find that the people concerned might be willing to talk. If you get my drift?' They smiled in return and made their goodbyes, thanking him for his help.

Once Reith and Cooper were a good thirty steps from the front of the building, he said. 'You know, I really couldn't take, you know, much more of that, you know?' Cooper laughed out loud. 'Oh my days! I'd started to count them. Please God, someone will tell her soon. But very useful to get Chloe Antoine's suspicions almost confirmed. We can talk to the PA's now and get more detail.'

'Right,' said Reith. 'Over to Paddington. Let's see what we can find out about our Mr Patel.'

This was easier said than done. On arrival at his home address, a tall, narrow terraced house with a neat garden to the front, they found a large gathering spilling out of the house. Both officers recognised a traditional family and friends' response to a tragedy. On enquiring after nearest relatives, they were introduced to Irfan Patel's wife, Rusia, and his son, who introduced himself as Al. Clearly Westernised but with a protective eye to his mother, Al professed absolutely no knowledge of his father's property development activities. It was obvious that Rusia was about to protest at this, but was shushed by her son. Surrounded as they were by a throng of interested bystanders, all ready to witness police brutality, the two officers simply passed on their regrets for their loss and told them that they'd be asked to make formal statements in the next day or two. It was clearly going to be more productive if they shifted the venue to a local nick.

TWENTY TWO

Dear Diary

We had to write a story about our trip to the castle for our homework. Our teacher marked them while we were doing silent reading. She read us bits from different ones. When she got to mine she read a few bits and then she said she would give 10 pence to anyone who she thought had written a better one.

That was amazing. She thought my work was good. She gave the 10 pee to Katy, because she'd written about the castle mint and I hadn't.

I didn't care. She said mine was good.

All day that felt like a hug from Granny.

TWENTY THREE

Sunday trailed onwards through the misty, cold dampness of a cheerless January day.

Reith returned to his office and worked his way through a pile of memos and email updates. He noticed in passing a short note about a potential bird-flu type issue in China, but that wasn't anything unusual for the time of year.

Fleur Cooper made the rounds of the team members she considered to have key tasks in hand. Brent she couldn't find, but when chatting with Daisy, now elbows deep in sorting Edward Horbridge's paperwork, she learned that he'd headed off to a garden centre in Chelsea. Daisy herself was rather upbeat.

'Actually Gov, Mr Horbridge might have been a nasty twonk, but his filing system is a dream. It'll only take me another hour or so to create an overview and identify the really relevant stuff.' She paused and then grinned. 'But it's quite tempting to get lost in other things, because I have *never* read such incredibly rude complaint letters. They're really entertaining because it's almost impossible to believe that someone actually wrote them!'

Fleur then made her way back into the sergeants' lair, finding Kurt Groehling in his corner empire, both computer monitors alive with data. Kurt seemed to be creating a database on one screen. Fleur looked at him with a raised eyebrow, enquiring.

'What time is it Gov?' He peered at the bottom right corner of one of his screens. Fleur glanced at her wrist – one of only a few people in the nick who still used a watch rather than a mobile. 'Just gone one.' Kurt nodded. 'I thought I was hungry, definitely my lunch time, but I wanted to get the skeleton of this built up. Listening to Maze last night, then picking up on what you and the Super got this morning, I've logged on to the Land Registry.' Like many forces, the Met paid subscriptions to access external information. 'Every one of our victims has been buying and selling property. Some for quite a few years, others more recently. I've started plotting in the amounts involved and I don't want to worry you but we're talking many, many millions.'

Fleur grimaced. Kurt was capable of great exactitude. When he used looser expressions like this, it meant he was concerned.

Cooper nodded. 'Make sure you log your progress so far, so the rest of the team can see it.' She was just turning away when Kurt said,

'I'm getting info in from the digital research into the other victims. Do you want that now, or later on, at wash-up?'

Cooper considered this. 'Is there anything that needs immediate action?'

'No, not really. Just general stuff.'

'Right, at wash-up then. I'm setting that for 4 o'clock, so we can try for some sort of evening. The babies might not be back, but we can always ring them if necessary.'

Both she and Groehling knew that Fleur meant Don and Ajay. Don would have been mildly peeved to hear this. He'd been hoping that Ajay's temporary attachment might have promoted his own status away from the newbie category.

Fleur's next call was a quick text to that very man, Cervantes, who reported that they were now in Guildford and about to make their second visit. She headed for Reith's office, partly because she wanted to share her findings but mostly because, in his PA's area, he had a rather lovely coffee machine which he didn't mind sharing on a quiet day. She chose the stairs, conscious as ever that her exercise routine would yet again be dictated by her caseload.

TWENTY FOUR

Dear Diary

It's quite exciting. I've only been at this school for a few months but we're getting ready to go up to big school and it's different here to my last school. Here there's something called a two tear system and you can take a test to see where you can go. There's something called a Comprehensive and something else called a Grammar. The test is called an Eleven Plus.

Some of us got a letter to take home. I thought I might be in trouble again, but I'm not. Apparently he went to the Grammar too and he's pleased I might be going. But I am a bit afraid now in case I don't pass the Eleven Plus. Apparently the Comprehensive is for ignorant losers.

TWENTY FIVE

Cervantes and Murthi had taken the decision to drive to Basingstoke and Guildford. It hadn't taken long for Murthi to use his system access to identify the reduced relevant services on a Sunday so, much as Don in particular enjoyed a train journey, they agreed to use Don's beloved Mini Cooper soft top. He rarely used it for work, recognising its potential for criminal targeting but on this occasion, if time got away with them, it would be easier at the end of the day to drop off Ajay before himself heading home, obviating the need to return to base to swap a pool car for his own.

The traffic out of town had been fairly painless and they'd made good time to Old Basing, which appeared to be a rather lovely village adjacent to the newer town. Neither knew Basingstoke, though Ajay had heard it called 'doughnut city', because of its many roundabouts. They'd barely touched the town itself, Old Basing being to the north east.

Their target address was a quite stunning double fronted house in warm brick, though as the two men walked towards it, both found themselves thinking of the same thing. Murthi said,

'No-one cares about this house.' Cervantes nodded, and the two of them stood for a moment and surveyed the evidence. Rotten window frames, dirty glass, peeling paint on what could be a magnificent front door, an overgrown garden. Even the two police officers, neither of whom knew a bean sprout about gardening, could see it had once been a beautiful space, left to ruin.

Don sighed and said,

'Well, we'll never own anything like this, unless the six numbers come up…..anyway, let's see if there's any sign of life and then try the neighbours.'

Despite some vigorous bell pushing and knocking, no-one presented themselves. The two made a circuit around the property, at the rear of the house finding themselves in a space that, neglected as it was, still lifted the heart, even on this drizzly day.

Back outside the front drive they looked in both directions, debating which way to go first. The house to the left was the closest, although still a good three hundred metres away. Leaving their car in Ken Bell's drive, Don and Ajay walked towards this property and turned into its open drive. Ahead of them stood another attractive house, in what would be described as the Regency style, four tall windows on the ground floor, in the middle of which stood a porticoed door. Two storeys above that, with the same number of windows, slightly diminished in size on the top floor. But this house was clearly loved and cherished and it gleamed in its setting amongst borders of evergreen plants, with trees further away from the house, marking the boundary.

Ajay looked to his right, back towards the Ken Bell house and was gratified to see that the treeline didn't completely mask the building.

As they walked down the drive and stepped past a large bed of tall shrubs, a building appeared to their left, set back against a fence. It was a double garage, with what appeared to be a workshop space to one side. In here was a man holding a screwdriver and what seemed to be an instruction sheet. On the floor a large carboard carton and on a bench sat a pile of pieces. Both men recognised the Swedish company's logo and both, without recognising it, felt relief that someone who lived in a house like this still did normal things. Cervantes coughed, and the man looked up, put down the tool and paper and stepped towards them.

'Hello. Can I help you?' All the polite caution of a middle England property owner defending his territory.
The two formally introduced themselves and were told in return that their host was Steve Rodney. In what they judged to be his early sixties; he was a tall, good-looking man with an impressive head of white hair. Having learnt their identities, he tilted his head in question. Don responded.

'We're here about your neighbour, Mr Kendell Bell. Would you be able to spare us a few minutes?'

A shadow passed over his face, but he nodded and said, 'Look, come into the house. My wife's off at the hospital – first grandchild due any minute.' He grinned, 'That's why I'm trying to build a crib – we're going to be looking after the baby for two days each week, while our daughter goes back to work. Not for a couple of months though...which is just as well because it'll take me that long to work out the bloody instructions!'

As he said this he ushered them into the front of the house and then through an overdressed hall into a large and airy kitchen diner, part of which was obviously an extension. He headed straight for a coffee machine and opened the drawer beneath the work surface, displaying a neat array of different coffee pods, signalling them to make their choice. They did so, complimenting him on the house and the coffee machine as he worked, neither of them keen to start their real conversation until they had his full attention.

Despite a choice of available seating – a dining table and chairs at one side of the room and two wing-backed chairs and a sofa in an alcove overlooking the garden, the three men leant against the worktops and sipped their drinks.

'So, what has our Mr Bell been up to?' This was said with an air of exasperation and resignation that both officers recognised. Good, Steve Rodney might be able to shed light on something or other. Don started,

'Mr Rodney, we're…'

Steve Rodney cut him off. 'Rod – no-one ever called me Steve and now I'm retired there's no need for the Mister anymore.' Cervantes nodded.

'Okay. Thank you. Rod. First, we're sorry to tell you that Mr Bell died, in London, a couple of days ago.'

Rod raised an eyebrow. 'Not going to pretend I'm anything but relieved. None of us knew what to do about the horrible bastard. Problem solved. Except, I suppose I hope no-one else was involved, got hurt or whatever?' The two men removed this concern in swift order. Ajay took up the thread this time.

'Horrible bastard? How did that manifest itself?' Cervantes smiled to himself. Plenty of coppers 'talked down' their intelligence, reducing vocabulary. He was never sure if that was to reach the lowest common denominator in the nick, or to fool their clientele into under-estimation. Either way, Cervantes liked a good turn of phrase and didn't belong to that particular club. He was pleased to see that Murthi didn't seem to either.

Rod regarded them in silence for a moment, obviously marshalling his thoughts.

'Well, it's just a long line of irritations really, right from the start. Stupid things, annoying things, rudeness.'

It was the officers' turn to offer a quizzical tilt of the head.

'Look, shall I just start at the beginning and give you examples?' They nodded.

'Right, well, when he moved in we both walked over, me and Claire, my wife. We took a little hamper of stuff Claire had put together, some wine, some cheese, crackers, nibbles, that sort of thing. Well, he came to the door in his underpants – two o'clock in the afternoon it was – didn't ask us in, thank God. We introduced ourselves and it was really obvious he wasn't listening. He took the hamper, ripped the cellophane off the top, took the wine out and gave the hamper to Claire. 'Waste not, want not,' he said and then 'See you around.' And he shut the door. The outrage was mild but still apparent. He continued.

'The neighbours on the other side, Lewis and Roger, they got much the same thing when they went to say hello, but this time he said something about them being gay. Fairies, or something dismissive like that. This was back in the summer, two summers ago, and we always have a neighbourhood barbecue in August, in aid of our local hospice. So he was invited. He didn't RSVP, but he turned up, about half ten in the evening, already way over the limit. He made really unpleasant sexual remarks to any woman with a strappy dress or top and taunted a couple of other women who were more covered up, making remarks about what they were hiding. A lot of us took him to task but he didn't give a damn, just put his face right in ours and shouted, like a fat little playground bully. Lewis and Roger got a grip, literally, and frogmarched him out and back down his own drive, with him ranting and cussing the whole way.

'And it went from there. Rubbish left out in the street, loud parties, the house left to rack and ruin. One of our neighbours waved at him once; he was walking along the road and saw Ken in his car, and without thinking just waved to say hello, you know, as you do. Ken drove his car right at him, onto the kerb and only swerved at the last minute, laughing his head off. Our neighbour, Neil, rang the police about that one, but there were no witnesses. Same with the parties, because although they were disruptive, the noise levels weren't sufficient for action, because we're all too far apart. He'd throw rubbish into other people's gardens – ours, Lewis and Rog, any old property he was driving past. The council warned him about that, so he'd stop for a few weeks and then start up again.' He paused for breath.

'You get the idea?'

Don nodded and said, 'Thank you – bit of a nightmare for you. Can I ask, did you ever meet his wife?'

Rod looked a little taken aback. 'Someone married *that*? Occasionally there was a woman who came over, maybe for a night or two, but we never got close enough to learn her name or anything. Taller than him, dark hair?'

Cervantes nodded slightly at this description of someone who could be Lauren Greenwood. Murthi carried on.

'Rod, is there anyone else you think we should speak to? Perhaps with different experiences of him and his behaviour?'

Rod shook his head. 'No, I don't think so. He's a topic of conversation at every event round here, from bonfires to port after dinner. We all know everyone else's tales, and they're all the same kind of thing. But I could ask around for you, if you like, and let you know if anything different comes up?'

Don Cervantes considered this and judged it to be a constructive offer. He pulled out a card and handed it over, saying as he did so,

'Obviously you can let people know he's dead. All we can say at the moment is that we're investigating his death. I know it's a long shot, but someone might have heard him say something, at some point.' He pushed away from the kitchen worktop and put his empty coffee mug in the area where he judged the dishwasher might be, Murthi following suit.

'Thank you very much for your time Rod. We're going to just go over to the neighbours on the other side, just in case, then we'll be heading off.' Rod responded.

'Lewis and Rog, you mean? They're away, skiing. Not back until next weekend. But I tell you what, I'm going to text them. I doubt they'll have anything to add, but, sad to say, they won't be sorry. In fact, I think it'll make their bloody holiday.' He laughed, a sour note. 'What a crappy epitaph – glad to see him gone. I wonder what'll happen to the house.'

He ushered them back out of the house, coming with them, obviously intent on continuing his battle with the crib. Murthi stopped him just as their paths were about the diverge.

'If it's any use, my Dad always reads the instructions aloud to himself. He says it helps.' Rod laughed, an unforced, merry sound now, adding to the few clues they'd garnered that indicated this man was usually a genial, decent bloke. 'I'll give it a go, but I think it's my understanding that's defective, not the instructions!'

TWENTY SIX

Back in the car, by mutual agreement, Murthi listed all of the key points in his notebook. These would be transcribed later that afternoon or the next day, depending on what time they got back to the Smoke.

Once they were on the next stage of their journey, heading east towards Guildford, conversation became less formal, the two men swapping backgrounds and interests. Murthi admitted he still lived at home and wasn't looking to leave just yet.

I've been well lucky. Mum and Dad have a big house and about fifteen years ago they built a granny annex in the garage, for my grandad, when he couldn't manage anymore. We've never really been one of those Indian families that likes to have everyone under one roof, but Grandad really needed help, and it did work. He only died three years ago. I'm the oldest so I got to move into the flat. I know I'm a jammy dodger – Mum puts meals in the fridge for me every day, does the washing.'

Don glared at him, a quick glance away from the road.

'You lucky git. I haven't even got a washing machine – no room. It's the launderette for me.'

A smug grin from Ajay. 'Told you. Jammy dodger. There is a drawback though – I've never dared take a girlfriend back. That'd start the next Inquisition. We're pretty westernised really, until weddings and children come up...'

This time Don laughed. 'Glad to know there's a downside to paradise!'

It took just over 45 minutes to make the journey to Gordon Szabo's address in Guildford. As they pulled up outside the address, Don got a text from Fleur Cooper, who was checking on his progress. Conscious that someone was already at the door waiting for them, Don texted back that they were about to start an interview.

This time their surroundings were quite different. Now they stood outside a modern town house, three storeys high. Quite obviously high-end and designed on the spacious lines of the Regency townhouses found in cities like London, Bath and Cheltenham.

At the front door stood a short and dumpy woman with bright eyes and wild, frizzy hair and the look of someone holding herself together as best she could. She was dressed in what Fleur Cooper would have called expensive boho, with a flowing dress and long-line waistcoat, topped off with a wide array of beads and bangles. As she ushered them into the house, she created a light, musical tinkling as she moved.

'I didn't know what time you were coming, but the police here said that you were on your way. I rang them because I wanted to know what was happening.'

Don apologised for keeping her waiting, without really knowing why. He said,

'Can I just confirm that you're Elizabeth Szabo?'

'Oh yes, Lizzie please.'

She led them up the stairs to a dual aspect and very pretty sitting room, with lovely views over the river. She offered them coffee and both accepted, knowing that it often helped, working through familiar tasks. She set off back down the stairs and they could hear her moving around in the kitchen. She was back in a matter of minutes, bearing a large tray with a coffee pot, mugs, side plates and an array of sandwiches and obviously home-baked cake.

'I know it can be really hard to find time to eat in your job, so I thought this might help?' She looked enquiringly at them and both young men nodded enthusiastically. They also, Don from his work experience and Ajay from many years of family training, recognised that Lizzie would be happier if they accepted her kindness.

For the first time in the case, their victim was not about to be portrayed as a villain of the piece. Lizzie was clearly thoroughly overthrown by her loss.

'I just don't understand it. The police here say that you, in London, that you're treating his death as suspicious. But why, our police said it was a heart attack? No-one would hurt Gordon? He was so kind, so thoughtful. I haven't told the children yet – I don't know what to say. They're staying with my sister while I work out what to do.' She looked at the two policemen, eyes wide in confusion and fear. They both offered the standard and utterly useless 'we're sorry for your loss' refrains, but as ever this was meaningless noise. Both men judged that it was time to get what they'd come to find. They'd agreed earlier in the car that Don would lead at their first call, Ajay at this one. He cleared his throat and said,

'Mrs Szabo – Lizzie. Do you mind if we ask you some questions?' She nodded, mutely.

'What was Mr Szabo doing in London on Wednesday?'

'He'd gone up for a meeting about work. You know what he did?'

Ajay replied, 'Not exactly.'

'Well, he worked in property, we both do, did…for the past few years we've been buying up property in up and coming areas, or doer-uppers in good areas and flipping them…you know, renovating them and then selling them on. Some people do it and keep the houses to rent them out, but that didn't interest us. We like….liked…oh God…' she gulped 'we liked to sell them on to people who wanted the house, wanted to love it. Gordon did all of the property purchasing and selling, the paperwork and so on, we agreed the renovations together and then I'd project manage the work. I've been thinking about it over the past couple of days. We've got two in hand at the moment, and I know I can finish those, but I don't have any idea how I could do it long term without Gordie. It was fun together, you know, not just work.' She stopped and regarded them sadly, large blue eyes misted with pain.

Ajay prompted her. 'So, Wednesday?'

'Oh yes, sorry. He does some work with a group of other property developers, running courses showing interested people how to get into the work. It's not as easy as people think. You need a really good grip on financial controls, as well as the experience to roughly work out what a building might need, what its potential profit margin is, where the target market sits.'

Ajay picked up the topic offered. 'So can you tell us about this group? Is a formal thing, a company or organisation? Who's in it?'

Lizzie shook her head, rather vehemently. 'Oh no, it's not formal. Gordie didn't really like the others. He only stuck with it because he enjoyed the presentations. They always featured our projects and Gordie loved to talk about those. I went to a few of them, and I loved watching him capture the audience. And I put together a slideshow, a PowerPoint, you know, showing the transition from wreck to treasure. And charts and tables that stressed the business aspects.' She paused, and thought for a moment. 'The others, Gordie didn't have much to do with them, aside from the presentations. He always said to me that he thought they were dodgy geezers! I met a couple of them at the talks. There was a man called Ken who needed a rolling pin to the face and a woman called Green something who was a cow on legs behind the scenes but all plastic charm in front of the audience. She's a solicitor.'

The two officers glanced at each other, knowing it might now be necessary to update Lizzie on the demises of Mr and Mrs Bell. It would likely come out in the next few days, when the newspapers and wider media got involved. They parked that thought for the moment.

Again, Murthi prompted. 'And the meeting? Was it with them?'

'Yes, they've got a presentation coming up. I think three or four of them were meeting up in Fulham for a coffee, to finalise numbers and so on. But also, Gordie wanted to drop into his solicitors, they're in Fulham too. It would have been better, I always thought, to use a solicitor here, but the Green thingummy woman offered a good rate to go through her firm, so we stuck to that. He didn't have an appointment or anything on Wednesday, he just wanted to pick up a copy of the Land Registry search on a potential new property. And then, then, none of that happened. The local police turned up here around lunchtime to tell me what had happened. They say I've got to wait for an autopsy, but that it looks like a heart attack.'

This put the two officers in a quandary. She did deserve to know, and others had been told; it was only that the Surrey police hadn't known about any of the discoveries subsequent to the initial request to inform Mrs Szabo of her husband's death. They looked at each other, a glance that was quickly picked up by Lizzie Szabo.

'What? You know something?'

As gently as he could, Ajay explained that a number of people had died in the same way and that Gordon's death was being treated as a murder.

She stared at them, dumbfounded. After quite a few seconds of shocked silence she went straight to the salient point.

'What other people have died?'

At this juncture it became obvious to Cervantes and Murtha that they had little choice but to run through the names and see if they were known to her. They began by stressing that this was extremely confidential. She understood immediately.

'God, I don't want the media to pick this up. How horrible to be watched while we go through this. But who else has been... has been murdered?' She stumbled over the unlikely word.

Murthi looked at Cervantes, who picked up the tale.

'Well, Kenneth Bell and Lauren Greenwood – we've already mentioned them. Did you know that they were married?'

She raised her eyebrows and said acerbically, 'Well, I didn't know that. But how good of them to marry each other and save anyone else from having to live with them.' Lizzie Szabo, in normal circumstances would appear to have a cutting wit.

Cervantes continued. 'There's a retired dentist called Edward Horbridge; he lived in Wimbledon?'

She shook her head, and Ajay continued. 'Calum Grant? He worked in PR and lived in Kensington.'

This time she nodded and said, 'Yes. I met him at one of the presentations. I didn't dislike him exactly, he was kind of charming, but I wouldn't trust him, if you know what I mean? His suit was too perfect, his attention when talking to you was a tiny bit too much – does that make sense?' They both nodded but said nothing.

'Finally,' said Cervantes, 'a Mr Irfan Patel. I'm afraid we don't have any information on him yet.'

Lizzie Szabo shook her head at the name. 'No, I never met him, and Gordon never mentioned him.' She considered for a moment and then said, 'so at the moment it's the property thing that connects the people I know. Does it also connect the dentist and Mr Patel?'

Cervantes was cagier with this one. 'Possibly – I'd have to stress that we're still investigating.'

Lizzie Szabo clearly accepted this, but it didn't stop her continuing her theme.

'The thing is, I don't know what the other two are like, but I want to be really sure that you understand, there can't be anything dodgy that connected Gordie to them. You'll never get me to believe that.'

She pursed her lips and leant back in her chair, obviously relieved to have stressed her conviction.

After all the necessary farewells and the sharing of Cervantes business card, on which he wrote his personal mobile number, the two policemen beat a sad retreat, conscious for the first time that someone had been so negatively impacted by their loss. Cervantes had met Caroline Horbridge and, whilst she was shocked, he reckoned she was set fair for a far better life without her husband. Lizzie Szabo was a different kettle of fish.

TWENTY SEVEN

Further north, in London, Mick Brent had used a pool car to get across to Chelsea, much as he hated it. Driving in London was no pleasure for a man who enjoyed actually driving, rather than practising the braking and queuing required by the capital city. And the weather was cold, wet and miserable, so staying out of it as long as possible wasn't a bad thing.

The garden centre was enough to lift his spirits though, with the colours and smells of the very best of its genre. He wasted a few minutes identifying plants and ornaments he thought Maisie, his wife, would like, noted their prices and stored them mentally for discussion later. They'd laugh about the unbelievable rates at the very least.

Then, squaring himself to his task, he looked about for the coffee bar area, spotting it through what appeared to be a department of upmarket gifts, candles, pictures, china and the like. He thought as he strode through that he and Maze should make a trip to this place. It was admirably disability friendly.

He found the café to be thronged with visitors and grimaced to himself that he hadn't thought through his timing, but he was here now, so what the hell. He quickly identified what seemed to be a manager and showed her his warrant card, explaining that he wanted a few minutes with the waitress who'd raised the alarm over Calum Grant's collapse. The manager looked a little harassed, but then checked her watch and said,

'Oh, it's OK. It's Phoebe you want, and she's due her lunch break in ten minutes, so I'll get her to bring you a drink and she can start it earlier. What would you like, and would a sandwich help you at all?' Mick blessed his lucky Chelsea stars and asked for a cup of tea and any meat-based sandwich. He was all right on artisanal breads, but he didn't fancy any of your quinoa and tofu affairs.

The manager said, why don't you use the staff office? There's no-one in it on a weekend, especially a Sunday. She shepherded him behind the serving counter and through a swing door to a short corridor. At the back of this she unlocked another door and ushered him into a space with three desks, as ever kitted out with computer hardware. There were some comfortable looking, almost informal seats and she pulled two of these alongside the largest desk, placing them at right angles so they wouldn't feel cramped. 'I'll send Phoebe through to you, if you don't mind waiting a minute or two?'

Without waiting for his answer, she was off, leaving Mick to explore the office. He amused himself by reflecting on Phoebe's name, reckoning that it probably dated to the days when the US sitcom Friends was still producing new episodes. Then he mentally disciplined himself. He was in Chelsea, he was lucky she wasn't called Damson, or Fruity-Loopy-Su-Zu. Then he thought again. A young woman working here was unlikely to be a Chelsea resident.

In a matter of a couple of minutes a young girl with very pale blonde hair was gingerly backing through the door with a tray of sandwiches, a pot of tea, mugs and two slices of what looked like lemon drizzle cake. He jumped to his feet to help her and cleared some filing trays from the desk to make space. The necessary pouring of tea and distribution of sandwiches – ham and red onion for him and brie and grape for her, broke any initial shyness on her part and she happily subsided into the seat he gestured her towards.

He started, in the way of all interrogators seeking to relax their targets, by asking her to tell him a little about herself.

She grinned at him and swallowed a mouthful of her sandwich. He was amused to see that she'd extracted all of the grapes and left them to one side of her plate.

'Well, I'm Phoebe, I'll be twenty next month, I'm studying Robotics at Heriot Watt in Edinburgh and I'll be going back there at the end of the week.' She looked at him, clearly interested to see if he needed more. Brent asked,

'Can I ask where you live?'

She nodded, 'Of course. About two minutes' walk from here, in Lordship Place'. He whistled involuntarily and she grinned again.

'I know, it's outrageous, isn't it? And did you know, it's the only street in the UK called Lordship Place, so it's unique?' More soberly she said, 'I'm really not a spoilt Chelsea brat. Dad's a surgeon with a rich patient base and a conscience, so he's always made sure my brother and I have a good grip on reality. Which is why I've worked here for years, at weekends and school holidays and now college breaks. He says I'm responsible for all my personal purchases now, clothes and stuff.'

Having finished her sandwich, she now dispatched the grapes one at a time, clearly relishing their flavour.

Mick Brent judged it was time to get down to brass tacks. While he'd been waiting for her, he'd slightly chastened himself when he realised that this girl would be about the age of his own child or children, if things had gone differently for Maze. He was a favourite uncle with his two nephews and his only niece, but otherwise silently and forever internally regretted the lost opportunity. He might have been proud to have a daughter like this.

'Well, you know why I'm here, about Mr Calum Grant? I think you were the first person to get to him when he collapsed?'

She nodded, clearly still distressed.

'It was horrible. There was absolutely nothing I could do. Dad makes sure that we keep up our St John's Ambulance qualifications, every three years, but none of that was any use. He was unconscious when I got to him and it only took a half a minute or so after that. And the ambulance got here really quickly. They said there wasn't anything I should have done that I didn't.' This was clearly for self-reassurance.

Brent pressed on. 'Did you see him go over? Was there anyone else nearby?'

She shook her head. 'No, it was the noise of his chair and the china that made me turn.' She thought for a moment. 'There was a man who went past me just before that, coming from the same area. Oh. I hadn't thought of that. None of the other tables were in use in there, not at that time on a wet weekday morning. So I don't know if he was with Mr Grant, but there was only coffee for one on his table.'

Brent was interested, far more than he could show. 'Can you describe him?'

'Not really, I didn't see his face. So I have an impression of him being quite tall, with a hat, a kind of Stetson cowboy thing, do you know what I mean?'

'Like those leather ones?'

'Yes, it might have been leather. I'm really sorry but that's all I've got.' She leant back in her chair and looked at him, considering. 'I know I watch too much TV, but whether there was someone else with him doesn't seem to tie up with a heart attack?'

It was Brent's turn to smile. 'Well, I can't say a lot, but we are investigating. But I'd be grateful if you'd keep a lid on that if you can.'

She looked quite shocked. 'I live in Chelsea! I've seen enough cameras and gangs of reporters to last a lifetime. Dad says on a personal level that it's only the stupid, the spiteful or the truly desperate who talk to the media.'

Brent looked at his notepad, assessing what he'd learned, little as it was. He gave her his card and asked if she could make herself available to give a formal statement if needed. She reminded him that she was heading to Scotland within a few days, and he promised he'd get it sorted before that, making a note to himself.

Having satisfied the professional requirements he then turned his attention to the cake, checking with Phoebe that it actually was for him. She laughed out loud as she waved him on, and then picked up her own plate with obvious alacrity.

For a few moments they enjoyed their sweet treat, with Mick asking questions about robotics and what a career in that discipline looked like.

'Well, to be honest, it's a kind of make up your own mind sort of field. The possibilities are endless. Obviously, there's all the automation we're used to, cars, assembly lines, factory management and so on. Then there are defence applications, space travel, underwater research, all of that. But I'm interested in the medical side. It's not just about replacement limbs, now tiny robots can be sent inside the body to find things, take images, collect specimens, even remove things. I've got another year and two terms to go. I'm hoping I do well enough to go for my doctorate, but that'll be in a placement somewhere. Dad says he can't help, that I've got to make my own connections.' She sighed. 'I do get it, and one day I'll be grateful that I'll be able to say I did it myself, but sometimes I wish he'd slip up on the good guy front!' Since she was clearly proud of her father and his principles, Brent just toasted her with a teacup.

'Maybe one day you'll be able to get my wife out of her wheelchair?' He was only half-joking. Unlikely as it was, he would always hope. Phoebe looked interested and

151

sympathetic. She asked about the injury and Mick explained. She responded,

'I'm not an expert yet, but I do know there's a lot going on in that field. The hard thing for the two of you is that real breakthroughs could be made tomorrow or twenty years from now. Has Maisie signed up to a trial database?'

Mick didn't know such a thing existed, but after a few minutes of discussion gave Phoebe his card and said, 'Obviously use this if you think about anything else from last week. But if you hear of a trial or whatever that might be good for Maze, please let me know.'

Phoebe checked how he'd travelled that morning, then walked him back through the café, then the garden centre to a staff entrance at the side. 'This is the closest to where you've parked.' Brent had become aware of the hammering of heavy rain on the structure's roof, once they'd emerged from the office and thanked Phoebe with warmth. Yes, a daughter like her might have been a fine thing.

TWENTY EIGHT

Dear Diary

I PASSED!!! (I've learnt that journalists call it a 'screamer', when you use lots of exclamation marks.) He was pleased but it won't last, because in the letter there was a list of what I need for the new school.

But I'm not going to worry about that now. I expect there would have been a list from the Comprehensive too.

TWENTY NINE

Some quick texts around the team ascertained that everyone could get to the station in time for the proposed

4 o'clock meeting, with the exception of Fletcher, who'd assumed radio silence.

Variously, team members filled the gap with admin or travelling, with all of them making it to what Cervantes insisted on calling afternoon prayers in good time. Even Reith had been able to descend from the gods. As ever, Groehling had unearthed a family pack of biscuits and they settled in to review progress. He also relieved everyone by taking control of the HOLMES inputting as they worked.

Fleur marshalled the meeting into order and asked for everyone's updates in turn. The team members who'd been out to play were the first to kick off, and Brent and the two younger officers rounded up their experiences. Fleur asked Reith to outline what they'd found at Lauren Greenwood's firm, knowing that the Super had a very low boredom threshold in meetings – better to keep him occupied. Daisy went next, summarising her explorations of Edward Horbridge's paperwork.

'I did say to the Gov earlier, it would've been easy to get lost in all of his complaints. They're ab fab – I've never seen anything like it. If you published them in a book, they wouldn't let you, if you know what I mean?' She settled to her task.

'Anyway, it wasn't difficult to explore his financials, which was what you wanted me to look at,' she glanced at Fleur for corroboration. 'And he was really well off. There's no mortgage on the Wimbledon house and over the past five years he's bought and sold twenty two properties. Six through Lauren Greenwood's company, eleven through another company that I'm researching now and the rest through a solicitor called Lauren Bell...I'm guessing that's who we think it is. She's registered as a sole trader.' She looked at Groehling, 'Kurt, does the Land Registry show who acted for a purchase or sale?'

Groehling looked interested. 'Well, there's a yes and no to that. Historically, it sometimes showed up if the searches were all paper-based, but sometimes not. But now, they're digitised, and it's possible to see which registered users accessed the Registry to request data. It's generally a company name though, not an individual. What's particularly interesting is the gap between purchase and sale – it's really short for virtually all of the transactions, except for the Szabos. So there can't have been much serious renovation going on. But every single property, again, apart from the Szabos, and one of Edward Horbridge's, have two things in common. They sold for substantially more than they were purchased for and they were all sold to companies. There's a lot of work for me in there – at the moment I can't get behind the first layer of businesses to see if they have a common root.'

Fleur nodded. 'OK Kurt, let's stick with you. What else have you got? You've already touched on the digital dive, and I know you've got some financials?'

Kurt Groehling looked serious. 'Let's take the digital dives first. All of our victims have been purchasing and selling property for varying periods of time. Gordon and Elizabeth Szabo are the longest-servers. Interesting that; they used a city centre solicitor in Guildford until six years ago, then they switched to Lauren Greenwood. All of the others have used Lauren Greenwood and Lauren Bell, no-one else. Irfan Patel's the new boy on the block. Just activity over the last five months.

'Everyone's done well out of this, whatever this is. The Szabos are probably the least profitable, even though they're the longest in the tooth. Don't get me wrong though, they've got nearly £7 million in assets, including property, cash and investments. Lauren Greenwood is the jackpot winner – she has accounts all over the shop; so far I'm around the £40 million mark with her and I honestly think I'm scraping the surface. Ken Bell is the next in the Premier League, but you want to see his outgoings – some really dodgy phone line subscriptions and escort services. Edward Horbridge is around the £11 million mark.' He turned to look at Fleur.

'I told you Gov, very concerning.'

Cervantes chose this minute to butt in. 'The thing is, so far no-one has seemed to be particularly popular. But today, we met Gordon Szabo's widow and she's blown apart. But you're saying that he might have been the trailblazer on this?'

Reith intervened. 'Not sure if that's what's being implied or not. Being naughty or nice isn't necessarily any indicator of criminality....Hitler loved dogs apparently...but I do see what you mean. But there's another way of looking at it. What if Gordon was the 'hook' for the con? At the moment it's possible that his work has been legit. And if you were a little criminal consortium, running property development presentations would be a good way to identify possible co-conspirators. The Szabos were able to present a genuine history of success. But I'm guessing that some people might think that property is an easy route to profit, and some of those attending the seminars might be easily tempted down a side road.

'It's the main issue that's still occupying me though. Were these people killed because they'd fallen out with what might be organised crime, or is it something else?'

Cervantes had no opinion on the 'what if' question, but nodded in gratitude. He'd liked Lizzie Szabo and had felt for her. As a police officer he still had some finer feelings and some element of natural trust rather than disdain. It was one of the reasons that Cooper and Reith rated him. He was sometimes able to better understand scenarios exactly as they appeared, rather than laminating them with cynicism, prejudging.

The team agreed necessary activities for the following day. Groehling would continue to develop the database he'd started, showing the property transactions, Fletcher would be put to work on identifying the solicitors, individuals or companies, involved. Nothing was said about his non-appearance at the meeting, but the very absence of comment highlighted the fact. Brent was to focus on the Solicitors' Regulation aspect, and would try to get an appointment with them in Birmingham. He also needed to reconnect with the Bordeaux police, to see if Chloé Antoine's alibi held up. Reith was concerned that they were trespassing on the Fraud Squad's territory and felt he needed to touch base with them. He was also conscious that money-laundering was not a strong experience area for any of them. He didn't want to pass the investigation over to another team – this was a serial killer, after all – but he didn't want weak knowledge to undermine them. He began to construct possible scenarios and then reminded himself of something unconnected.

'I've just remembered that it's David Jerman's memorial service tomorrow. A few of us really have to go. Any volunteers? It's 11am tomorrow, I'll email details once I know who's going. We're invited to a buffet lunch after. I'm staying for that.' Fleur Cooper and Mick Brent were cautiously optimistic on hearing this. They'd felt that Reith had made a connection with a witness, indeed a victim of their very public case from the previous summer. He hadn't made any moves since then, but maybe this was the opportunity he needed.

Brent replied first. 'I'd like to go Sir, but it depends on the Solicitors' Regulation whatnot. Maze wants to go, so I'll join her if I can.' That remark hid a multitude of organisational nightmares. Maze had lost her driving licence because her physical condition meant that her breathing wasn't always under complete control. So to get her and her wheelchair to an unknown venue was no mean feat. But over time the couple had built up a strong network of support providers and Maze would work it out. The pair were constitutionally unable to ask for help from their friends, but they both worked and were well enough off to pay for specialist taxis, and one of Maze's carers would accompany her.

Cooper said, 'Peter is going, and I said I'd meet him there.' Fleur had met her partner during the course of their previous large-scale investigation and, whilst she was reluctant to move forwards as swiftly as he, she was nonetheless happier than anyone in the station had ever seen her.

Groehling summarised the information he'd fed into the computer system and the meeting dispersed, Fleur Cooper stressing that the day was over. None of them knew how long this investigation would take; they didn't even know if the killing was over.

No-one mentioned it, but everyone, even the newbie Ajay Murthi, was wondering when the other shoe would drop – when would the media pick up on the story? It seemed remarkable that they hadn't, but this was an unusual case. None of the victims had died in what appeared to be suspicious circumstances to the bystanders who'd been present. Fingers remained crossed.

THIRTY

Monday dawned slightly less wet and miserable than the weekend.

Brent was in particularly early; he had some admin tasks to perform and he wanted to ring the Solicitors' Regulation Authority. Wise in the ways of government and regulatory bodies, he guessed that some key staff would be in the office from as early as 7am. Switchboards tended to turn on automatically at some point around 8 or 8.30am. Dialling in before that recognised that some 'phone systems were routed out of hours to a couple of key staff. If so, he could possibly cut to the chase a lot faster than having to start with a telephone gatekeeper.

His luck was in. His natural charm served him well and the person answering the 'phone was clearly a member of the leadership team. As expected, he wouldn't talk over the 'phone, but it swiftly became apparent that they'd already got Lauren Greenwood on their radar. Brent was both surprised and pleased to be offered an appointment for that day, late afternoon. Even better, it turned out that there was a satellite office in London, and it was possible to meet there, giving him plenty of time to get across town after the memorial service.

He and Maze had a bit of a plan in mind; they'd both felt a strong attraction between Reith and Leonie Merton, a witness and unwilling participant in their major case from the previous summer. Nothing seemed to have come of it and Mick was inclined to put it down to diffidence on Reith's part. Maze thought there was more to it, a mix of bitter experience and concern about Leonie's earning power. Today they both thought they might try to engineer something

He added notes to the system and also tapped out an email to Fleur Cooper, as Senior Investigating Officer, then rang his wife to let her know he'd see her later. He'd donned a decent suit that morning, in case he could get to the service and now it meant he'd be appropriately garbed for his meeting at the end of the day.

Fletcher appeared on the dot of 8am, scowling at the chairs and files that were not in line with his rigid internal grid. It sourly amused his colleagues, who watched him try to impose a regimented pattern of desks and chairs in the sergeants' area, to absolutely no avail. He would never understand that his disdain for the majority of his colleagues was fully reciprocated. They knew what he was trying to achieve, so they subverted all of his attempts. He fired up his computer and then began to construct a to do list from the instructions relayed to him by email.

Groehling wasn't far behind. He amused himself for a minute or two winding up Fletcher about what he'd missed over the latter part of the weekend but then settled into his tasks.

Both Brent and Groehling were conscious that the brass, in the first instance probably Cooper, would be taking Fletcher to task over his weekend disappearance. Fletcher was too often guilty of deciding his own priorities and in this case his colleagues thought he'd seriously misjudged the situation.

It would have been untrue to say that Mick and Kurt, individually, regretted the bollocking heading Fletcher's way. He was a constant thorn in everyone's side, even if he did have a good logistic brain. Fletcher's colleagues were however protected in one way. They knew he would be challenged and disciplined as necessary. Not for them the irritation of watching colleagues get away with murder and the loss of respect for senior officers as a result.

Mick turned his attention to the telephone again. He wanted to talk to JP Marchand in Bordeaux and judged that, just after nine continental time, he might find his French colleague in the offices. Again his luck was in and he spent a few pleasant moments chatting with the Procurateur. Wise in cross-Channel politics he was careful to exchange personal greetings and enquire after JP and his team before enquiring as to progress. The two men quickly resumed their easy discourse from Sunday morning and JP had plenty to report. He confirmed that Chloé Antoine had certainly attended her interview and stayed at the hotel she'd referenced. He'd seen her hotel account and interviewed a waiter who had served her breakfast on the morning that Calum Grant was killed. No doubt that she was out of the picture. Mick relayed his gratitude, quite clearly sincerely, and repeated his invitation to meet up if JP was ever in London. There was the merest hint of hesitation before JP confided that he was actually booked for a two day course in central London in mid-

February...perhaps they could share a glass of wine? Mick assured him that they could do better than that, and made a mental note to follow up on something later in the day. They made, for policemen, a major step forward by sharing personal mobile numbers and rang off, wishing each other the best of days.

Reith and Cooper arrived in the suite together, obviously having been released from the same meeting. Fleur headed straight to her office, but Reith wandered around the large investigation team area, and then the sergeants' space, exchanging pleasantries. He was exceptionally good at remembering points of interest, so sports' affiliations, children's progress, holidays were served up for quick reviews. It contributed to a team which might not understand his wish to climb the slippery slope, but which thoroughly appreciated his approach to them as colleagues. Fletcher however was the one exception to this today. He received only a curt nod.

Cervantes came into the office at some speed, closely followed by Murthi; Mick grinned to himself, it was like watching two Labrador puppies let off the lead.

'We've got another one, I think. The Forensic people have just rung in from Chelwest.' Even those not involved in the case looked up at this, but Groehling, Brent, the two youngsters and Reith were quick to crowd into Cooper's office, Reith shutting the door firmly on Fletcher's outraged face.

Cooper snapped out. 'What do we know? Who, what, where?'

Just as concisely, Cervantes came back with. 'Chap called Neville Humberstone. Found by his apartment building manager in the lift, late last night. Ashok Khan, the Chief Forensic guy at Chelwest, started the autopsy this morning and spotted the injection mark straight away. He rang me direct.' He looked around the room, 'I met him on the first case, or at least, the first one we heard about. We don't know a lot about Mr Humberstone. Apparently he was a financial advisor, whatever that means.'

With varying degrees of personal experience of the breed, everyone in the room recognised two things. Financial advisors ranged from thoroughly impressive to decidedly dodgy, as in virtually every other field of employment. And secondly, property and finance went hand in hand...

Cervantes and Murthi were dispatched to follow up and get more info, Cooper nodding to Groehling to check that he knew he'd be needed to get the background work started.

As the team trooped out of her office, Fleur straightened her shoulders and steeled herself for the encounter with Fletcher. She stepped outside of her door and called him in, politely and quietly asking him to take a seat. The occupants of the sergeants' office were treated to Fletcher beginning a protest about his exclusion and a very tight, 'Stop at once, Mr Fletcher. Sit down and...' The remainder of the discussion was nothing more than a quiet hum of Fleur's even and measured tones and louder, more shrill inputs from Fletcher. Frustratingly, no-one could hear the words, but Fletcher's appearance some forty five minutes later left the interested audience in no doubt. His flushed face, his trembling hands and his rigid walk through the office and out the other side told a clear tale.

Cooper left it for a few minutes then began to gather her belongings for the memorial service. She'd brought a decent coat into the office today, rather than her more serviceable ski jacket, and she donned this and collected her Radley bag from one of her filing cabinets. She was a shoe and handbag girl, but without the resources to truly fulfil her likes, so she settled for Radley and Staud rather than the Mulberry she really wanted. She'd looked at knock-offs, but couldn't bring herself to do it. Conscience could be a terrible affliction. She met Reith on the stairs on her way down, and updated him on her confrontation with Fletcher.

'He says he's entitled to time off. I told the annoying little twat that he only had to discuss it, not behave like it was a God-given right to do whatever he likes. He didn't raise any personal issues before or today, and I've finally drawn the line. We were all a bit thrown by him last summer, with the Rain Callan case; it almost looked like he was trying. But he bloody isn't. His contempt for everyone except himself is mind-blowing. So I gave him a lot more than two barrels. I told him that he's disliked and looked down on by virtually everybody. He wanted to know who's complained about him, but it upset him even more when I said he wasn't important enough to anyone to bother complaining. He started on about how nobody respects him, mucking up his desk and so on, but I told him that you earn respect, by doing a really good job and by supporting colleagues. I said he was like a bee in the middle of a hive, waiting for everyone to be good to him, with no mutual reward. And then I said that even the Chief Constable doesn't do that.'

Reith muffled a snort of laughter.

'And he actually said, 'why would he, he's useless?' I didn't lose my temper, but that did it. I told him that I'm putting him on the Disciplinary Process for constant disregard for protocols, communication channels and basic human interaction levels. He's incandescent and he's gone off to find a Police Federation rep. Don't reckon they'll be happy. He despises them too.'

Reith stopped halfway down the final flight of stairs and calmly regarded her. She stopped, two steps ahead and looked back up at him. She took a deep breath and then grinned.

'Sorry! I can calm down now. Any conversation with that man is like talking German to a Spaniard. Total incomprehension.'

Reith laughed. 'It's been long overdue, and the team needed to see it was in hand, especially after him going

AWOL yesterday. It's not on. You know I've got your back and if we have to kick him out, then we have to. He's got that one ability to see flaws in a process or argument and he can drill down deeper than anyone I know. But it's always on his terms, and that's got to reduce.' He looked glum for a moment. 'I'm not daft. We'll never get it to stop completely.'

THIRTY ONE

The memorial service was, surprisingly, a lively affair. David Jerman had been divorced, but evidently amicably so and his ex-wife was there, part of the tribute to his life, along with friends, family and colleagues. The minister made a good fist of bringing David to life in the proceedings and both Harry Wilson and Leonie Merton spoke movingly and humorously about working with him and being his friend. It turned out that David had been a true whisky aficionado and owned shares in a couple of Scotland's very few privately owned distilleries. Both Harry and Leonie used this to great effect. Talking about maturity and depth and bringing into the cold church the real flavour of a man the police had only seen in one dimension. Fleur thought how sad it was, that they'd never had the chance to know this other, fuller character.

Steve Reith, seated two thirds of the way toward the back of the church watched Leo Merton with self-aware interest. He recognised that her attraction for him had not abated and he wondered if what he was about to do was wise on the personal front.

They met, just outside of the church doors and she said to him 'Where did you go?

'In what sense?' he asked.

'I wanted you to ask me out. I thought you would. I thought we shared something, I'm not sure what.'

She looked up at him, unsure of herself. He smiled down at her, and took her arm to walk down the path, away from the dark and echoing church.

Leo had travelled to the church with Harry Wilson and continued on her journey to the subsequent lunch in Knightsbridge with that arrangement, but she was obviously pleased that Reith and Fleur were also heading that way. She'd spotted the Brents too and was looking forward to catching up with them. She'd reflected after the events of last summer that she'd been thrown into an intense and very focused relationship with some of these police officers and that, after it was over, it felt as if the world had shifted somehow. People who had been incredibly but fleetingly important were suddenly gone, on to the next thing.

At the lunch, around fifty people chatted happily over a more than decent buffet. Leonie made a point of coming across to Reith and reintroducing him to Chris Boyd. A very talented businessman with a range of properties, a catering company and a highly acclaimed Knightsbridge restaurant, he'd gladly handed the restaurant over today for the event. Though it had undergone a significant renovation, the officers and many of the guests remembered only too well the bomb damage here the previous June. Chris Boyd had initially thought of moving on, but it went against his native Yorkshire grit to give in. So The Green Velvet was now Arizona Dreaming. A few people cottoned on that it was a reference to Phoenix, and the bird emerging from the flames, though most visitors initially expected some sort of American cuisine. But it now held a Michelin star and a table was hard to come by.

The Brents, seeing Chris Boyd, joined the small group and updating and banter was shared around. Mick Brent, mindful of the conversation with his French counterpart earlier that day confessed to Chris Boyd that he'd promised JP Marchand 'more than a glass of wine'. He grimaced at Boyd and said 'I know I probably can't afford the full a la carte, but I'd really like him to see that we have world class restaurants here too.' Chris Boyd laughed at him, frankly pleased with the compliment and equally certain that Mick hadn't been asking for a favour. 'Just let me have a date and I'll do something that won't break the bank. Maybe we could make it a bigger group?' He cast his eye around the cluster of colleagues and winked at

Maze. Clearly the Brents weren't the only conniving pair in the room.

Fleur Cooper and her partner Peter Howard were in time to hear this comment as they came up to their colleagues. If a meal here was on the cards Fleur's conscience wasn't going to trouble her for long. Brent assured Boyd that he'd agree to just about anything if he got to eat here twice in a lifetime.

Maze, framed as ever in her wheelchair smiled warmly at Chris and said, 'So often when we're out, people talk to Mick and not me. You know, the 'does she take sugar?' thing. But your team have been lovely. The whole place is accessible, really accessible and no-one has talked down at me. They all step back so I'm not peering up and they're not staring down.' She laughed. 'There was a woman at our local Italian for years who kept kneeling down to talk to me. I know she thought she was being lovely, and she sort of was, but I always wanted to gurgle and coo like a baby!'

Chris nodded in pleasure. Only he and Maze really understood how much work had gone into training staff to automatically do something that might be needed just once in a while. It was one of the reasons the menu prices approached breath-taking. Though it was sad that society didn't just do it naturally. But then, he reflected, many folk would always think of him as a Yorkshire upstart, just as they'd see the stunning Fleur Cooper as an immigrant and the disabled, talented Maze Brent as less than perfect.

Steve Reith chose the moment to draw Leonie Merton slightly to one side. 'I wanted to ask you something.' He continued, quickly. 'Professionally.' She blinked, her bright gaze dropping slightly, and he was aware that he'd disappointed her and himself. He added, 'For now, at least', and smiled warmly at her. She looked up again.

'I remember when we met last summer, you told me that you'd done some work with us in the past, with Art and Drugs.' He shrugged nonchalantly. 'They really rated you apparently.' She giggled and he remembered how much he loved her warm, low, pleasing voice.

'So, might you be interested in a project with Major Crimes? Without giving you details, it's urgent and we think it's money-laundering at its root. But it really is time critical. We'd need you right away, and until you have a look at what we've got, I don't know how much of the working week we'd need, or for how long.' He looked at her, trying hard to conceal his eagerness for a positive answer. He was nervous that he wanted this, because he fully understood that this feeling was only partly driven by a professional imperative.

She looked thoughtful. 'Actually, that does sound interesting. But am I going to get blown up?' She wasn't totally joking.

'Hopefully not this time. The targets seem to be connected by the money, not anything else. At least as far as we can see. But I'd need to know today, tomorrow morning at latest.'

She nodded. 'I'll talk to Harry. I'm actually finishing up a big project at the moment, and my next major one is a couple of weeks off.' He started to say. 'That may not be anywhere near enough time', but she continued, 'But I want to use the new project to train one of my team leaders up to another level of compliance, so I'm going to let him lead, with my oversight. If I'm with you for a period, it won't be so obvious to him that I'm doing it. Can I ring you first thing tomorrow?' Reith handed her his mobile.

'Ring yourself now and I'll have your number and know to answer it.'

Across the room people were settling into smaller groups, ready for longer chats, and Harry Wilson and Leonie Merton reassumed their duties as co-hosts to keep that working. The police officers had no such luxury and began their polite extrications from conversations. Promises were made to stay in touch, and Reith followed the Brents towards the door. They passed Fleur and her partner on their way, overhearing a remark about meeting up for dinner later.

In the car on the way back to the station, Reith prodded what he thought was a sore point. Only fair after all, he'd been only too conscious of everyone focusing on him and Leo. Bloody cheek!

'So, is it going all right with you and Peter? Hard work, when both of you have jobs that can derail any kind of planning'. He waited.

She nodded at him, then quickly turned her concentration back to her driving.

'It's only that he's ready for the whole meet the family thing, merge friends and all that. That's a bit speedy for me. And he's really top drawer material. Winchester, Oxford. Classic upper class. I can't imagine he's going to please Mama when he produces me.'

Steve Reith tilted his head in acknowledgement. 'Even if that's true, give him credit for not caring about that. My dad', Reith's Scottish accent was a little more pronounced as he spoke, 'my Dad thought all police officers were bent, miner-bashing thugs. Clearly doesn't mean I agree with him.' He thought for a moment.

'I don't know much about your family?'

She waggled her head. 'Not much to say. My father died a few years ago now. My mother and I aren't particularly close, but I get on really well with my nephews. I had a brilliant aunt when I was little; didn't get to see her much, but she was kind and funny – she did the best presents in the world. I still remember my Post Office set – I loved it. So I decided to be that kind of auntie.' She laughed aloud. 'I get a lot of pleasure buying them *very* noisy presents!'.

Reith laughed out loud. He enjoyed discovering new levels of mischief in his usually far too buttoned-up inspector.

He coughed, ready to confess to his conversation with Leonie Merton, but Cooper beat him to it.

'Did I see you talking with Leonie? I'm not going to bother asking you whether you sorted out a date, but I did wonder if you might have thought of asking her for a professional consult? I know she's cleared with us as an expert.'

Reith was grateful for the easy run in. 'I did. I think she'll do it, but she's going to ring in first thing tomorrow.' Without noticing that he was doing it, he patted the mobile in his pocket, reassured by his now more direct connection with the attractive Ms Merton.

Cooper was pleased, on both the personal and work levels, though she only commented on one. 'Great. It's just not our expertise, even though Kurt and that plank Fletcher can get right into the bowels of virtually everything. But I'm afraid we're wasting precious time because we don't actually know what signs we should be looking for, or whether there are key players that we ought to be finding. I'm sure we don't want to hand it over to another team, because at the end of the day it's murder, but I don't want us to balls it up.'

Reith could only agree. He might worry that he'd opened a personal can of worms, but he was reassured that they were bringing on board someone with potentially the much needed credentials.

THIRTY TWO

Dear Diary

I start at big school tomorrow. I'm scared but I'm excited too. We'll get different teachers for different subjects. I can't wait to do Science. Granny says there's something called English Literature. I like the sound of that.

Granny and Grandad have been amazing. They told him that they wanted to give me my new school uniform for my birthday. They said they wanted to help him, so he didn't have to worry about it. I think Granny knows he wouldn't have worried at all and I just wouldn't have had a proper uniform. I sort of think he didn't know whether to be pleased or insulted, but Granny was clever and I think he ended up feeling pleased. So Granny took me shopping and I've never had so many new things. And we went to a tea shop in the middle of the day and I had a hot chocolate and a toasted cheese sandwich and a caramel éclair. And then Granny took everything home with her. She properly lied to him. She said she'd bought mostly second-hand stuff, except the shoes. He was pleased by that I could tell. She washed all the clothes and put them in supermarket shopping bags and brought them round here this morning.

I don't understand how someone as lovely as my Gran had someone like him. I never talk about him with her, but I think she wonders too.

THIRTY THREE

Back at base Fleur sped around the office, catching up. She started with Kurt Groehling.

'Anything to report?' No-one took offence, because it was never personally meant, but sometimes Fleur forgot the niceties in conversation, when pressure was up.

'Yes and no', came the guarded reply. 'I've got down to three companies that seem to be at the end of the majority of sales and purchases we know about so far. But then it's a dead end for me; I don't know how to get any further. Interesting though, not a single one of the Szabo's properties have taken that route. They've all gone on the open market. So the Super might just be right about them being the patsies.' He looked up anxiously at his line manager. 'I'm a bit stuck, Boss. Where do I go from here?'

Fleur recognised decidedly unusual signs of concern in her generally unflappable digital detective.

'Well, some good news, maybe? The Super's asked Leonie Merton to consult. She's got a big background in this and we're hoping she'll say yes. We'll know in the morning.'

Although Groehling had encountered Leonie the previous year, he hadn't got to know her or picked up much about her professional life, since that hadn't been particularly pertinent to his area of the case. He made a note of her name on the large tear-off blotter pad he kept on his desk, intending to do his due diligence once Fleur moved away. Fleur noted, as she often did, that Kurt always looked awkward with a pen in his hand, and that he still had the smallest and most illegible writing she'd ever seen. She turned to Cervantes.

'Don? Anything?'

He nodded. 'I've found Rose Horbridge. She's a teacher and she actually lives in Norbiton, so she's not really far from her parents' house. Am I OK to go and interview her, with Ajay? I thought it'd be better at home, after school finishes tonight.'

Fleur agreed. 'Make it after 7 o'clock. My neighbours are teachers and they never seem to get home until later than you'd think.'

From the good guys to Fletcher. She straightened her shoulders again, ready for the ice-cold reception she was sure to receive, but when she turned round, she saw no sign of him at his desk. She glanced out into the larger office but no Fletcher there either, so she headed into her office to see if he was logged into the system elsewhere, or if he was noted as attending a meeting or an event. Nothing. She checked her emails and found one from HR, asking her to contact them. Heart sinking, she closed her office door and rang the extension number provided. After being connected to the required person, a Fred Gregson, it didn't take long.

'I'm afraid that Simon Fletcher has just been signed off with stress.' Fleur sighed, obviously audibly, since the HR rep responded with,

'I know, it's a total pain. I think you know the system, but I don't think that you've had a process underway here before?' Fleur agreed, saying, 'No, but I did email your team this morning, asking for support in taking Mr Fletcher through Disciplinary.'

'Yep,' came the reply from Fred. 'I'm your man on that, and because it's related, I'll work with you on anything that comes up re the stress thing now. Mr Fletcher will be assigned one of our team too, and they'll provide advice if required.' The humour and warmth in his voice became apparent as he said, 'Not sure we'll be doing a lot of that for him, as our entire office was treated to a full tirade from him this morning. Apparently we're all a bunch of totally over-qualified idiots with pointless sociology degrees who couldn't get proper jobs. Apparently he has a detailed log of just how incompetent and stupid everyone in the building is, including us, and we're all going to get full specifics.' Fleur half gasped and laughed at this.

'Do you let that pass, or does it need to be acted on?'

Fred responded swiftly. 'Oh, it gets acted on. It becomes part of the narrative now. He receives a letter from our team summarising his comments, noting their offensiveness and warning him never to repeat the behaviour. It'll also note that the record will be included in his file for future consideration in the eventuality of related matters. Which we already know will come to pass, of course.'

Fleur sighed again and Fred was once more quick to come back. 'Look, I know this is the worst part of any manager's job, but honestly, I can't see that there's anything here to worry about. It's not like we're not all aware of Mr Fletcher's world view. We've had plenty of run-ins with him over the years. We've seen his detailed logs before and they're petty beyond the point of childish. If it ever went to a tribunal he'd be a laughing stock – I can't believe a barrister would even let him start.

'And on the stress front, he's being referred to our Occupational Health team for an assessment. I don't think they're going to come out of left field with anything new from him, and you'll get the chance to provide a summary of your perspective. And if it's of any interest, he hasn't yet got a Federation rep; between you and me, everyone in this building has refused to act for him. So he's got to go further up the chain, and they'll certainly understand what's being implied by that, even if he doesn't.'

Fleur thanked her new best friend and hung up. Ah well, she mused. At least the daily irritation of his presence was removed for a while, but it was bloody typical of the little twonk. Just when they needed his skills. She turned back to the matters in hand, and texted Cervantes to report in. He appeared at her office door in short order, accompanied as ever by Murthi.

'Hello Gov. Did the memorial thing go OK?'

Cooper replied in the affirmative and got down to brass tacks.

'Neville Humberstone. Any info?'

'Yes Gov. As said, he was a financial adviser. Self-employed, used a virtual PA service. Got all the right qualifications, but,' he looked at this notepad, 'apparently there was a big change in the requirements a couple of years back and a lot of FA's left the job, because the new exams were really hard. Mr Humberstone took three shots to get through. He only ever worked on property issues, mostly mortgages and loans. I've spoken to the PA service he used and they've already emailed me to confirm that they'll forward everything they've got digitally as soon as we let them have the warrant. I've filled it in for you and emailed it for authorisation,' he offered helpfully.

Throughout this conversation Fleur was conscious of Murthi hovering near the door, still uncertain of his role in the case. She looked up at him.

'Ajay.' He stiffened slightly and looked enquiringly at her. 'How's it going? Are you finding it interesting?'

He nodded. 'Yes Ma'am. I mean, the systems are the same, but it's fascinating seeing it from another perspective.' He waited, aware that she was about to say something else.

'Right, good. Look, there's always a choice in these swaps and placements, and most of that is down to you. Do you want to observe or muck in?'

'Muck in Ma'am, definitely.'

'Right, good again.' Fleur looked over at Cervantes. 'Don. Divvy up your task list. You don't need to double-hand everything now – we need all the help we can get.'

After they'd gone, Fleur fired off a quick email to Fred Gregson, asking for guidance on what to tell the rest of the team about Simon Fletcher's absence. She knew that they'd read between the lines with perfect clarity, but she thought there'd be some protocol about communications and so on.

Out in the sergeants' area, Brent was whizzing quickly through emails, just before setting off for his meeting. One took his particular attention and he read it carefully. He placed a call and, once finished, leant around the door post to Fleur's office.

'Gov. Just got an interesting email from Chloé Antoine, you know, Calum Grant's widow?' Fleur nodded but remained silent.

'Apparently her friend, Harriet Brand, has arrived, come to stay to help out. She's told Chloé something that Chloé thinks we need to hear. I'm going to drop in to see them after I've done with the Solicitors' thing.'

THIRTY FOUR

Mick Brent strode out happily. The day was cold now, but not wet and this wasn't paper work, so all was good in his world. He reflected as he walked that a year ago he could never have guessed that one of the worst cases in his experience would have resulted in his being able to move into Major Crimes and Homicide as a full time member. His wife, although a highly-respected Forensic Psychologist, was also afflicted by the effects of a serious road accident many years previously. Confined to a wheelchair, she nevertheless held down an impressive consulting service, largely dealing with risk assessments for the criminal and prison services. Until the previous year, the fact that her breathing was sometimes precarious had led to all support services asserting a preference for residential care. Whilst they'd avoided this, no-one was prepared to offer overnight support. But the high profile nature of their last major case had included a spotlight on Maze Brent and her predicament, and mountains had been moved. Embarrassing it had certainly been at the time, but with so positive an outcome they both found it hard to resent the public focus they'd had to endure for a while. So now Brent was no longer constrained by the office hours he'd previously had to negotiate.

By nature he was a detective. Things *interested* him. Usually they were relevant to a case, sometimes not, but he loved to *know*. He was efficient at administration and organisation, but most of all he relished getting out and about, looking, questioning, puzzling. It was only a brisk fifteen minute walk to his meeting; the weather being as bone-chilling as it was, ambling along was out of the question anyway. The day was already turning to dusk and he enjoyed the lighting up of the city around him as he paced his route. Maisie always laughed at him; she said that he walked like a copper, ran like a rugby player and sat like a lump of potato. He guessed she was probably right, though he always re-joined with a spirited denial.

Arriving at the venue, Mick reported to a helpful receptionist and was soon ushered into a pleasantly furnished office.

Twenty minutes later he was outside again, slightly bemused and certainly amused. He doubted he'd heard quite so many 'should that prove to be the case', 'allegedly' and 'should further investigation confirm' caveats in his entire career. But one thing was clear. Recently someone had contacted the Solicitors' Regulatory Authority about Lauren Greenwood. And not her employers; they had certainly been in contact, but more recently. Brent had the impression that the discrepancy in timing and order of these two notifications was one of the things currently in the category of 'should further investigation confirm.' With the home turf issue of Simon Fletcher in his mind, Mick Brent was sorry for this. The chances were that an entire firm was going to pay a price for one rotten apple. He knew only too well that the normal clangers and slips of working life could be seriously magnified by a focus on someone else's wrongdoing.

He shrugged his shoulders back into what his mother would have called his 'good' coat and stood for a moment, getting his bearings. The District Line, he thought, and headed towards the Monument tube steps. As a driver who loved cars and driving, he saw no way that he'd ever enjoy driving again in London. He amused himself as he squeezed into a space on the platform and then the tube, thinking, in the style of Yoda. 'Broken it is, our London. Shame, it is.' Congestion charges hadn't helped, just made the frustration more expensive. Public transport was cramped and uncomfortable and not always efficient. But most of all, his fellow passengers seemed to have become so bloody arsey over recent years that the camaraderie he recalled from his earliest days on the beat had long gone. In his ear, Yoda said, 'Responsible, the Americans they are. Do this they did, talk of work ethic they must.' He thought Yoda might have a point.

Outside Chloé Antoine's apartment block he leant back to look up at the pleasing façade. His arrival was anticipated and his buzz answered immediately. He was ushered once more into the beautiful kitchen, where he found a woman he assumed was Harriet Brand sitting on one of the sofas in the window area. She stood to greet him and Mick was shocked by her gaunt appearance. He knew from his previous conversation with Chloé that Harriet was ill, but he hadn't gathered just how seriously. Privately, he thought that he saw many signs that the end of the road was close for this poor woman and he worried briefly about making what was clearly already a difficult life more so. But then, it depended on what she had to say.

Chloé, having gestured him into the sofa opposite her friend offered him an 'apero', guessing that he'd understand both the word and the meaning. He did. The after-work drink was often an important one in France during the week, and became a signal of the evening at weekends. It also meant that Chloé wanted this interview to be a civil one, so he glanced at his watch, noted it was past 6pm and gladly accepted a glass of white wine. Unidentified by Chloé as she handed it over, he was delighted to find himself the custodian of a really good Chablis. He leant back and smiled at Harriet Brand, who had watched the proceedings with a calm but alert air.

'Ms Brand. It's good to meet you.' She nodded, and Brent continued. 'But I hope you don't mind me asking – are you well enough to cope with a chat with a clumsy London plod?'

She laughed, clearly as amused by the unlikely description as he'd wanted her to be.

'I'm fine, thank you. And it's Harriet – Harry – if you please. If nothing else, I'm so angry that I've got some extra energy for a while. What's best to do? Do you want to ask questions or should I just do a sort of round up of what I've found out and then you can interrogate away?' She smiled at him, her head tilted to one side, her beautiful bone structure evident regardless of the ravages of the cancer.

'The second I think. Until I get an idea of what you need to say, my questions will be cack-handed at best.'

Chloé Antoine interrupted him at this point, her delicate French accent a pleasure to the ear. 'I am so sorry, but I cannot resist. Cack-handed, this is a new one.'

Harriet laughed and was quick to provide a couple of examples. 'It means clumsy, not refined. Like my cooking or your singing!' Satisfied, Chloé settled herself in a corner of the same sofa as Brent and withdrew. Harriet rubbed her neck with both hands and leant forward slightly.

'OK. This started yesterday when Chloé and I started to talk about Calum and what she's been learning about him. Specifically, about the property stuff. You see, he arranged my mortgage when I bought my house in Manchester, or at least he put me in touch with a chap that did. And he also introduced me to the same solicitor that Chloé knows, Lauren Green something or other. Anyway, when I was going through it all was also the time when I got my cancer diagnosis. I've got two children, they're six and eight. My husband died four years ago. Aneurysm.'

There was no self-conscious distress as she pronounced this, just a matter-of-fact announcement. 'You don't have to declare cancer after you've had a mortgage approved and it's started. But what was relevant for me was that I had critical life cover. I got it when James, my husband died. It'll pay my estate an income and cover the mortgage. Because I didn't take out a huge loan, the house would be paid off in a couple of years. But this Neville Whosit thought I ought to have an additional policy. He said it was against the law to prevent me from getting that sort of policy – I suspect now that that's a bare-faced lie. So anyway, he sorted that for me too. Really easy, done on line, not a huge premium or anything, and worth it to have a good property outright, to leave for my kids.

'The fact is, I knew early on that my chances weren't good. It's ovarian cancer.' She paused. 'The silent killer, they call it, because doctors miss it. Even bloody female doctors, like mine, rabbit on about irritable bowel syndrome or gluten intolerance. So, it was Stage 4 before they found it. At the time I thought Calum and this Neville bloke were kind and supportive, you know. I mean,' she glanced apologetically at Chloé, 'I never liked Calum, he just wasn't good enough, but in this I thought I'd found a bit of human decency.'

She looked directly at Brent, temper blazing now in her eyes. 'I hadn't. Indeed I hadn't. Do you know what they did?' She didn't pause for an answer.

'It was yesterday. I don't know why, but I began to think about the insurance policy. The more Chloé and I talked the more it worried me, so I pulled it up – I've got digital copies of everything. And I read through it all. Like all policies it's long and it's got loads of fine print. There's a sort of summary page, where my kids get the house transferred to the trust I've set up for them, but for the first time I read past that. And in there I found it.' Her voice rose, and shook slightly. 'In the event of my death the policy covers Calum and Neville Wotsit – they'd get my house. The insurance didn't protect *me* at all. I don't know whether to be most angry with myself or with them. It's just a standard policy, even down to its usual ten day change of mind clause, which of course I didn't. So then I rang the insurance company direct and got them to send me a copy of the policy. And in that version, the summary page assigns it all jointly to Calum and Neville.' She leant back, tired.

'Chloé's printed copies for you,' she gestured to a large envelope lying on the table between them.

Brent became aware that his fingers were rigid around the stem of his glass. He looked directly at Harriet Brand and said, slowly and distinctly.

'Mrs Brand, Harry, I couldn't be more sorry for everything that you've been through, that you're going through now, and what you've just found out. Is there anything specific you want us to do?' He added, 'and have you cancelled this bloody policy?' He couldn't help it. He was flat furious and almost cross with the two men for being dead.

'Oh yes, I've cancelled it. I've had a long talk with the insurance company. To start with they wouldn't accept any responsibility, because Neville Thingy dealt with the all of the correspondence from them, but I kept pointing out that, whilst that can be helpful, maybe a system where both parties get original copies would reduce the temptation to do what these two sods did. But your question, do I want you to do something? Oh yes. Because what if they've done this with other people too? Calum knew, they both knew, that my kids only have me for financial support. They'll be loved and looked after by my husband's parents, they're still young enough to do it well and they'll be properly cared for. But my parents-in-law aren't well off and it would have been really, really hard without the money from my house and the estate. So, if Calum and his nasty mate had no compunction about screwing me and my kids, who else have they done over?' She regarded him bleakly.

Brent took a overlarge swig of wine. Not a delicate savouring of the French vintage, just a deep hungry need for comfort.

The conversation didn't take much longer, at least with the focus beaming onto Calum Grant and Neville Humberstone. Neither Chloé nor Harry had any more information on that topic, so the three of them chatted amiably about Harry's children, with her describing their antics with obvious pride and a sort of buried frustration at what she was never going to see of their futures. She said,

'Noah, he's the 8 year-old, he's certain he wants to be in the police, if he can't be a footballer, like his hero Salah. 'Course, we live in Manchester, so that doesn't make him popular at school.'

Brent, ever helpful, said, 'Well, if you're ever down here with them, I can give him a tour of our station, get a photo with some uniform and all that.'

Harriet Brand looked sad but pleased. 'I don't think I'll be able to do that, but Chloé could?' She looked enquiringly at her friend, who nodded, and then continued, 'I haven't said, but my husband's parents are down here, and the kids will come to them soon...' she tailed off, 'soon...anyway. The kids are young enough and they don't need to hang around with the old memories. I know my parents-in-law would move if I asked them, but they have support structures and friends here and we all think it'll be easier. And they adore their Aunt Chloé, so they'll get plenty of silliness too. And, you know, they only speak French with her, so they've already got better language skills than you could imagine.'

Brent was firm. 'Then Chloé must let me know when the children are here and ready for the canteen pie and peas!'

It was gone 7.30pm by the time he took his leave, and he rang Maze to let her know he was on his way. As ever, he felt his heart lift when he heard her voice and they chatted about the evening ahead, such as it was, as he made his way towards the nearest tube station.

Across town, Don Cervantes was making his way towards a small terraced house on the edge of Norbiton. He and Ajay had split up, as advised by Cooper. She was right, the to-do list was lengthening by the minute.

The house was dark as he knocked on the door of the tidy little cottage, but as he turned away he almost bumped into the woman who was stepping up the small path. With her face lowered, attention on her 'phone, she hadn't seen him and his appearance made her jump back in shock. He had time for two quick reflections before he said anything. First, there was no doubt that this was Caro Horbridge's daughter. With the same fine bone structure and petite frame, he could see how stunning the mother must have been in earlier times. And he felt a pang of regret that people in London, so often women, felt threatened by people. He quickly pulled out his warrant card.

'I'm sorry to startle you Ms Horbridge. I'm Detective Constable Cervantes, from the Metropolitan Police. Would it be possible to have a word with you?' He handed her his card. 'If you want to check with the station that I'm genuine, I'll gladly wait out here for you to do that.'

The young woman made a quick decision. In her job she worked with the full range of youth, and had as good a grasp on character as any intuitive experienced copper.

'No, come on in.' She ushered him into a tiny hall and said,

'Just bear with me a minute while I get some lights and the kettle on.'

She left him standing in the hall whilst she stepped into a room to his right. He saw the lights come on and he heard her pulling curtains. She called out,

'Come on in Constable. Have a seat. I'll just get the kettle on and make us a drink. Tea or coffee?'

He opted for coffee and then sat patiently, scanning her full bookshelves with interest. He was a keen reader, often getting through two or three books in a week, even with his crazy hours. He could see an interesting mix. There were clearly some school text books mixed in there, mostly music, but also some mathematics, which puzzled him. There was a far greater number of travel books, but even that was superseded by a very eclectic crime writers' collection. Strong writers like Reginald Hill and Ian Rankin rubbed shoulders with their American peers and some French names, he thought. He made a mental note of the authors' name. He'd read many of her selected British writers, so maybe the continental ones would be worth a look.

He could hear her bustling about in the kitchen and detected a kettle coming to the boil. He turned his attention to the room. There was a television in one corner, a small dining table that could seat four at a push in the bay window. It was a pleasant space, jauntily furnished in a background beige but enlivened by cushions and throws in jewel colours.

As he settled back more comfortably in the only armchair in the room, Rose entered with a tray holding two mugs and a plate of digestive biscuits. She handed him his drink then sat opposite him, perched on the edge of the sofa.

'You must think I'm so stupid. I let you in and stuck you in here and I didn't even ask what it was about.' Cervantes just smiled politely. That was far more common that people would believe. Despite the TV programmes that showed combative, argumentative encounters between the police and the public, that wasn't often the case. Most people were keen to make a good impression, going straight into 'host mode'. The vague sense of guilt that most felt was slightly lessened by the familiar routine of making a drink, emphasising their home turf.

Cervantes said. 'Don't worry – that's perfectly normal.' She looked sceptical. 'No, really.'

He swallowed. This was his first time breaking the news of a death to a family member on his own. He'd watched it done a few times, but now it was his turn. He'd learnt from his observations that pussyfooting about was crueller than the 'rip off the plaster in one swipe' approach.

'I'm really sorry to have to tell you that your father died last week, on a train coming back from Manchester.'

She looked surprised but not shaken.

'Oh. Was it a heart attack or something? He was usually angry enough to bring one of those on, most of the time.' She regarded him with clear, bright blue eyes, calm and controlled.

'It wasn't natural causes. I'm afraid there's a very strong chance that it was deliberately done.'

She leaned back into the sofa. Paler, she nonetheless maintained her composure. She smiled.

'Well, it wasn't me. Though I'll tell you, from about the age of seven I thought about ways to make him go away. I suppose I'm a bit surprised that someone actually did it. He was always careful to choose employees that were very subservient. He didn't really like people to have opinions. How's my mother?' For the first time, some animation.

He was a little taken aback at how quickly she'd shifted reference to her father into the past tense, but then realised that he'd been in her past for over a decade now. It was probably how she always thought of him.

Cervantes judged that honesty was probably going to get him more than tact.

'Well, she's shocked. But I truly think she's just beginning to understand that her life is going to change an awful lot, for the better. I got the impression,' he hesitated, 'I got the impression that she was very much given clear, um, parameters, for her life.' He upped his inflection at the end of that comment, almost making it a question. Rose Horbridge took it as such.

'She wasn't allowed to breath without permission. It used to make me so angry that she didn't stand up to him. I tried, you know, after I'd qualified as a teacher. Even when I was just at college, I thought I could encourage her to leave, be near me. But I think he changed the 'phone number, quite soon after I left. I wrote, and wrote, but she never answered. Once, I went round there to see her. Just my luck, she wasn't in. But a neighbour must have told him – the old bag next door thought he was the bee's knees – and he turned up at my college digs and told me to keep away or he'd make her suffer. And he told me not to bother writing, because he'd set up for any mail addressed to my mother to be redirected somewhere else. To his office, I expect. ' She took a breath. 'Nasty, mean-spirited, spiteful, bullying old bastard. I wanted to tell him that, the last time I saw him, that day in college. But I didn't dare, because he was quite capable of making Mum pay for it, for days or weeks.

'Back then, I just couldn't understand why she put up with it. Now I realise that she stood between him and me as much as she could, arranging after-school activities that kept me out of the house, things that he would think were acceptable. Mostly music. And I do get it now, that it's possible to be so worn down by somebody that you can't see a way out. I thought, after he'd been to warn me off, that I'd give it a while. So, about six years ago, I started writing a couple of times each year, just giving her a 'phone number. I thought maybe he'd have stopped with the mail redirection, because he really didn't like spending money on anything. But I guess I was wrong, because I never heard back.'

Cervantes said, quietly. 'She never received anything from you. It doesn't seem to have occurred to her that your father had intervened in that. Perhaps he encouraged her to see it his way.'

She nodded, sad but resigned. 'I've got a different life now. I love my work, I've got good friends. I'm getting married next year. But I would like to see her again. We used to be so close. Do you think that she'll be OK if I get in touch?'

Cervantes had no doubt as to that and passed on her mother's 'phone number. She thanked him, then looked him in the eye.

'Well, you've probably spotted my favourite reading material, so you can guess that I know you have to ask. When do I need an alibi for?'

Cervantes gave a genuine smile. 'Last Thursday, most of the afternoon.'

She nodded. 'Well, I was at work all day. Thursdays, I don't have any free time in the timetable, and I do a lunch club and then orchestra after school. I'll talk to my deputy head in the morning and tell him that you're going to ring to get corroboration. Is that OK with you?'

He thanked her and took the details of the contact he'd need for follow up. Picking up his coffee mug he said,

'So, it's music that you teach?'

'Yes, though I also do a bit of Applied Maths, with the sixth form, just to keep my hand in.' Her visitor looked surprised.

'Ah. Lots of people don't realise that many mathematicians are quite musical, and vice versa. It's a matter of patterns, you see.'

As a bloke with virtually no appreciation for music beyond what was belting out from the radio in the car or in any pub he frequented, he dimly saw the comparison, but parked it in his memory as interesting but not relevant to the here and now.

She bid him farewell at the door, kindly wishing him a safe journey. He wondered if, when, she'd contact her newly widowed mother.

THIRTY FIVE

Dear Diary

It was my brother's birthday today. He got a train set. He's four, so he can't really play with it. *He* does though and holds up my brother so he can see it. I'm not allowed to go into the room when it's all laid out. He says I'm a useless waste of space.

One of the trains has steam coming out of the top. I'd like to know how that works. Sometimes I can ask him a question and he doesn't get mad, if it's a subject he's interested in.

He likes reading action thriller books. Alistair McLean, Bernard Cornwell, Len Deighton, Wilbur Smith. I've read all of his books. He lets me but he checks every page afterwards, in case I've done something stupid like turning a corner down. I'd never do that. But I think he does like it that I've read them.

They've never been to a parents' evening at my schools. I bring the letters home but they go in the bin. They went to the nativity at my brother's nursery though.

I've got to choose my subjects for my exams. It's hard to pick. I know I want to go to university but I don't know if I can. My form teacher says you can get a grant, which is like money to pay the college and to eat and everything. But she says that the parents have to pay too and it depends on how much money they have. They won't pay. My teacher says I'll fly through my exams and then my A levels. I do like learning.

There's a big world out there.

THIRTY SIX

Tuesday dawned dry and viciously cold. The entire team was in the building well before 8am, Reith in particular facing an avalanche of paper and emails. A broad range of things to note, others for response, some for urgent action. There was an issue with an upcoming freedom of speech conference and an expected right-wing protest, something going on at one of the Scandinavian embassies which looked like espionage but, reading between the lines. he thought could easily be some careless international love affair – did they never learn; the Chinese virus thing was still a way off on the radar but he did note that more health bodies seemed to be getting involved. He remembered the effect of SARS, and the whole bird flu thing and thought that it would probably be no worse than that.

Unconsciously he'd been checking his mobile since he'd arrived, and at eight prompt it rang; of course, he'd forgotten it in that moment and it made him jump. He took pleasure in seeing Leonie Merton's name on the display and answered it quickly, breathing in her voice and aware that he was far too invested in wanting a positive response from his request of the previous day.

At 8.30, Reith, Cooper, Brent, Cervantes and Kurt were in one of the small briefing rooms. Although the major incident room which was theirs for the duration of this case was at their disposal, Fleur had a few things to say that needed to be kept rather more quiet. She began with,

'Right. You'll be aware that Simon Fletcher isn't with us. I can tell you, formally, that he's now off with stress for the foreseeable future.'

The core team regarded her balefully, saying nothing. She continued.

'There are guidelines, so please be aware that we can't talk about this outside this room. But,' she pulled a wry face, 'you're all going to be interviewed on another matter, which some of you may feel is related. I would just ask you to be fair and honest. As regards contacting Mr Fletcher, the HR team say that it's appropriate to do so as long as any messages are supportive and don't relate to any ongoing issues.'

The silence continued. Not one of them would be tempted to contact Simon Fletcher, secure in the knowledge that it would be both misconstrued and certainly never reciprocated, should the tables be turned.

Content that the right points had been made, Cooper looked towards Reith, who gladly provided a more positive note.

'I'm delighted to tell you that Leonie Merton will be joining us later today, to work on the money laundering angle.' Reith took rigid care to ignore the smug expression on Brent's amiable face.

'She's very experienced in this area, which we're certainly not, so it's a relief. It's murder, and multiple ones at that, so I can't let it go out of house, but I'll admit I've been stressing about it.' He looked at Kurt Groehling, 'You too Kurt, I think?'

Groehling nodded. 'Oh yes. You know that feeling you get, when you know there's so much that you don't know? Anyway, Ms Merton is really impressive.' Without realising, he betrayed the depth of his previous concerns and subsequent research, 'Fraud and Art both say she's the best they've ever worked with. And,' he produced with the air of one making the key point, 'apparently not up herself at all.'

Those two issues dealt with, the group transferred itself to the large incident room, where almost twenty people awaited the start of day briefing and their assignments. The depth of investigation on something like this was profound, and a key part of the session was identifying two officers to work with Groehling and Leonie Merton, as well as assigning them at least one admin person. Groehling was keen to have Daisy and after a brief skirmish with Brent, who liked her for her interview skills, was successful. Cooper chipped in.

'Don and I've been talking. I didn't realise that Ajay has a degree in economics and accountancy. So does it make sense to everyone else to put him into the new group?'

Ajay looked up from his place at the end of room, surprised to hear his name and then keen to hear if he'd get the chance to be on the 'inside' of this latest development. Since figures and finance weren't high on the priorities or interests of most of the others in the room, his wish was granted, and he was exchanged with Daisy, who was delighted and a little relieved to return to Brent's tutelage.

Cooper took centre stage again. 'I'm just going to ask Mick Brent to take us through a conversation he had last evening. I think it's, finally, going to give us a direction.'

Mick stood up from his seat at the end of a row, turned and leaned against the wall so that he had a good view of all of his colleagues.

'Right; you'll all know from the briefings and the case notes that Chloé Antoine is the widow of Calum Grant. Not so much a grieving one, I'm glad to say. Anyway, I met her friend Harriet Brand yesterday.'

Succinctly, Brent told the vicious tale. Many of the team were parents, but all were human. The depth of emotional betrayal shocked them all and there were general murmurs of distaste from across the room.

Cervantes chimed in after this, summarising his visit to Rose Horbridge. 'I've checked with the school this morning. She was definitely there all day, no opportunity to get away. The deputy head seemed really keen to stress that she's highly regarded. Says she works with the whole range of abilities and that even the hardest nuts don't want to upset Miss Horbridge.

Cooper pulled them back to her agenda.

'Right, so it's now become obvious that there are two sets of crimes to be explored. The murders, obviously,' she offered a wry smile, 'and what we think is the money laundering. There are obviously overlaps, because if what we're beginning to suspect is true, the murderer is also in the data somewhere, quite possibly as a victim of the sort of thing that almost happened to Harriet Brand.'

From there, the session moved to task allocation and then out of the door into action. Kurt Groehling hung back for a moment, keen to talk to Cooper on a practical note. Reith gestured to him to continue, and stood to one side for a moment.

Kurt said, 'Gov, I know we usually keep everything going in the main incident suite, but I'm a bit worried about that with this little financial team. We're going to be accessing some really sensitive data, and it isn't that I don't trust anyone on the team, but when it comes to big databases and passwords, and then personal file printouts, I'm not keen on the open doors.

Cooper glanced at Reith, but he was already nodding. He said,

'It's a good point Kurt, and I think Ms Merton will feel a lot more comfortable.' Reith turned back to Cooper. 'Any ideas?'

She was swift to respond. 'Well, the Chief Inspector's office is empty; no-one's likely to be in there for the next few months. The door locks, there are decent blinds and there are marker boards all the way down one wall. We can get a couple of extra desks in there; we can probably sort it before Leonie even arrives.'

Reith nodded again. 'Make it so, Number One.' Their ongoing joke about Cooper's enjoyment of the old Star Trek series resurfaced for a moment.

Kurt departed to secure the furniture and support he needed to create the desired office space, leaving Reith and Cooper alone. Reith slid his bottom on to a nearby table and gestured Cooper to sit down.

'Now is as good a time as ever to tell you. The CI's office isn't going to be vacant for that long. Graham Dyer has submitted his retirement papers and that'll all go through over the next few weeks. Do you want it? I've pretty much got carte blanche on this, but I didn't want to assume.'

Fleur Cooper was taken aback.

'But I've only been here five minutes.'

Reith snorted. 'It doesn't feel like that. You've brought in more practical, positive things than anyone else I can ever remember, you already know absolutely everyone in the nick, even the bullet-heads find it hard to say you're a crap officer. And, most of all, for the past few months you've been doing Graham's job and your own. My only concern,' Fleur looked up, slightly perturbed, 'is that you'll get some flak for the speed of it. But I think you'll cope.'

Fleur reflected on the flak she'd already survived and grinned at him, for once her natural diffidence and reserve pierced by her delight. The chance for promotion, albeit to a job she already did, was a gift, and to stay working with Steve Reith was something she'd fight hard to do for as long as possible. She laughed aloud.

'I hate the film, but please can I have some more Sir?'

Reith was quietly pleased. He'd been a little worried that she'd see the politics as more important than the practicalities.

'I can't make the formal announcement yet – HR first. But I did think I might persuade Mick and Maisie to host a takeaway night with the core team, plus Leonie, and just mention it then. Tonight or tomorrow? You, me, Don, Kurt. What do you think?'

Fleur reflected. 'It's not quite the usual formal structure, is it? We've sort of formed an odd little team in the middle of the bigger team. I don't think that matters so much, because it does happen across the whole group, when we all pick up on different directions. I'm just wondering, since we're not sticking rigidly to the command shape on this, whether we ought to have Daisy and Ajay in there?'

Comfortable with anything that worked, Reith was fine with this. It was a social thing, after all. He was keen to get Leonie Merton embedded with the core group and thought that a pizza night be the fastest way to do it, Maze Brent permitting. He went in pursuit of Mick, who he found back at his desk in the sergeants' lair. He outlined his thinking to him. Brent was keen, but said,

'We don't actually know if Leonie can do either night. Shall I wait till she arrives and check it out before I ring Maze?

The plan agreed, the two men parted to pursue their hectic days, Mick continuing the construction of his to-do list and Steve Reith to marshal the papers and his thoughts for a contentious finance meeting.

THIRTY SEVEN

Dear Diary

I don't know what to do. I don't think I can tell anyone. I can't tell Granny, it's too bad. I can't tell a teacher at school, because I think they'd have to tell someone. I don't know what to do.

It was last night. He's very angry with Mum about something. I don't know what, but he's been punishing her all week. Not physical stuff, but nasty comments and stuff. And then, after we'd all gone to bed, he came to my room and made me go to their room. He pushed Mum outside the door and locked her out. She started crying. I heard my little brother with her, he was crying too.

And then he started touching me, on my neck, on my chest. All the time, he was yelling at Mum, telling her what he was doing. I didn't know what to do. He's strong, and he was really angry. I only had my nightdress and some knickers on. He pushed me onto the bed and he started to pull my nightie up and touch my legs. All the time, he's shouting to Mum about what he's doing.

When he hooked his fingers on my knickers, I started to scream and he punched me hard, in the tummy. I didn't stop screaming though and that seemed to break through somehow. He bunched my nightie into a knot around my neck and pulled me off the bed and held me up against the wall, by the light switch, while he unlocked the door. When it was open, he shoved me, really hard, across the landing and against the opposite wall, and then he let me go. He grabbed my mother and pushed her back into their bedroom. Just before he slammed the door, he looked at me and shouted at me to look after my little brother.

I put him to bed and read him a story until he was asleep. Then I went to my room. I have big bruises on my arms, some at the front of my neck and a very big one right across my tummy.

I couldn't sleep. I thought and thought but I can't see how to escape yet.

This morning, nobody asked if I was all right.

I don't know what to do. I'll have to hide the bruises. We've got PE today, and they can't see them.

THIRTY EIGHT

By 10.30 Leonie Merton had presented herself at the main Reception, been collected by Kurt and escorted to her temporary home. The general plan was that Cooper, Brent and Groehling would brief her on the case and then await her thoughts. They'd all previously worked with external consultants, with widely varying levels of success. Some had been useful, but limited, others totally disconnected from the reality of the world of policing and just one or two of real and long-term value. They all hoped, but no-one was counting any chickens.

Coffee was sourced and the four huddled around the main desk in the newly commandeered room. Leonie listened intently, asking questions as they went along, saying,

'It's no good if I make a list of questions and save them up. We'll all have forgotten the flavour by then.'

She made a number of notes as they talked, sketching what seemed to be a loose diagram, adding arrows and question marks as the discussion deepened. She was visibly impressed by the scale of the finances involved and clearly horrified by the deal dealt to Harriet Brand.

When the three officers had reached the end of their outline it was gone 2pm and no more questions seemed to be forthcoming. All four leant back in their chairs, Leonie looking down at her notepad. She turned her gaze on the three of them, her green eyes alight with enthusiasm and energy.

'Well, it's not going to be boring, is it? So, what do you want from me?'

They all looked taken back at this. 'Sorry?' said Cooper.

Leo smiled.

'It's in your gift. How hands-on do you want me to be? We can go from me doing every task you've identified as necessary right through to me identifying key areas for investigation and setting you the parameters. I've learned,' she said carefully, 'that some people prefer to be totally in charge...'

Fleur snorted and, without realising, set their future relationships on exactly the right path.

'At the level of your fees, I'd like you to put your knickers on over your trousers. There aren't any big egos here, we need your expertise and we need it fast. You tell us what you need'

Leo roared with delighted laughter. 'Great. Then I need an hour or so to lay out key activity. How do you want it handed out? Through you, or can I talk to others in the team?'

Fleur thought for a moment. 'Use Kurt to start with – he'll introduce you to people so that in the future you can go to the right person. But we've also got a briefing at 5pm – I think it'd be good if you could talk to the full team. Maybe a few minutes on what money laundering really is? Then a broader view of what we're going to be examining? So then they'll understand what's coming their way?'

Cooper didn't say it, but both she and Leo knew that this would be a key point in the team recognising her professional credentials.

That agreed, the three police officers rose to leave Leo to work on her tactical plan. Mick remained for a few moments and outlined Reith's plan to get them all together of an evening. Leo seemed both pleased and amused and readily offered either evening, dependent on Maze's wishes. Brent departed to check with his wife, who was in turn delighted to get a catch-up chance with this investigation. The Brents agreed between them that the following day might be better; it gave Leo more chance to meet people in the station, took some pressure off her first day and allowed Maze and Mick the chance to plan a menu. No way was Maze going to permit a takeaway supper when she had a clear shot at her romantic target for Reith and Leo.

Mick sent a quick email round to the team, but also stuck his head round the door of Reith's outer office, asking Reith's PA, Claire, to get him to check for an email from him 'about tomorrow night'. Brent thought that would be sufficient to avert any chance of Reith missing the key email in the raft of information he received every day.

Back in her new project base, Leo regarded her notepad. It was clear what needed to be looked at; now it was just a question of how deep they'd need to go. Whilst she was a commercial animal by trade — after all, the company could only keep people in work if it made a profit, she was also keen never to take advantage. She and Harry Wilson, her co-director, preferred repeat contracts based on mutual respect, rather than the serial fleecing of easy targets. So, for this project she needed to bear a number of things in mind. Keep the costs down for the Met, but also ensure that they were provided with cast-iron evidence for any possible prosecutions. On top of which, she needed to provide a framework for them. People worked best if they understood why they were doing something. Leo knew that was going to be easier said than done in this case. If you just started with the thorny topic of mathematics, many, many people turned off before they got anywhere. Add the financial aspects to that and almost everyone assumed it got even worse. Leo didn't expect to get many people to see the wonderful world of puzzles and patterns that she visited each day, but she at least needed to open the door to its possibilities. She bent to her task.

At 5pm the main room was fuller than it had been in the morning, partly because of the normal ebb and flow of people in and out of the building and partly because there was a curiosity as to Leo Merton. Many recalled her from the previous summer and their odd, terrible protagonist.

At the front of the room, next to Fleur Cooper, stood Leo with her shining auburn hair attractively pinned in a sort of loose bun at the back of her head. She was wearing black trousers and silk shirt under an emerald green blazer. Reith, slipping into a row at the back – a movement not missed by Leo, thought that she looked like an exotic bird in the midst of his tired officers, most garbed in duller tones. Even the shining Fleur Cooper faded a little in this company.

Fleur dealt with a couple of practical issues then introduced Leo. She said,

'I know you're going to make her welcome, but for the love of Mike, listen to her today. I've asked her to explain some key stuff, which might just help us move forward faster than we have so far.' She nodded at Leo Merton, who then stepped to the side of the room and picked up a large box. She placed this on the front table and opened it, watched with interest by the cohort in front of her. Out came a very large bowl filled with fruit and mini bars of chocolate. She smiled and said,

'Bribery 101. I'll keep this filled on two conditions. First, that you bear with my questions, no matter how daft you think they are and second that all the fruit as well as the chocolate goes before I do a refill.'

A brief smattering of applause, which she ignored.

'Right, Money Laundering 101. Is it OK if I do the absolute basics? I know some of you'll know more, but Inspector Cooper has asked me to lay down some groundwork.'

A general murmur of approval came from the room, though no-one could be said to sound particularly enthralled at the prospect. Leo continued.

'Right. Someone tell me, in a sentence, what they think money laundering is.'

A couple of hands went up and Leo selected a tall officer at the back of the room, who said. 'Well, is it a way to hide dirty money through more legitimate sources or outlets?'

Leo nodded, pleased at the precision.

'Exactly. So let's just take that a bit further. When we say dirty money, where's that coming from?'

It didn't take long to establish that the most common sources were trafficking – drugs and human, fraud and theft and increasingly digital crime. Not to be forgotten was the increasing evidence of dirty money in and out of the terrorism arena.

'OK. So how big a problem is it? I mean, you know and I know that it's a *significant* problem, but that's because we see if before and after, as it were. But how relevant is that to the big wide world?'

Interested, but uninformed, no-one said anything.

'Well, the estimate here and in the United States, which we can therefore assume will be roughly reflected globally, is that between 3 and 5 per cent of GDP is dirty money travelling.'

Now unsure, the room still didn't react and Leo smiled.

'I'm so sorry – this won't hurt for long! The GDP is the Gross Domestic Product, which is just a technical way of saying it's all of a country's income, expenditure and production, of services or of products delivered within in a year. So what I'm saying is that between 3 and 5 per cent of everything is dirty money on its travels. So we've all unwittingly touched it, used it, been affected it by. It's caused prices to rise, insurance premiums to increase and complicated all of our working and personal lives because now we have to try to prevent it happening. If you've bought a new house, you know about the documents and evidence you have to produce, if you're interviewing for a new job it's the same, and so on. If you inherited some money and paid it into your account, it will have been reported and scrutinised. So in reality it's not just about a small bunch of bad guys doing the dirty on each other. It's quietly invaded all of our lives and it's costing us. So do you want to know how it's done?'

The room was beginning to warm up and responded positively.

'Well, let's start with a simple example. Let's imagine that you run a very profitable but highly illegal business - say a drug distribution ring. Your profit is too high to conceal from the tax people without arousing their suspicions. You want to buy a nice house, and cars, and send your kids to an upmarket school, and you can't pay for all of that with cash from your back pocket. So, you begin putting the funds into a legitimate-seeming enterprise - let's invent a pizza restaurant owned by you or a loyal mate, who'll no doubt take a cut for his trouble.

Your restaurant might look like a perfectly normal one, complete with regular customers and good pizza. But it's actually a front for your primary economic activity, which you, of course, can't list on your tax returns or bank account applications. You route most of the money you make selling drugs through the pizza restaurant, spending it on kitchen equipment, food products, supplies, services, advertising, even staffing.

Once on the restaurant's balance sheet, the illicit funds merge with legitimate gains from paying customers. It's difficult or impossible to determine whether a given expense involves legit or illicit funds — the answer is now both, which is the whole point.

To untrained observers, you're running a very successful, totally above-board restaurant and nothing more. And of course it's successful, but the restaurant didn't have to pay for anything from its own profits. So what's on the balance sheet is *all* profit – what people like me call the 'bottom line'. Because the provenance looks straight up, you now feel safe extracting income from the business, even though much of it came from an activity that would normally land you in prison.' Leo paused and said, 'there's been a very, very high profile case in the States recently. Anyone care to guess at it?

Ajay raised a slightly nervous hand. 'Are you thinking about the Russian political interference thing?'

Leo smiled in approval. 'Absolutely. So let's cut that down to its bare bones. Basically, the two men involved were shown to have funnelled Russian money through US and foreign companies, on behalf of Russia. That money was then spent to secure political influence. Or what real people like us would call bribery. So, are we all happy now that money laundering is a way of channelling money to make it look like something it isn't, and then to use it to do what we really want? Sex, drugs, rock and roll, world dominance, whatever?'

By now, the topic didn't seem so dense and the room was fully engaged.

Leo carried on. 'The actual doing of it, the getting it in a door, washing it and sending it out again can be very complicated, because it's essentially a game of smoke and mirrors. They're trying to get things past the authorities, the tax man, the police, Customs and Excise, whatever. So it's a sort of conjuring show – what you see isn't what you get. But in essence, the principals of money laundering are very clear.

The way I like to think about it is musical. To make music you need an instrument and some musical notes and you're away. The music can be very simple – three blind mice. Or it can be Tchaikovsky's Nutcracker Suite,' She hummed the familiar 'Cadbury's fruit and nut theme, to laughter.

'Money laundering is just the same. It can get very complex, but the bare bones remain the same every time. So let me give you the memory trick for it. PLI – Please Leave Immediately!

P is for Placement. This is your criminal mastermind getting the money into the financial systems. The risk here is high, because, as you know, financial institutions have to report large deposits, so questions get asked. So generally, a sensible miscreant will go for a drip feed approach – hence things like car washes and restaurants and so on. You probably already know this is called 'smurfing'. And we use the same name for the low-level criminals who are often tasked with paying small amounts into a range of different accounts; they're smurfs, and they can actually spend five or six hours a day paying in small amounts.

I'm going to mention cryptocurrency here, but not in depth, because at the moment there's no sign of it in this case. But watch this space; things like bitcoin aren't subject to the full range of scrutiny, so my world is expecting to see more of it. And just to frighten you a bit, my world is, to a very large extent, exactly the way you imagine it. People with calculators in dusty offices, adding up and taking away. Yes, lots of my colleagues are tech savvy and use computers well, but we were slow to get out of our offices and into the virtual world. There are still relatively few of us comfortable in that context, and it means there's a very big door very wide open. And my final note on that topic – it ain't new, either. There's been something called 'fei ch'ien' in China – that means flying money, for hundreds of years. In the Middle East, it's 'hawala' – and that means transfer. Both of these work internationally, and there's no paper trail. Think about money under the mattress, on a huge scale, but exchanged down to promises made with enormous price tags, like 'I commit to paying one million dollars on your behalf, no questions asked', through to property gifts on immense scale.'

Leo looked around the room. 'Any questions on that bit?'

Heads shook, though it was apparent that the group were still interested.

'OK, so L is for Layering. This is when the money that's been dropped into the system gets moved through a whole series of transactions. That's simply designed to complicate the paper trail and make it hard to follow. So some practical examples are electronic transfers between bank accounts, in multiple names, in multiple countries. Or property transactions with shell companies – we think that's what we're looking at here. The companies concerned only exist on paper and have no legitimate function. Or – my favourite, purchases of high-cost goods or commodities – yachts, diamonds, luxury cars, gold, large-scale building developments.

Going back to the American case and the Russians – the first indictment listed 17 US companies allegedly owned or controlled by the two men, plus 12 in Cyprus, and three others in the United Kingdom and the Caribbean. Not a small operation. And there's a reason I'm using it as an example, because it highlights why our not so local criminals are doing it. Offshore companies were crucial to the political enterprise, but are equally so to a commercial criminal. Many countries, including Cyprus, have very loose bank secrecy regulations – so that allows bank account owners to hide their identities and, it therefore follows, to obscure the source of funds paid into their accounts. There's something called the Financial Secrecy Index – I know – who knew? On that, Cyprus is the 24th most secretive banking destination in the world — not quite as opaque as the famous havens of Switzerland and the Cayman Islands, but it's not good news to have even more of them in Europe.

If we ever get a minute over coffee, feel free to ask me about the one million dollars of antique rugs that were purchased as part of the American political story…

And finally to I, for Integration. Here's what our criminals feel is the safest stage, because it's when the transactions are all legal. So, for example, the sale of high-value items originally purchased with the dirty money – as we're thinking in this case. The yachts are sold, the houses likewise. And sometimes it's not a sale – it could be a transfer. Or it could be the purchase of stocks, shares. Whatever it is, it's now clean, and can be sold again, lived in, sailed on, driven or worn. There's now a paper trail that makes it legit.'

Again she stopped and regarded her audience.

'Before I go on to what we need to look for in this case, are there any questions?'

The officer who had given the earlier definition of dirty money raised his hand.

'It seems really dense, I mean detailed. How do you get all the way through it to prove what's happened?'

Leo nodded in appreciation. 'That's so true. It's incredibly difficult. But I'll be a bit big-headed and say that I'm hoping that's why I'm here. If this was a normal murder case – if there is such a thing – you all know exactly what to do and you work your way through it. Look, let me go back to saying that I think of it as musical. You do too, if you think about it. It's built on years of experience, and you might call it the copper's nose. I just know that when I look at some financial trails the music isn't quite right, there's a bum note or more in there. I know you get it too. I'm not exaggerating when I say that's something that saved my life last year – one of you 'heard' a bum note and stopped me being badly damaged or killed by an acid device.'

The room all knew the story, but the reference to it and their understanding of parallels between their work and Leo's began to align. She wasn't out of the woods, but this was a straight talker who seemed to know what she was doing and, even better, could explain it to the uninitiated.

Leo began again. 'So, enough theory. What does this all tell us about our next steps? I'm going to be honest, because I think you'll recognise it too. It starts like a funnel – there are a lot of questions to start us off, but the more answers we get, the narrower the funnel will get. Or we might end up with two or more narrower funnels – we don't know yet.'

'That's where I've started. There are some financial queries that our team need to look at,' Leo smiled towards Kurt and Ajay, who were sitting together. 'There's around 800 questions I've listed there.' The room gave a collective gasp. They knew she'd only had the afternoon to look at it. Leonie smiled inwardly. In fact there were exactly 823 questions for 'her' team.

'We'll be looking at direct financials, bank accounts, loans, insurance policies, spending patterns, credit arrangements. Mucky little world sometimes,' she said cheerfully.

'More urgently, I've got another 650 queries that need answering that aren't directly financial, but they'll really help our little money team narrow the funnels. So, for example, for everyone murdered, for the property sellers and purchasers already identified, I need to know about children, private schools, holidays, vehicles, post codes – quickest way to estimate a house value. And things like Facebook, Instagram, Tik Tok – priceless. A photo in front of a yacht – we want to know. To quote a good mate of mine, 'nowt so daft as a big-head'.'

Fleur quickly broke the larger team into its two main constituents and Brent marshalled the larger group, sorting Leo's requirements into smaller teams and sharing out the neatly detailed tasks. Kurt did the same with the more technical ones and the small core financial team withdrew.

Steve Reith sat for a moment at the back of the room, watching the ebb and flow around him and recognising his peril. He'd been utterly entranced, again, by Leo Merton. He'd been aware of it last year, on the case where he'd met her, but he'd been able to park that. The situation had been tense, unreal. But now he was seeing her professionally and realising that he was deeply attracted.

THIRTY NINE

Steve Reith rarely talked about his past, particularly his emotional one. He had a couple of really good friends from his teenage years, and they remained close. He had the same level of closeness with three people he'd got to know in more recent years, two from the rugby world and one from work – or at least he hoped his friendship with Fleur Cooper was going that way. But with none of them did he share his inner self or the core part of the years between the development of those two groups of friends. He wasn't sure any more if he could. Walls had been built, emotions controlled. He was empathetic and sympathetic to others and highly resistant to it when directed at himself.

It wasn't a pretty story. In his mid-twenties he'd met and quickly married Laura, a woman he'd met at the gym. They liked many of the same things, from sport to TV and films. They'd spent some happy, adrenalin-packed holidays. They'd made love in thrilling, slightly dangerous venues. It was only over time that he'd realised that she was a seething mass of neuroses. Life wasn't full for her unless it was also full of drama, excitement, argument and friction. The arguments were endless, spurious, furious, draining. If things were too peaceful she'd engineer catastrophe around her, drumming up attention and support.

Skilled in her marketing career, Laura nonetheless moved ceaselessly from job to job, spectacular fallings-out in her wake. Reith saw before her that her options were diminishing in the world of employment as her reputation spread and began to precede her. By the time she noticed, the damage was probably irreparable. This too was laid at Reith's door, his absence of support, his absence at work. More long, pointless, hysterical tirades followed by urgent, angry sex. Absolutely not what the ambitious young new sergeant needed to come home to after a difficult and challenging day. The young Steve Reith had begun to think of divorce and, with hindsight, he realised that she'd picked up on this.

One night he arrived home to be greeted with the classic table set for dinner, candlelight, his favourite menu. She was pregnant and he saw no escape, nor would he have chosen one at that point.

All was well for a few weeks. The busy-ness of medical appointments, of telling people, of planning, kept her engaged and fulfilled. But it couldn't last, and by the fifth month her natural character was at full throttle, maybe even worse with additional hormones aplenty. Steve, up to his elbows in an immensely difficult child protection case, had little time to identify the oncoming crisis, though he believed he could and should have done so. It stayed with him to this day, a heavy weight of guilt and regret.

It began with small incidents, a bump, a fall, not feeling well. He was called at work twice to collect her from hospital after fainting episodes, for which no cause other than the normal blood pressure fluctuations of pregnancy could be offered. The rows became louder, longer, more hysterical. He was accused of so many things, not caring, having an affair, even of not being the child's father. That, he'd never know.

It culminated in the last call to work, but this time a colleague had to take him to the morgue, where he identified the body of his wife and the small, sad bump that would not now be his child.

When he heard the tale, he knew it had been a miscalculation on her part, just another escalation in her attention-seeking campaign. She'd stepped out in front of a car – bystanders all said it seemed that she wasn't looking. He was sure she had been – the car wasn't moving fast and would probably just have pushed her to the kerb. But she never saw the motorbike weaving, very fast between the slower vehicles, and the impact from that threw her into the air and over the bonnet of another car. She'd died on the way to hospital, her last words making no sense to anyone but Reith. 'He should have listened. He should have listened.'

It broke something small and precious inside Steve Reith. He'd begun to think of the baby as a person, would have conversations with it in his head, planned to take it to rugby matches, girl or boy. The fact that he'd missed what Laura has degraded herself to, the desperate actions she was prepared to take, ate at him even now, in the pit of his stomach in the dead of night.

So in recent years he'd dated, but never loved. Liked but never laughed.

But he had a sense that his world had shifted, and yet he had no sense as to what it might mean for the future.

FORTY

Dear Diary

I've just got my GCSE results. They're good. He's pleased because he can boast about them. I'm really hoping I can stay on to do my A' levels, but I think it's going to be difficult. Granny is working on it. She hasn't said it directly, but I've sort of guessed that he's always regretted not staying on at school himself. When he's talking about it, he makes it sound like my aunt was given the choice and he wasn't, but I think that's not true. So I've got my fingers crossed. I wonder where that expression comes from? I must look it up, I use it a lot. And I've just ended a sentence in a preposition. I know you're not supposed to, but sometimes I can't see a way round.

FORTY ONE

Wednesday continued hard and cold and the other shoe dropped, possibly. Fleur took a call from the station's press officer, saying that he'd had a call from the switchboard saying there was a reporter asking to speak to the senior officer on the 'murder' case.   The press officer had parried it for now, because it could easily be the usual fishing for tidbits, but that wouldn't hold for more than a couple of hours if they really had something. Max.

Fleur discussed next steps with him, then legged it up the stairs to alert Reith, or his secretary, if he was unavailable. Finding his inner door firmly closed and his PA on guard, she passed on the sad tidings and asked that Reith let her know if he had any particular opinions on next steps with the media.

Back at her desk she reflected. It was a dual-edged sword. Going public with some of what they knew might bring them more information, especially from people affected by the money-laundering and property development thing. On the other hand, the murder was now only part of it, and they were just as keen to catch the financial criminals too. And behind them, maybe even the people cleaning their dirty money through this very large washing machine. Going public would alert them.

So now time was absolutely back at the top of the agenda.

In the office next door to Fleur's, Leo had been at the computer since just after 6 am. Sleep had been fitful for her as she wanted to get into the guts of the problem. Clear sighted as ever, she knew a part of that motivation was her very real wish to impress Steve Reith. There was something about him that called to her. He was certainly intelligent, a key requirement for her, but he also had a solidity, a dependability, about him that was attractive. And she suspected some emotional damage in there too, because she hadn't been wrong about the mutual attraction, so there was something else holding him back.

She stretched her neck and returned to her task. The real skill in financial detection was in identifying the approaches that would provide the most information without causing ripples that might alert the people at the centre of the transactions. There were more overt tools available, like an Unexplained Wealth Order, but they were only useful when you thought you'd got as far up the chain as possible. That was some way off, and Leo needed to climb up a long way yet.

What non-mathematicians could only guess at were the patterns that Leo and her peers worked within. She hadn't been joking when she said that for her it was a sort of music, a set of chords and rhythms that could be beautiful. In this sort of case she was looking for the breaks in pattern, the bum notes that would alert her to another door and take her further up the dirty ladder. She suffered no illusions; although she'd jokingly made reference to getting blown up when talking to Reith earlier in the week, once she'd seen the scale of money movement she knew they were dealing with serious crime. The fact that Lauren Greenwood had well over forty million pounds in assets told her that the scale of the money she'd been moving was way, way over that. The faster they got to the head of the snake the less likely she and her police team mates were to become personal targets. From the discussions yesterday she knew that the media hadn't picked up on it yet, but without any knowledge of the world of homicide detection, she still thought that was inevitable. So, time to dive.

Over the next hour she was joined by Groehling and Ajay; they were promptly supplied with a list of online investigations to pursue. Leo herself took a break from the computer screen and turned her attention to the notepad into which she'd been scribbling notes as she worked. There were a few 'phone calls that could save time, if she could just prevail on people to be helpful. The first was to a branch manager at a high street bank. She'd encountered him when working a case with the Metropolitan Police on a series of Art frauds, also in the money laundering arena. His bank had been used by the criminals concerned and he'd come under fire for not registering the drip-feed influx of large amounts of money. Leo had been instrumental in demonstrating to the bank that the chances of anyone spotting it, outside her category of specialist, was virtually non-existent. She didn't want him to break any rules or regulations, but she did reckon that he might be open to introducing her to the technical people within the bank who could help her pierce a few more layers.

She was right; he still felt significant gratitude for her previous support. He listened carefully and understood what she needed, though he cautioned her that they'd need warrants. That she recognised, but approaching the right people in the first place short-circuited the convolutions she would otherwise have encountered. A name and direct 'phone number now on her pad, she referred to Groehling and Ajay.

'We need to meet with this chap, Rick Oserji. He's head of digital security at the Shires Bank. I already knew about him because he often presents at conferences on the topic and I have a suspicion that he's going to understand where we need to go better than most. I think we need to go armed with all the necessary paper work, because we're going to make a trail. We need that as part of our chain of evidence and he needs to be able to prove that it was legitimately requested and provided.'

Kurt took the contact details from her and started the warrant application process as he simultaneously picked up the 'phone to make an appointment.

In the larger incident room, other tasks were being followed through. Irfan Patel's son had been located and instructed to report to the station. Daisy reported that he'd been disgruntled and aggressive on the 'phone, but she felt this was just displacement activity. If his father had been doing what they thought, and he knew about it, he'd know his options were limited.

Don had turned his focus to Calum Grant, Lauren Greenwood and Neville Humberstone. These three he felt to be the king pins within the group they were investigating. Irfan Patel was new to it, Ken Bell seemed to be a bit over the hill for this kind of leadership, the elderly dentist didn't date all the way back to the start and Don was still hoping Gordon Szabo was just the unwitting face of it all. He headed for Brent and said,

'Mick, I think I need to get further into Grant, Humberstone and Greenwood. Do I need warrants for their homes and office premises, since they're definitely murder victims?'

Brent pondered the point. 'I think you do, because they weren't the crime scenes. Dotting the i's, you know? There shouldn't be a problem. It's murder and they're the deceased. And I think you'll find Chloe Antoine will be helpful, with or without the warrant.'

Cervantes nodded, accepting the answer he'd been expecting and heading back to his desk to get the applications started. Lauren Greenwood was probably the one to start with. She lived in Kensington, no apparent house mates and she'd clearly been the one manoeuvring the legal hurdles for this complex web of deceit. He thought as he worked, wondering what they'd find. Anything from nothing to the motherlode. Who knew? He headed back to Brent.

'Mick, do you want to come with me for this? I can't get Forensics out fast enough and we don't know who else might have access, especially if they know she's dead.'

Brent nodded. It wouldn't be appropriate for a lone officer to search; any findings could then be queried and this was too important.

'Let me know when the warrant is through.'

Daisy was looking at Edward Horbridge's files. She'd separated them into the financials, which were clearly relevant to the case and the more personal, complaint folders. Those were fascinating but at present not pertinent, so she began returning them to one of the large plastic crates in which they'd arrived. Each of them had been clearly labelled by Edward Horbridge, all beginning with 'Issues relating to…' and then the company or individual to whom it referred. It was as she did this that she spotted the tab that said 'Issues relating to LG'. She put her filing aside and took the folder to a work table in the corner of the room, where she had the space to lay out the file contents.

Daisy was taken aback but delighted to find copies of notes made by Horbridge relating to transactions with Lauren Greenwood on the sale of each of his properties. The properties were listed in date order, identified by address. He'd neatly recorded monies coming in to his property finance account, each one of them assigned with either the initials LG, CG or NH. The next column showed the property purchase price, then a column for personal fees, another for professional fees and finally the sale price of the property, with the purchaser name listed alongside.

The personal fees seemed to be 15% of the final sale price. The professional fee was identical for each, at twenty five thousand. Daisy surmised that the flat rate fee was standard for handling the property, and the sale percentage a negotiated fee that reflected Horbridge's efforts to increase the value of the asset. Bearing in mind that the average property sale price was around the two million pound mark, it didn't take a numbers whizz to see how lucrative this was.

There were a number of things to grab Daisy's attention, not least the purchaser names. Only three were listed, spread fairly evenly across the transactions. Daisy thought they were all company names. Stormforth, Cavaletti and Renton. They would certainly be useful to Leo and her team.

Just as intriguing was the final set of sheets she extracted from the file. Each page was headed with a property address and under each one Edward Horbridge had listed a series of what seemed to be complaints regarding Lauren Greenwood. These ranged from criticism of poor time-keeping to inaccuracies in accounting. On three of the sheets Horbridge had also added a name, as a foot note, followed by a question mark. Andeslev. As Don had done only minutes previously, she headed to Brent to run her findings past him.

Brent whistled. 'Bloody brilliant. Get in to the money lot and share it.'

Always pleased to be the bearer of good news, Daisy made for the commandeered office next to Fleur's. The door was open and the three occupants all bent over their laptops. They all looked up as Daisy appeared in the door frame. She quickly took them through her findings and handed a photocopied set of documents to Leo. Leo smiled in pleasure. Getting company names helped enormously. She was sure they were shell companies, but that didn't matter. Money went in and out, which made them interrogable. As she read each sheet she passed them on to Kurt and Ajay. Ajay looked up and said,

'It might be nothing, but the company names that Kurt's already identified are different to these, but the initials of their names are the same – S, C and R. Might that be an easy way for them to group and track what they're doing?'

Both Leo and Kurt concurred. Leo said, 'That wouldn't be unusual, but well spotted. Whoever's behind this has substantial funds; it would be easy to lose track. But I can't imagine any of his co-conspirators had any idea Edward Horbridge was keeping this kind of record. They'd have lost the plot. And if anyone further up had found out, I think he'd have been terminated. Not being dramatic or anything.' She looked at Kurt.

'Is that what you think might have happened?

Kurt shook his head, less in disagreement as in uncertainty. 'It's a possibility, but so is the revenge angle from someone who'd been harmed by them.'

Daisy said. 'And what about this Andeslev?'

Leo, who hadn't yet finished the property sheets, swung her chair abruptly towards Daisy.

'Who?' she asked, quite sharply for her. Daisy explained, pointing to the name on a couple of the final sheets. She noted Leo's expression and said 'Do you know him?'

Leo shook her head and said. 'Not personally, but it does help, in a definitely 'I wish it didn't' way. Can we get Fleur for a few minutes do you think?'

Daisy leant around the door frame that served this office to one side and Fleur's to the other. Fleur was on a call, but Daisy gestured to her to join them as soon as she could.

For a couple of minutes the small finance team explored Edward Horbridge's handwritten notes, each adding actions to their personal to-do lists, Fleur joining them just as Leo was about to speak. Now she did so, addressing Daisy.

'Daisy, can you just give the Inspector a summary of what you've found?' This was done in swift order, Fleur whistling quietly as Leo noted the possible connection with the companies' names. Once she'd reached the name Andeslev, Leo took back the baton.

'Right. This is why you needed to be made aware right-a-bloody way. Your Serious Crime lot have a great deal of info on this guy, and I've come across his work on a couple of occasions. He's an accountant to hire, if you like to call it that. Russian originally, I think, but apparently lives in Switzerland now. He arranges funding on a grand scale, and he's not picky. They suspect him of having working links with Al Qaeda, with Isis, with Boko Haram and half a dozen other terrorist organisations. And that's only the half of it; he's certainly responsible for a lot of the money laundering that goes on around Europe. He doesn't do it himself, his speciality is setting up effective, efficient teams to wash out the dirt. But that's not his only skill set; I know from the last Art case that I worked on that he's what's called a concierge. He can make other things happen, like bumping people off.

'I'm frankly concerned. If he was unhappy with this group, he would have had no compunction about taking them out. But if he didn't, and he becomes aware that they're dead and we're involved, then he'll close down all of the ends that we can currently see. I don't think he's done any of that yet. From our investigations yesterday evening and this morning, the smurfs are still paying in across all the high street banks. So our urgency factor just got multiplied.'

Fleur closed her eyes briefly, reflecting. 'Right. Briefing room in twenty, get round everyone please and make sure they're there if possible. No discussion about the topic.'

Cooper departed, ringing up to Reith's PA and requesting that she be put through to him, only to be told that he was already on his way down to their floor. As Fleur cradled the handset, Reith appeared in the sergeants' area, heading her way. She updated him then said,

'Look, now we've got a real problem. The press are on to something, albeit not the whole thing. The Press Office say they actually only know about Calum Grant dying, so they were chancing their arm. Now, we do know a lot more about the money chain, even if we haven't got the names yet. But if this Andeslev becomes aware of our scrutiny then he'll close it down. I think that means we can't go public asking for help. But then again, if he bumped them off he'd also be closing down exactly the same things – in fact, would have already done it. Leo says there's no sign of that yet.

'So, on balance I think we can assume that Andeslev is not our killer, but is a part of the laundering operation. Is that how you're reading it?'

Reith stared at the ceiling, thinking. 'Yes. With his apparent expertise, he'd surely have shut it all down by now, so it doesn't seem likely that he's our killer. Leo is right, I've seen his name a few times and I'd rather not meet him in a dark alley. So, what are you thinking?'

FORTY TWO

I'm allowed to stay on at school, as long as I pay him as much as I would if I'd got a job. He found adverts for trainee secretaries and I've got to match that.

I've found four things. Monday to Friday, I'm doing a milk round in the morning and a leaflet drop in the evenings. On a Saturday and a Sunday in the day I've got a job in the kitchens at a café on the seafront. On Friday and Saturday nights I'm washing up at the golf club. He hasn't really asked where I'm going to be, just checked how much. I know I can beat the amount he wants from me. I haven't told him how many jobs, because if I'm lucky I can save a little bit, maybe for university. I've told Granny about two of the jobs, but not the other two. She'll worry too much.

FORTY THREE

In the briefing room a few minutes later, Fleur made a point of shutting the door and explaining the sensitivity of their latest intel, taking them through the findings from Edward Horbridge's papers.

'I am totally trusting every one of you not to take open discussion of this out of the room. We have some sort of chance at getting him, and maybe some of the others in this particular operation, but only if we can move swiftly and silently. An Interpol representative is on the way, someone with first-hand knowledge of Mr Andeslev, and the finance team will work on that angle with him or her, with the rest of us providing backup or input as needed.

'But for the rest of us, our major job now is to narrow our focus on the murders and any suspects. The work you've all been doing with Leo's list of questions is bearing fruit – Mick, do you want to take us through that?'

Brent gathered up two sheets of paper from the pile in front of him and came to the front of the room.

'First, kudos to those of you who've got hold of all of this data in such a short period of time – I know it was painstaking and not always interesting, but here's what we've got so far.

'From the first 169 property transactions examined we've identified 24 forged insurance policies assigning post-death benefits to either Calum Grant or Neville Humberstone or, in half a dozen cases, to both. Those activities don't relate to the apparent money laundering properties but to individual property purchases which the buyers subsequently lived in. But we can't afford to ignore them, because they're potentially just as likely to be well and truly pissed as the other group. We've got 12 properties where Lauren Greenwood falsified ownership documents on collateral. For example, a yacht was provided as surety for a mortgage, but the yacht didn't actually belong to the person buying the property. We've found cumulative income into all of our victims bank accounts that fully cover the property purchases. Oh, with one exception. With Gordon Szabo, there's absolutely no evidence of involvement in his finances. He's used the same building society for years, and his accounts show no unexplained income at any level.'

'Our financial Avengers,' Brent smiled as the room laughed at this, 'have got a lot further on the task of breaking through the ceiling of what we knew. They've been able to map connections up to the ones listed on Edward Horbridge's list. Knowing the likely initials helped a lot with that, and for each one there are four or five shell companies in between. Now they're trying to get above that, but already some patterns are emerging as to the geography of the company registrations and some commonalities in names and registered addresses. That's almost exclusively international, and out of our control, but the more information we can provide, the more likely it is that we can run at least some of these people off the road,'

Brent paused and regarded his audience. 'I know it's not as sexy as feeling his collar ourselves, but if Leo is right about this Andeslev bloke also being tied in with terrorism funding, I for one will be glad to contribute to his downfall.'

His audience, who'd been feeling exactly the same dip in interest as they watched their direct involvement dilute, accepted the point and voiced it with a low hum of approval.

Fleur Cooper took control of the meeting again and said,

'Right, back to it. We've all got a lot clearer view on the finance side and I think we can leave our experts to that. For the rest of us, let's refocus on the murders. There has to be a common thread somewhere, so it's time to start mapping.'

Fleur was referring to the system used to interrogate connections between different people, in this case, the victims. A large board was already set up with pictures of all of the victims. Under each person, a list of what was already known, connecting lines being drawn between them where evidenced links existed.

As the majority of the room emptied, Reith, Cooper, Brent and Cervantes stood in front of this board. Reith was the first to speak.

'I'll be honest, my worry is that there's nothing yet, no obvious connection that leads us back to a source. There are so many potential victims that might have hatched this lot, but virtually nothing to suggest an identity.'

His three colleagues silently acquiesced. Cervantes said,

'I know it's lack of experience, but I don't know what to do next.' Brent barked a laugh.

'None of us do mate, none of us. This is unusual for us, even for a serial killer. Usually there's an obvious pattern. It might not make sense to us, because we're not as twisted as our killer, but in this case, nada, rien, zilch.'

FORTY FOUR

Dear Diary

It's hard, doing my A Levels. I mean, the work isn't very hard, that's just interesting and everything we learn makes me want to go and find something else to explore a bit more.

No, it's at home it's even harder than usual. I know he's really just very, very angry that I'm still at school. I think he thought I'd pack it in, or not keep all of my jobs, but I'm still going. I can't give in. But it's hard to work at home, because he makes sure the TV or the radio is on wherever I'm working. It doesn't matter if I move, he'll just move the radio. I can't say anything or turn it off because he'll lose it, and he still hits me sometimes. Not as hard maybe now, because once I hit him hard back on his arm with my school bag full of books and told him, really quietly, that I'd tell people what he was doing. So that slowed him down a bit, but I know that inside it just made him even more angry.

He does stuff to cause trouble. He's used black ink markers in some of my textbooks and blocked out whole paragraphs. I can't accuse him, but I know it wasn't there when I went to bed. Last week he poured a whole teapot of hot tea into my school bag.

In Psychology, we've been learning about self-awareness. I've realised that I've always wanted him to care about me, but I know he really, truly doesn't. He loves books, so the fact that he hates me enough to damage them is hard to accept. I think he loves my brother, but even that doesn't feel like the kind of family my friends seem to have.

I had to apologise to the teachers at school and offer to pay. The odd thing is, I'm beginning to think they know more than I thought. Sometimes my teachers give me photocopied sheets from the books, so I don't have to take the whole book away. They don't do that for everyone. And they're not being sarcastic or anything, usually just quietly giving me the sheets.

I want a good job, where I don't have to rely on anyone. Where I can shut my own front door and just be safe.

FORTY FIVE

Reith, Cooper and Leonie Merton sat in his office, enjoying a decent coffee from his much-envied machine. They were all due at the Brent house for dinner in a couple of hours, but Reith wanted a quick review before that happened. He cleared his throat and began.

'Right. Let me see if I've got this right. First, we've now got a clear line of sight to Andeslev, though not yet to the people behind him, funding this property circle?'

Leo nodded. 'Yes, that's true, but I am nearly there. What I said yesterday about my profession not being totally clued up about the concealment of moving finances is right but, thankfully, it's also true that the criminal world is just as patchy. Often, they use very skilled hackers, which is frustrating for people like me, but also rather helpful.'

The other two looked at her, puzzled. She continued.

'Because they're hackers. Not financiers. They know how to hide the transactions but they don't know about the patterns that someone like me is looking for. I've already found half a dozen breadcrumbs that seem to be leading in the same direction. I really don't think it'll be long before I can give you the end-user accounts.'

'Seriously?' said Reith. 'Why don't they use people like you then?'

Leo laughed. 'I have been approached, twice. I'm sure a few people have been tempted, but then they fall down on their low hacker skills. For me, it's just not elegant. I've always loved the purity of numbers, the clarity as they fall into the right place. And I'm not designed for subterfuge. I could never remember what I was supposed to say.'

Reith and Cooper laughed, and he continued.

'So, there are two possibilities as to the murders. The first is that it's someone in the money-laundering chain, for some reason. Maybe they were skimming or something?'

Again, Leo responded. 'You know, I can't speak to the criminal side of that, but from my perspective there are a couple of reasons that doesn't sit well with me. First, I can categorically say that the Szabos were not involved in this; they're squeaky, squeaky clean. Surely that would be known? They didn't receive any fees or cuts. And Irfan Patel is very new to the gang; I guess he wouldn't have been pulled in to some inner circle of creaming off the top so quickly?'

Fleur Cooper was quick to chip in. 'That's very true.' She shook her head. 'No, I think we have to accept the sad fact that it's related to someone who had the dirty done to them, or someone close to them.'

Reith nodded his agreement. 'And that makes it a bloody nightmare. Because the potential number of victims to the financial malpractice is both complex and widespread. At the moment the only options we have for uncovering that are Leo's very detailed questions. Which is good in one way – at least it is an avenue to pursue – but it's also producing so many possibilities that we're drowning. I don't know yet how we can narrow it down.'

The early evening briefing was a low-key affair. Nothing further had been heard from the journalist, for which thanks were given and fingers crossed. The detailed work coming out of Leo's questions was highlighted, with the same caution as Reith had expressed earlier. The volume might be overwhelming and budgetary constraints didn't allow for endless research. Ironically, the absence of media scrutiny also lowered the pressure on Reith's bosses to up the budget. So less stress, but less resource.

The little group heading for the Brents' bungalow was invited for 7pm, and Reith offered to give Leo a lift. He thought she might find it easier arriving with him, as well as saving her the trouble of navigation. She accepted with grace and winked at Cooper, out of sight of Reith's eagle gaze.

So, mused Cooper, *she's* interested. And I'm sure he is, so what's holding him back?

In fairly quick order from seven o' clock, the odd little cohort arrived at the Brent's smart bungalow, Reith and Leo the first to arrive, four or five minutes ahead of Cervantes. Leo took the opportunity to compliment Maze on their beautiful home and, as ever, Maze was quick to explain that they'd been able to buy it from the proceeds of her injury compensation. Leo rode over that and remarked, 'Well, it is a beautiful building, but I didn't really mean that. It's so beautifully decorated, what a wonderful eye you have.'

Nothing could have pleased Maze or Brent more. Mick Brent because he loved to have his wife's many accomplishments recognised and Maze because she was proud of her home and always pleased to share it with an appreciative guest.

By this time Cervantes and Ajay were hovering just inside the door and Maze propelled her wheelchair towards them, conscious of Cervantes' self-doubt and Ajay's initial shyness. Maze absolutely understand that Cervantes' natural ebullience hid an equally natural diffidence and he'd hesitated outside on the doorstep for quite a few seconds before he pressed the doorbell. Maze had always understood that about him, and respected him for it, so she dealt with the issue in the best possible way and gave him the task of opening and serving the Prosecco she'd been chilling.

By the time that was achieved, the full group had assembled and was gathering around the huge kitchen island, a lower level than most as it doubled as a kitchen table. Bar stool height would have been too elevated for Maze's wheelchair, so the island was made up of pillars and foot space, with the pillars holding cook books and a range of glassware behind glazed doors. Leo regarded the room with delight. Her friend Chris Boyd, the restaurateur, would love this kitchen. It had all the signs of a household that loved to cook, and if Mick Brent's apron was anything to go by, this was a couple who each enjoyed preparing food.

Maze gently nudged her guests into sharing their individual, personal news. She got Fleur to provide an update on her partner, Peter Howard, and got Daisy talking about her up and coming holidays, Reith about the rugby trip he hoped to make in the autumn and Cervantes to admit that he'd joined the station's quiz team. Ajay was quickly prodded into describing his family and his garage apartment, receiving some good-natured teasing, which he accepted with a smug grin. 'Jammy dodger!' he laughed. Kurt was the easiest to kick start, his twins had just been given their first child-level computers, much to his wife Sandy's irritation and to the twins' delight. They'd both taken to the new skills with alacrity; not unexpected, as they could already navigate the TV remote, the central heating control and the room radiator controls with facility.

As for herself and Mick, Maze happily shared their latest news; she'd been invited to speak at Harvard in the autumn and she'd agreed, subject to Mick being included in the visit. Part of what they wanted her to describe was the case from the previous summer, when her involvement had both aided the investigation and placed her in the firing line. Maze thought that including the police perspective would be interesting for a roomful of academics who sometimes lost sight of the wood for the trees. Much good-natured joshing resulted from this, with Fleur laughingly noting that Brent had to get permission first. Maze didn't forget Leo and extracted from her that she'd got a kayaking trip planned for the summer, with her friend Chris and a couple of other canoeing mates, travelling through the Ardeche in France. She explained,

'It's very organised. We take our cases to the starting point and unpack each evening, then pack up the next morning and our stuff's taken to the next hotel. We're all knocking on a bit these days and we're not so keen on the camp sites and bottles of cider now. So we stay in fabulous hotels, drink gorgeous wines and work off the calories during the day. We take the heavier water, the level threes and fours, so it's a challenge some days, which makes it a lot of fun. And we run a sweepstake on the most capsizes. The least flips gets dinner at Chris' restaurant. The most pays for it!'

Reith coughed, discreetly, then a little louder, until he'd got their attention. Fleur, who guessed what he wanted to say, regarded her knees in solemnity, afraid she would grin ridiculously.

Reith looked at the group and said, 'This is absolutely on the QT for now, and I need your word that it goes no further?' Unsure but ever willing to support the best boss they'd ever had, everyone nodded.

'I think those of us who worked at the nick before Inspector Cooper joined us last year know just how many systems and approaches she's quietly improved in that time, both for us and uniform. I've rarely worked with a better officer, which is why I'm pleased to tell you that, once the paperwork is complete, we'll be moving Leo and her team out of the Chief Inspector's office, so that Fleur can move in.'   He raised his glass and said imply, 'Fleur.'

Fleur's colleagues burst into happy congratulations, clearly delighted for her. Her smile and her slightly brimming eyes spoke volumes and Leo was the first to give her a congratulatory hug.

From then the evening took a route that all but Leo and Ajay recognised. Mick placed baskets of hot, cheesy garlic bread at each end of the table and the talk turned to the case. Fleur encouraged everyone to summarise their work to date, with Maze insisting on exploring perceptions of each topic.

Reith shared the headlines the three of them had discussed earlier that afternoon and then, prompted by Maze, also broached his concern that they had too broad a field.

Kurt was more sanguine, since he understood what HOLMES could do, as well as the database he'd been building for the past two days. He'd created enough fields to allow some meaningful interrogation and he was hoping that would make it easier to group lines of enquiry. Daisy, although not on the finance sub-team, had already been populating this database and she was beginning to see that it would be, if not easy, at least not impossible to pursue distinct lines of enquiry, such as anyone who'd had an insurance policy which might have been hijacked.

Cervantes had been quietly working his way through Leo's questions and was able to provide three other lines of enquiry – near relatives of the deceased, colleagues and what he called 'interesting' connections. He explained.

'It's mostly Kendall Bell, though Neville Humberstone and Calum Grant have a bit of it. Very interesting club memberships, some quite disgusting expenditure streams, all pretty much illegal. With Bell I think there's a child porn angle.'

The officers in the room nodded in grim recognition of something only too familiar. Leo shuddered at the thought and wondered how these decent people slept at night.

By the time these topics had been gnawed over, Brent was producing a magnificent pastry dish from the oven, followed by tureens of potatoes, vegetables and a couple of gravy boats. Mick said.

'We're highly honoured. Maze has done her world-famous beef en croute and I'm telling you now, there'll be no leftovers, no matter how much I'd like there to be.'

Their guests regarded the Brents with various levels of awe, Leo probably the most aware that it took real skill and some bravery to produce the famous pastry dish. Cervantes and Groehling ever grateful for good food and Daisy keen to watch and learn.

Conversation slowed somewhat over the next few minutes, as plates were emptied and refilled. Reith was happy to note that Leo was certainly not a picky eater and had gladly accepted a second helping.

FORTY SIX

Dear Diary

I've started applying to universities. I had to be honest with one of my teachers. She's the Deputy Head, and she runs a sort of debate group for Year 13 students. It's really interesting, and she says it'll prepare us for the kind of interviews we'll have at college. But the thing is, you need parents' signatures and stuff and I had to tell her that my father doesn't agree with me going to college.

She just looked sort of sad and said that there was plenty we could do. The school will handle the postage issue - I'm allowed to give their address instead of mine. They'll include a letter in every application, explaining the problem. It's embarrassing but I can get over that if I can just get away.

He's made a list of all the universities he's thought of and why only idiots would apply. Mostly communists, apparently. Also, real people don't go to university, they get proper jobs.

My Deputy Head is brilliant though. She made a better list. I didn't know that you could get sponsorship to get a degree – so I might be joining the army!

FORTY SEVEN

The group split up around 10pm, everyone only too aware of the next day and all that needed to be done.

Reith opened the passenger door of his car for Leo and waited for her to settle before he closed it, regarded watchfully by Maze and Brent from the open doorway, light spilling out onto the brick-set drive.

When Reith was settled beside her and they were pulling away, Leo looked at Reith and smiled.

'So, what's it to be?' she asked.

He paused at the junction of the drive and the road and looked at her. 'In what sense?' he queried, unconsciously echoing his phrase from the memorial service earlier that week.

'Look, I don't want to be a bunny boiler, so I'd rather clear the air. I had the feeling that there was something between us last year, but then it went nowhere. I'm not a stalker or a grudge bearer, so can I just ask you if you feel it too? If not, I'll never say another word and I promise not to make anything awkward.' She waited, conscious of how much she wanted a positive answer.

Reith, similarly, was aware of how much he wanted to give her the answer she wanted, but also hemmed in by his years of constraint. He answered her, carefully.

'Yes. I feel it too. But I need to be honest. My last serious relationship was hellish and it ended even more badly. If we do try this, it'll be slow and you might find it too difficult, waiting for me to catch up. But,' he paused for breath, 'but, I do want to catch up.'

Leo exhaled and put her hand gently on his thigh and left it there. They both understood the commitment from each side.

Reith was heading back towards the station where Leo had left her car. He'd offered to take her directly home and collect her in the morning, but she'd declined, saying that she wanted an early start. They were expecting the Interpol representative sometime during the morning, and she wanted to be as prepared as possible.

It was as they were turning down one of the many one-way streets at the edge of Wimbledon that it happened. A large, unmarked dark van parked on the left-hand side of the road suddenly turned its lights on and swerved hard, straight into the side of Reith's car. Reith's left hand flew protectively across Leo and the two of them were shaken violently by the collision. By the time the car had settled back on all four wheels both doors had been yanked open, a flash of knife visible in the street light on both sides, the seat belts sliced free, and heavy, gloved hands had clamped sweet-smelling cloths over their faces.

The two were unaware of their swift transfer to the dark van, slightly further down the street and their subsequent journey through the quieter night-time London streets.

FORTY EIGHT

The team reconvened at eight the following morning, each with a list of queries, tasks and ideas. Ajay was clearly on edge, which already seemed unusual for him. Fleur, marshalling her papers into meeting order, glanced at him.

'What's up Ajay?' He looked embarrassed.

'Well, I don't know if anything is, really...it's just that Leo asked me to be in at 6.30 this morning; there's something she wanted me to work on, but she needed to take me through it. But she didn't arrive.'

Fleur was nonplussed. Even this early in their professional association this seemed totally unlike Leo. She looked up from her papers to see Brent regarding her fixedly. Suddenly conscious of a possibility she jerked her head at him and headed out of the room. Outside she speeded up, heading towards the stair well, saying over her shoulder, 'Come with me.'

Two floors higher up she headed into the ladies' toilet followed, after only a moment's hesitation by Brent. Inside, Fleur headed for the windows, choosing one to the far right. She used her elbow to nudge the retaining bar out of its proper alignment, allowing the window to fully open. She slid her bottom on to the window sill and then leaned backwards, looking to her right.

'Leo's car is still there. The Super's isn't.'

The retraced their steps to the corridor and then regarded each other. Brent spoke first.

'Look, I know we'd all like to see it happen, and maybe it has, but I just don't believe that either of them are capable of dropping the ball like this. Leo's got the Interpol chap this morning. I really can't accept she'd forget that.' Fleur nodded and pulled her mobile from her pocket. Reith was one of her speed dial options.

She waited. 'No answer. Just the voicemail.' She tapped the phone then scrolled through to find Leo Merton's number, with the same result.

'Right, my office.' They quickly headed back to their floor and into Fleur's room. Brent carefully closing the door behind him. Fleur searched through her contact information and tried Reith's home number, reaching only his voicemail.

A quick Google search gave her the address of Leo's company and she rang this number, asking to be connected to Harry Wilson, Leo's co-director. She swiftly explained her concerns and he was equally rapid in meeting her in them.

'Just wouldn't happen,' he said briskly, 'she'd let you know if anything at all held her up. I'd hazard a guess that Superintendent Reith is the same?' Fleur murmured her assent to this, but he continued. 'But we have car trackers. We can use that.'

Fleur explained that Leo's car was at the station, and that Reith and she had left a dinner meeting last evening in each other's company. Harry Wilson pondered that.

'Right. Can you track his car or mobile? I can request Leo's mobile data from our provider, but I think you'll have speedier results, if I email you our permission?' He terminated the call.

Fleur, whilst inwardly quaking at the potential scenarios that might have prevented her boss from getting to where he needed to be, nonetheless had the time to reflect that Harry Wilson had exactly the right attitude for the situation. Assess, see what could be done, get off the 'phone.

She looked at Brent.

'We have to call it, I think.' Mick Brent nodded, sober faced. Fleur said,

'Look, get back down to the meeting. Shut the door and tell them what we think's happened. Start listing ideas for action and assigning those, but don't start anything until I get there.'

They departed Cooper's office at speed, Brent to re-join his colleagues and Cooper heading to the open plan Command Centre. Part of the Metropolitan's Metcall system, each borough nonetheless had its own base, linked in a variety of ways across the capital. Once there, Fleur paused at the threshold, visually seeking the most senior officer. She spotted him, a fellow Inspector that she knew slightly from shared attendance at a couple of the dullest procedural training sessions she'd ever attended. They'd bonded, to some extent, over the boredom and poor refreshments. She approached him and asked him for a private word.

'Phil, I'm sorry to bother you, but I need a word on the QT, then your advice.'

To his credit, he didn't bother trying to talk her out of her concerns. As they spoke he was tapping into the system, searching for Reith's motor. Once he'd retrieved the registration he then did a general system search, knowing that would bring up at least two options. The internal database would appear, as would the DVLA link option. The first would allow him to activate the onboard tracker if necessary, but he didn't have to use that tool. As he pressed Return on his search, an Incident Alert appeared. He read this carefully and then repeated it to Cooper.

'Superintendent Reith's car was reported abandoned this side of Wimbledon, just after ten thirty last night. It seems to have been involved in a traffic incident, with the side bashed in. It's been impounded.'

Fleur was conscious of the sudden swoop in her stomach. 'OK. Understood. What do you advise now?'

Phil, whose life was rooted in the network of systems designed to securely tackle, manage and monitor virtually every scenario, paused only briefly.

'Well, our first thought has to be for the safety of the officer and his passenger. We don't currently have any idea of their whereabouts so I can't recommend a city-wide alert. But the scene needs to be examined, local CCTV has to be interrogated, door to door if it's residential. I'm guessing that you'll want your team to handle that?' Fleur nodded. He continued.

'I can start the mobile 'phone tracing. Send me the permission from the accountant woman's company as soon as please. I'll also start on the overnight incident log – you never know – someone might have seen something that'll help.'

Fleur departed, knowing that she'd put in to play what she could, but also knowing that it was, as yet, woefully inadequate.

She opened the door on her team meeting to find a group of people clearly keyed up but very focused on what needed to be done. Fleur took a deep breath and then sat, updating the group on what she knew so far.

'So, thoughts please.'

Brent began. 'Well, we thought that we needed to retrace the Super's steps, but now that we know there was some sort of debacle and where, we need to get a team there, as soon as possible.' He raised an eyebrow at Fleur, who nodded in acceptance. He continued.

'We need a couple of good, discreet, uniforms on this. Daisy knows who to hijack and she'll go and sort it. I think Don and I ought to lead the team on that front. But we're also conscious of the broader investigation. I know there's no point in speculating, but it's possible, even probable, that this is connected. We've got the Interpol rep here in a few minutes. Kurt and I think that he and Ajay need to meet him and take him through what we have so far. What we were discussing just as you got back though needs your input. Do we tell the Interpol chap about this?'

Fleur Cooper leaned back in her chair are looked at the ceiling, clearly considering the options.

'Yes, I think we do, but obviously with the caution to keep it to themselves. It's relevant, and he might have intel on Andeslev that could give us links to whoever has done this.' She thought some more.

'Kurt, Ajay. If this is connected to the money stuff, can you process what Leo was going to ask you to do this morning? Put the jigsaw pieces together? Because if they're doing this to stop her, then we'd better carry on with what she wanted.'

Kurt nodded his agreement, but slowly, and said, 'What if that triggers them taking, well, taking more conclusive action? They took them, they didn't kill them – they'd have done that at the scene.

Fleur looked grim. 'I know that, but it still needs to be done.'

The others looked down at their paper work, accepting her decision but understanding, for a couple of them at least for the very first time, that heavy is the head that bears the crown. Brent and Kurt knew they'd have done the same thing. The others weren't so sure their nerves would have allowed it. Fleur pulled back their attention.

'I'm going to have to let them know upstairs.' She looked glum. 'That'll be fun.' She shook herself. 'Right – go. Keep in touch. The slightest thing that might help, let me, us, know. Go, go.'

The team scattered, the imperative they all felt evident in their pace, their faces, the set of their shoulders.

Fleur walked up the stairs to the management floor. Different in both decoration and atmosphere, here all was calm and decorous. It usually made Fleur smile; she often pictured this series of suites as a papier mâché of the 'ideal' leadership setup, but sat atop a simmering saucepan of boiling caramel, likely to boil over at any moment. No time for whimsy today though.

She squared her shoulders.   She'd thought about her approach on her way up and had decided not to exactly follow protocols. She headed into the little anteroom used by Steve Reith's PA. Pulling the door closed, she sat on the edge of the desk and told her what they believed had happened. Claire, the PA, was visibly shocked, and her hand shook as she laid down the highlighter pen she'd been holding.

'Oh dear God. What do you need?'

'Well, who up here needs to know, and what's the best way to get to them, get hold of them?'

Claire was decisive.

'All of them. This is a code, though I'm not sure what colour. They'll decide that. There's a Leadership Team meeting in,' she glanced at her watch, ' twenty minutes. So actually, they're all here. I think it's best if you tell the whole lot of them in one go.' Conscious that this was no small thing, she smiled slightly. 'Are you OK with that?'

'Of course.'

'Then I'm going to go and get them all together right away.' She slipped past Leo and down the corridor. Rapping smartly on the first door, she entered without waiting for a response and disappeared from Fleur's view. Over the following three minutes, Fleur became aware of a number of people heading down the broad central corridor towards the Board Room. Within four minutes Claire was back, slightly breathless.

This was partly why Fleur Cooper had chosen not to go straight to what Reith would call a 'High Heid Yin'. They'd cavil and want more information. That and the fact that Fleur knew that it would then have been only too easy to forget Claire altogether. She wasn't having that happen to the only true partisan Reith had on this floor. Clair said,

'I've told them it's an emergency, but no more than that. They're all yours. I'll bring some coffee in a minute – if they're eating you alive I can use the old custard cream offensive.' She smiled grimly. 'I'm here. When you've finished, please will you come back and tell me what I can do to help Steve?' Neither she nor Fleur even noticed that she'd been shocked into using his name instead of the rank she would normally punctiliously use.

Nodding, Fleur sped away towards the meeting room. Steeling herself, she knocked on the door and entered. She noted that the Chief Constable was at the head of the table. There were a number of seats unoccupied around the room and she chose to stand behind one of these, taking care to choose one in the Chief Constable's direct sightline.

'Good morning everyone. I apologise for this but I believe you need to be made aware of an issue we are currently investigating as a matter of urgency. If you'll bear with me, I'm going to give you the headline and then break that down into a timeline, if that's acceptable to you all?' The Chief Constable, a man whose own mother could never have thought him to have an approachable face, just nodded. Fleur recognised the 'get on with it' sub-signal of his body language. She took a deep breath and began.

'We believe that Superintendent Reith has been taken by force. At present we do not have any knowledge of his whereabouts or condition. He was not taken alone.'

The room stilled to attentive silence. Whilst all of these people - all men, Fleur thought abstractedly - were here in most part because of their political abilities, Steve Reith was respected by one and all. A pain in the side he might be on occasion, but they knew him for what he was. A committed, trustworthy officer who had pulled more irons out of more fires than most.

Fleur continued her tale, explaining the events of the previous evening. She'd been a little nervous of this aspect but then realised that these men were used to business over drinks and dinner. She outlined Leo Merton's involvement. Leo was known to two of them because of her previous work with the Met and there were nods of recognition. She provided the key points of their work so far and then gave an overview of their planned actions in the current circumstances. She stopped her summary and looked at the senior man in the room, waiting.

The Chief Constable cleared his throat. Fleur was aware that Reith, albeit with reservations relating to the administrative politics of the man, rated this senior officer. He felt that he was a man of his word, as far as that was possible.

'Succinct. Thank you Inspector.' He looked round the table. 'For those of you that haven't met her, this is the officer who'll shortly take up a new post as a Chief Inspector.' He didn't pause for unnecessary compliments or comment. 'So. Capable hands. I can't see anything we can directly do at the moment.' He cast his eye around the table, looking for contributions. There were none. 'Right. You have a plan.'

Fleur thanked the room then headed to the door. As her hand grasped the handle, the Chief Constable spoke again.

'Inspector. Do your best to bring him home safely.'

After a quick discussion with Claire, who was now working in Steve Reith's office, clearing his diary with the minimum of both fuss and information, Cooper took herself back to her own floor. There was no sign of Brent or Cervantes. She could see Groehling and Ajay Murthi next door, in company with a stocky looking man, all of them seated around the desk. Rightly guessing this to be the Interpol representative she joined them, briefly introducing herself and thanking him for his help.

He handed her his business card and she learned that his name was Franz Hartmans, from the Netherlands. His English was impeccable and he was quick to assure Cooper that if there was anything that could be done to help in the search for Steve Reith and Leonie Merton, he'd do his very best.

Groehling joined the conversation and said,

'Franz thinks that they have some quite detailed and recent information on Andeslev's UK contacts. He's already asked for them to be emailed through to him. That'll give us another direction to work from. I'm thinking that we'll be particularly interested in any property holdings or leases, stuff of that sort.'

Fleur winced inwardly. They were all so desperate that Reith and Leo were still alive, though they all knew that body dumping ought also to be a focus.

FORTY NINE

Reith gradually became aware that he was laying on a cold, hard floor. It was dark and when he felt for his watch the luminous dial found enough light to display the time as 5:11. He felt sick and woolly-headed, and was conscious that parts of him ached. He gingerly stretched his limbs and decided that nothing was broken and he could move freely. Good. He wasn't tied up. As senses returned he thought in a flash of Leo. He patted the floor around him and made contact with a slim leg. Orienting himself, he moved to her head and stroked her face. She was still dead to the world. His initial panic calmed a little as he realised that they must both have received about the same dose of whatever as each other, Leo was substantially less weighty than him, so it would take longer to wear off. He patted his pockets. No 'phone.

He relaxed his shoulders and tried to think. First, survey the terrain. He spoke aloud and decided that they were in a relatively small room, but possibly with quite a high ceiling. He could see a glimmer of light in one wall, well above his head. At this time of day it wasn't daylight, and had more of an orange tinge. So possibly a street light then. He turned his attention closer to hand. He stood and tried moving forwards with his arms outstretched, until he reached a wall. Feeling along this to his right he came to a door. There was a handle, but levering it he quickly ascertained that it was locked. As he moved along the wall past the door he scraped his cheek on what turned out to be a wooden coat hook. He couldn't feel anything sharp that might be useful. He continued his exploration. Continuing along the second wall he stumbled over some debris on the floor. Getting down onto one knee he gingerly cleared the objects and sat next to them, feeling them one by one, hoping to identify something useful. A pen. A plastic pack, filled with soft paper. Tissues, he categorised. Something soft and nylon in a small pad. He couldn't determine that. A wallet. No, a purse. He felt around him in a broader arc and felt a leather strap. Guessing this to be Leo's handbag, he pulled it towards him and felt inside, and in the side pockets. A brush, what felt like a cardboard nail file, but no 'phone. He began placing the loose objects back in the bag. A long, shiny-feeling tube. Mascara, he'd guess. A thin tube, perhaps lip gloss. Too thin for lipstick. A calculator. So definitely Leo's then. Unable to find anything else, he resumed his journey. On the third wall, below the light source he found a pile of blankets or sleeping bags, maybe towels, he couldn't be sure, there was a mix of textures.

Back along the rest of the wall and then down to the fourth one, estimating where he'd initially joined this and turning away, back to where he hoped he'd find Leo. He wasn't far off. Like everyone, his sense of direction was impaired by the lack of vision, but he found his left hand on her long hair, now well and truly escaped from its neat and professional styling. She lay face down on the concrete. He headed back to the third wall, locating the pile of fabrics. He sniffed them suspiciously, but could detect nothing other than dust, so he judged them to be adequate and, clutching them, worked his way back to his fellow inmate. He laid some of the material on the ground and then did his best to move Leo's inert body onto it. The hard, cold floor would do neither of them any favours. He then lifted her head to rest on his thigh and covered her with what felt like a sleeping bag and then used the last of his haul to wrap his own shoulders. So far, so good.

Thinking next. He explored all of his current cases and concluded that he wasn't close enough personally to merit this. So, an old case then? Or more likely, Leo was actually the target. If she'd stirred up enough dust, her targets might have decided it was best to get her out of the picture while they sorted matters.

FIFTY

Brent and Cervantes examined the scene of the likely kidnap in detail, although there wasn't a great deal to be seen. The recovery operator who'd collected it had noted that the vehicle had been left in the middle of the road, with the front doors open. A small amount of broken glass near the middle of the long road gave some clue that this might be the exact location.

The two men stood, considering the street. About four hundred metres long, with the back wall of some sort of industrial building all the way down one side, punctuated every ten metres or so by a series of doors.. On the other side, a row of terraced houses, almost all in a parlous state of repair and most seemingly derelict and unoccupied. Cervantes grimaced.

'Bloody clever place to choose. They'd have to turn down here to get across to the road that goes down to the nick, so they wouldn't have been going really fast. And it doesn't look like there's going to be a lot of witnesses.'

Brent wasn't so quickly discouraged. 'Maybe, but there's a housing crisis. I bet we've got a squatter or two, and if Daisy's got the right uniforms, they'll get something. And look.' He pointed up to the top of the industrial wall. Three CCTV cameras stood above three of the doors. Cervantes regarded them hopefully.

'The street lights are all smashed here. I wonder if the bastards didn't see them?'

Brent nodded. The protective carapace of natural suspicion developed by all sane police officers was being pierced for both men by the desperate hope that they could find Reith and Leo. As he turned towards his colleague, Brent spotted a police car pulling into an empty space a little further down the road, and three officers emerging. He said,

'Don, uniform are here. Why don't you get started with them on working the houses? I'd try front and back, in case any likely lad gets away on his toes. I'm going to see if I can get to these CCTVs and any footage. I'll get back here as soon as I can.

He set off at a brisk pace, disappearing around the corner. Cervantes greeted the three policemen now heading his way, knowing all of them by name and recognising that Daisy had done well. These were some of the gentlemen of the nick, hard when necessary but still able to give the benefit of the doubt. The officer at the front of the small pack hailed Cervantes in return and said,

'Bloody mess this. Daisy told us what's what. Got a lot of time for Mr Reith, us. What do you want?'

Cervantes outlined the plan and the four split into pairs, using their radios to co-ordinate their simultaneous approaches to the front and rear of each property.

Meanwhile, Brent had found his way into the large industrial unit backing on to the road in question. Undoubtedly a 1950's construction, it turned out to house a most surprising business. Industrial diamond cutting. Brent found the Reception and then asked to speak to a senior member of staff as a matter of urgency. The slightly adenoidal girl asked him to 'Hab a seat and I'll get hib.'

Brent stood by the neat little seating area and waited. Within a couple of minutes he was being welcomed by a small, rotund man wearing a yarmulke. He introduced himself as Geoff Cohen, and ushered Brent through a door behind Reception. They emerged into an enormous atrium, filled with light from a spectacular glass ceiling, the floor space filled with enormous flower beds from which sprouted full-grown trees. From what Mick could see, the windows could all be opened with levers that came down to winding handles four feet from the floor. Geoff Cohen saw Brent's interest and said,

'This used to be a shirt factory, back in the day. So this whole area was filled with steam sewing machines, hence the window system.'

By now they were climbing stairs in the corner of the large space and Brent realised that there were offices and rooms built all the way round a gallery that circled the entire floor. They entered a substantial office, equipped with a large desk facing the wall at the back and an area with a coffee table and two sofas. Geoff Cohen ushered Brent to the more comfortable zone, sitting opposite him.

'So Mr Brent, what can I do to help you today?'

Mick responded with 'Do you mind if I ask what you do here? I saw the small sign that says industrial diamond cutting on the main door, but I don't really know what that means.' Brent needed to assess how likely it was that the CCTV system was going to be of any use.

Geoff Cohen responded enthusiastically. 'Oh, we cut diamonds for a lot of different companies. You probably have some of our work in your own tool box – diamonds are used for grinding, drilling, abrasion, polishing. These days it's mostly synthetic diamonds. Of course, when my dad started this business – there's a cliché for you – a Jewish diamond merchant – it was the real McCoy. But there aren't enough diamonds to meet need now, so here we are. Can I ask why you need to know?'

Brent responded readily, still hopeful. 'We think a crime took place in the road behind here last night. We spotted your CCTV and I'm really hoping, *really* hoping, that it's a good system?'

Cohen nodded, understanding the question.

'As it happens yes, but not because of the diamonds. Just because of the word.'

Brent allowed his puzzlement to show. Cohen smiled and continued.

'When we do use real diamonds, they're not the sort of calibre that you could turn into jewellery, so there's no decent value. And the synthetic diamonds, well, they come out at less than a quid a carat, but you can't tell the bloody burglars that. So in fact, we do have a very good system, because it's easier to deter the idiots than to keep replacing smashed door grilles and the like. It works in the dark, has automatic directional movement tracking and time stamped digital capacity. Would you like me to get our Head of Security to give you access? The quickest way is for you to nominate an officer and we'll issue them with full remote access to the system. Then they can copy, download, enhance, whatever.'

Brent reflected that this was one of the things that was often off about TV police dramas. So many interactions with the police seemed to be combative and unpleasant, but in reality most people wanted to be as helpful as they could.

Brent thanked Geoff Cohen very warmly and provided him with the contact details for Kurt Groehling, promising that Groehling would be in touch in short order. He took his leave and headed back around the building, calling Kurt on his way and setting the promised security link in process.

Rounding the corner he could see Cervantes and one of the uniformed officers in the window of a house not far up the road from where they were guessing the abduction had taken place. He stepped inside the front door, calling 'Hello!' as he did so. Cervantes put his head round the door frame of the front room and beckoned him in. The two officers had been talking to a young woman in hospital scrubs. Cervantes said, 'This is Marina. She's a student nurse at the New Albert.'

Brent joined them in a room half-heartedly warmed by a paraffin heater. There were candles in large glass jars, partly to protect them from breezes and partly to reduce any fire risk, Brent guessed. The woman looked nervous at the arrival of yet another representative of the law and seeing this, the uniformed officer chipped in . 'Don't worry Marina, this is Mick Brent, and I promise you he thinks that your pay rate is the crime, not a bit of squatting.'

Brent relaxed his stance to look as non-threatening and amiably enquiring as someone of his rugby build could and waited. Marina manned up and offered,

'Well, I was just saying that I got home about quarter past ten last night. I was the first one back. There are four of us...' She trailed off. 'But you don't need to know that. 'Anyway, I was just heating up some water for a hot drink,' she gestured towards the back of the property, through an archway in the middle of the room. On a wallpapering table sat a small camping stove, atop an asbestos mat. Brent ground his teeth at the unfairness of the system, but kept his eye on the prize. He said, 'And...?'

'Well, I heard a smashing from outside. A crash, like a car, you know. So I went to the window and I saw this dark van. It looked like it had hit the big four by four car, but I didn't see that, just heard it. It seemed to me that there were people in the big car but then they all moved to the van, and the van left. But there aren't any lights there anymore, so I can't be sure. Then the...the others came home and they said there was a car just sat in the middle of the road, engine running, doors open and everything. We weren't sure what to do, but we didn't think we could just leave it there, so…' She stopped, obviously marshalling her presentation. 'The thing is, we all need to stay here for another three months, until we earn enough for a deposit on a decent place, so we didn't want to risk it. But, you probably already know this next bit because I expect it's in the report somewhere. Anyway, so Tony went out and stood with the big car. Tony's parents live in North London, and he has a driving licence with that address, so we thought he could say he was just passing if the police asked. He put his gloves on and he took the keys out and then he rang the police. We were surprised how quickly a tow truck came, but then we guessed it was because it was blocking the road and that would cause problems in the day time specially. Tony did try to tell the driver what I thought I'd seen but he thought that the driver maybe didn't speak much English. Anyway, the car got driven away and that was that.'

Although they chatted with her for a few minutes more, Marina wasn't able to offer anything else, other than the direction of the van when it left. She was as sure as she could be of what she had described. The candles hadn't yet been lit and her night vision was as strong as it could have been. Assuring her that they weren't interested in her accommodation at the moment, they took their leave. Brent signalled the other four to go ahead while he rang Cooper and Groehling on a group call. He summed up their conversation with Marina, and Kurt picked up the point about the direction of the van. Cooper had been made aware of the CCTV access by Kurt and the two of them were about to start on that. Brent discontinued, then joined his colleagues as they worked their way down the road. Despite finding two other residents in situ, neither was able to offer any information from the previous night. Both were legitimate tenants and both TVs had been in use.

Trying not to be despondent, the small group made its way back to their station. It was now early afternoon and Reith and Leo had been missing for over fifteen hours. Without any communication or demands it was difficult to maintain positivity.

FIFTY ONE

It was gone nine in the morning before Reith felt Leo stir. The external electric light had gone, to be replaced by a dull, grey sunlight. He placed his hand lightly on her shoulder and waited for her to arrange her thoughts. He thought that she'd stretched her limbs, mirroring his own attempts to assess any damage. After a minute or two, her calm, caramel voice said, 'I really don't want to come out to play with you anymore. It totally sucks.'

He laughed and hugged her shoulders in pleasure at her humour and courage and attitude. He summed up the situation for her.

'It's just gone 9am. They've taken our phones. Your bag was emptied on the floor. There's nothing useful left for us to try anything with. We've got the stuff we're sitting on and wearing. There's no water, no food, no toilet facilities.'

She laughed. 'Don't sugar coat it, will you!' She thought.

'So they didn't kill us outright. Does that mean they might want something from us, or did they just need us out of the way? And if so, why?'

Reith had had over four hours to consider this. 'Well, I'm not currently involved in anything else on a personal level. Plenty of case oversight, but nothing that I can see would merit this. I was wondering...before we left the station last night, you said you were very close to accessing some key accounts in the money laundering?'

Leo grasped the point at once. 'I did, and I am...was. I thought I'd been exceptionally careful, but you can never be totally certain that you haven't triggered an alarm. Sometimes just logging into a bank's website can activate a bot that'll snitch on you to someone who's using the bank's facilities for illicit means. So yes, you could be right. We could be here just to stop me reaching the end of that road.' She thought some more. 'But why not kill us outright?'

Reith was reasonably certain in his reply. 'Killing a police officer is always a shoddy piece of work. Professional criminals tend not to see the point. It just riles up the police service, causes additional problems at airports and ferry ports and often brings an even stronger focus on the very activity they're trying to hide.

Leo pondered the matter for a while.

'So they might not intend to kill us, proactively? But have you seen any sign that they intend to keep us alive, proactively? No food, no water. And since you've mentioned it, I'm dying for a wee.' She sighed.

'I've been listening for noise, both outside the room inside the building, and outdoors, where you can see a bit of daylight. I haven't heard anything. No people, no traffic right outside, though I can hear the usual background hum. I shouted on and off for about thirty minutes, but zero response.'

Leo accepted this. 'And what about your team? Are they going to realise quickly, or are they going to think we're playing doctors and nurses and just forgot the time?'

His grin was apparent in his voice when he replied. 'I thought about that, but they know me better, and I'm pretty sure they already have a good handle on the unlikelihood of you doing that either. Be nice though...but still, no they'll have worked it out at least an hour ago. What I don't know is what there is to be found. I don't have my car keys, so is that because they have them, or because they got left in the car? And I can't find yours either.'

Leo was shaking her head. 'I left mine in the desk at the station. There was a file I wanted to check one last time before I went home. Didn't want to take it out of the station so I thought leaving my keys up there would remind me. Right, joking apart, can we please talk about toilets. Can we do something? I can't last much longer, can you? I'm not going to lie, this is excruciatingly embarrassing, but needs must. Did you find anything that we could use as a receptacle?'

Reith shook his head. 'Nothing. A big plastic bag would do for now, if we could tie it off at the top it'll save our senses for a while, but there's nothing like that.'

She shifted her weight to the upright position and leaned against him. 'I don't think my handbag will be any use, too

299

many zips and pockets. It'll probably leak like a sieve. Oh, but hang on! Did you say they'd taken everything useful? What about my shopping bag? Small, rolled up in a ball, inside its own little pocket.'

'Ah, that's what it is.' He bent backwards and scrabbled in the handbag, retrieving the little item. He passed it to Leo and she flicked it open.

'I think it's pure nylon. I think it'll do. It's just going to be awkward, but hey ho. I'm a kayaker and we have to wee out the side of our boats sometimes, and I know you play rugby, so gawd knows what you lot get up to.' She continued, musing to herself.. 'I suppose this is just horrid because we fancy each other but we're not ready for any of this.' She laughed. 'Enough. I'm going to find a corner and wee into my really quite expensive back up shopping bag and then you're going to, and then we're going to hang it on the coat hook. And while I'm weeing you're going to sing, VERY LOUD and I'll do the same for you.'

FIFTY TWO

Dear Diary

A level exams start this week. I am so, so frightened, but one good thing has happened. Granny says she needs me to come and stay and help with Grandad's bad knee. She doesn't really, she just knows that two weeks of peace and quiet will be really helpful.

But what if I don't get my grades? I can't stay here. I've still been thinking about joining the army. I can't join the navy or the air force because I get really travel sick and I guess that might be a drawback!

FIFTY THREE

Groehling had the control team at his full disposal; the word had gone round that something serious had happened to Steve Reith and people who might be able to help wanted to do so. As one of the older hands in the room said.

'He can be a hard bastard, but he's straight as a die and fair,, and he remembers what it's like out there. There's no-one I'd rather have at my back.'

The security CCTV had yielded surprisingly good shots of both the vehicles involved, and the incident. Groehling had played it back to the team before heading off to secure the follow-up he now needed.

The footage, although obviously filmed in the dark, was clear. The dark van, now identifiable as a Ford Transit, could be seen idling at the side of the road, lights off. The exhaust emission told its tale. The watching team all realised, much at the same time, that this had been a well-orchestrated event. The lights on the van were suddenly switched on and the van lurched out to the right and into Reith's Range Rover. The registration plate was easy to read.

Cervantes said, 'Someone had to be tracking them, alerting the people in the van to their route and then telling them when they were turning down that road. Can we see any sign of them?'

For the moment he was ignored, as they watched four people race from the van, two from the front seats and two emerging from the rear. In seconds they were pulling open the driver and passenger doors on Reith's car and, despite Reith quite obviously attempting to land a punch, quickly overpowered the two. It was also only a matter of seconds before Reith and Leo were transferred to the back of the van, leaving the Range Rover running in the middle of the road.

Groehling stopped the playback and they all looked at Fleur Cooper. She responded immediately.

'Yes, Don. They couldn't have done that without communication further back along the route. So there might be another car that doesn't come into that picture. Kurt, can you get anything from a camera further back down the road? They obviously didn't come right up to the scene, but they couldn't have driven past it anyway. We need to check other cameras from that diamond company, but also all nearby points, to see if we can identify a vehicle following the Super. And we've got a number plate for the van. I know we all get that it'll be stolen, but can we find it, draw any conclusions from where it was taken, where it was abandoned?' She sat up a little straighter in her seat.

'OK. The good news is that it wasn't an immediate hit. They didn't kill them. I'd say they were dosed with some sort of liquid anaesthetic, but there's no indication of anything worse.' She thought some more.

'And I'm beginning to think that this might well be funded by Andeslev, but I don't think it's Russian or East European involvement doing the actual work, otherwise Steve and Leo could've been dead on the spot. Whoever he might have used is more professional and possibly more local than that, knows the grief killing a police officer can bring. And the kidnap rather than something more permanent might be telling. It's over sixteen hours now since they were taken, and we, no-one, has had any demands for anything. Which makes me wonder if what this is all about is delaying Leo. She was talking to the Super and me last evening, just before we came over to yours.' She looked at Mick. 'She thought she was very close to the top of the tree, in terms of the money. That might have been their motive.' She turned towards Groehling. 'Kurt, is it possible that our targets could know that Leo was getting close to their accounts?'

He nodded. 'Oh yes. I mean, I watched what she was doing, and it was meticulous, but she couldn't have known if there'd be an automatic alert set up in any bank, or on any of the accounts further down the tree. It's why she wanted AJ in so early this morning. She reckoned a lot of the money was being moved in the States, which meant that if she got an early start today, the people concerned might still be in the land of nod, over there. And, like you said earlier, we've done everything that she'd listed for Ajay to do first thing this morning. Well before 10 am our time and a good chunk ahead of the American markets. Couldn't do it as fast as she would have obviously, but it is done. Doors locked, drainpipes blocked.' AJ nodded in acknowledgement of the point.

Another pause for thought and then Fleur spoke again.

'Right. Kurt and Mick, get the CCTV data down to the control room and then start on any other camera from the diamond place. Mick, stay downstairs and get some officers onto tracking Reith's route from Mick and Maze's to this street; you know what we want – a car that's following them. If we're truly lucky they might not have used a stolen car, because it wasn't going to be used in the actual take-down. And obviously we need a city-wide look-out for the van. '

'And AJ, get back to Franz Hartmans. Go through what you understand of Leo's work, see if he can add anything. Has he had anything back about known associates of Andeslev? If we can identify anyone at all that might be involved, it could give us two ends of string to pull.' The team all recognised one of Reith's favourite sayings.

FIFTY FOUR

Dear Diary

It's been quite a good summer, because once school was finished I got a full-time job and a weekend job, which meant I was out virtually all of the time. As long as I paid my keep everything was calmer at home, at least most of the time.

I heard a Beatles song the other day, one I hadn't listened to before. Some of the words were, "She's leaving home after living alone for so many years." It made me cry, a bit. I do try hard not to let it bother me, knowing he hates me, but sometimes I can't help it. I still do my best to please him, even if there's never any point.

It's results day tomorrow. We had to give stamped addressed envelopes to school, so they could let us have the results by post, in case we were on holiday or anything, but Mrs Lewis, the Deputy Head, said it would be better if I came up to school to collect mine, if I could. So I didn't do an envelope.

I feel like a musical instrument just after it's been played, like all my strings are still vibrating, but silently.

Whatever happens, I'm leaving here soon and I don't have to come back. If I can get in to college that's one way, but I've done a lot of research now and there are a lot of jobs where you can get accommodation, so I'll be OK. Mrs Lewis has been brilliant. She's never really discussed it but she asked me if I wanted to bring anything over to her house, for safety before I go. I thought about it and I took some of my books and Freddie, and some of the precious things from Granny. He hasn't touched those, because he wouldn't want her to know, but if I leave anything behind after I go, I think it'll disappear or get lost. Mrs Lewis put a suitcase in the spare room for me and I can add things when I want to. I keep my diary at school now, in my locker. Mrs Lewis says I can keep the locker until I'm ready to leave. I'm eighteen now, so I have the right to do whatever I want.

I'm trying to be mature, but often I spend time thinking about him and wondering if I could ever show him how much he's hurt me. But then, part of me knows that would please him, not upset him. I wonder now if he was always like this? I worry too that it's genetic. What if I have the same character really?

FIFTY FIVE

A small control room team, quickly assembled by Phil, w holed up in a miniscule viewing room equipped with half a dozen monitors. Methodically they were scouring the likely route choices made by Reith on the previous night. Each time they identified his vehicle they carefully searched the surrounding traffic, identifying potential tracker vehicles. It was after the third spotting of Reith's car that they began to believe their luck was in. They'd seen a pale Audi A5 about three cars behind Reith in their first encounter with the Range Rover. When they'd seen it in footage from two miles further along the route, they'd started to cross fingers. On its third appearance coincidence could be discounted. Too many route decisions had been made. They continued their careful examination of the many CCTV sources at their command and confirmed the shadowing of the big 4 x 4 by the Audi, right to the end of the road by the diamond factory. The registration number, although a little blurred by dirt in some images, was easily legible.

One of the team's fingers danced over their keyboard. She smiled.'

'It's not listed as stolen. Or at least, not yet. I'm sending the registered owner details to the printer.' She left the room and returned in less than a minute with a printout, which she handed to Brent. He practically snatched it from her and made for the door at some speed. Framed within the door space he stopped and turned back.

'Thank you all, thank you. I'm going to get on with this, but can you carry on tracking the van, to see if you can find where it went. And also if it's possible to see how, who took it in the first place? And also track that Audi after the incident? Where did it go?' He grinned wryly, 'Not a lot to ask, I know, but if we can get them back safe I promise you doughnuts for a week.' Before they could begin to share their eagerness to continue their search, to help in any way they could, he'd gone.

Upstairs, Brent crashed through the sergeants' room to Fleur's office, displaying every aspect of his many years as a rugby player. Anyone that had got in his way would have known about it. He brought his Inspector up to speed and she beckoned him to follow her next door, to where AJ and the Interpol officer, Franz Hartmans, were poring over a deep pile of financial printouts. Cooper was brisk.

'Mr Hartmans, please forgive my urgency. I know you have access to some information about contacts and known associates of Andeslev. Is this man by any chance one of them?' She thrust the printout towards him.

He flipped open the laptop on the desk near to his elbow and it flickered into life. He accessed his emails and opened a file that seemed to be an attachment. He was silent for over a minute, working his way down the list. Cooper and Brent, frustrated by their own inaction, respectively ground their teeth. Hartmans continued steadily, opening each line of his database and reading along. When he stopped he looked up at them and smiled, suddenly much younger in his demeanour.

'No, I do not have a record of this man. But I might have something useful, because I think your system is very similar to the one we use in the Netherlands.'

They regarded him solemnly, waiting for comprehension. He continued.

'In places like France post codes are very big areas – they can cover a whole suburb or even twenty villages. But not for us Dutch, and not for you, I think?'

Brent shook his head. 'No, that's true. Unless you're in the wilds of Scotland, a post code is usually very precise.

Hartmans smiled, pleased. 'Then that is good. Because I have a man on my list with the exact same postcode as this car owner, although it is not the same man. So that must be the same street or even the same building, yes?'

Fleur could take no more. 'Oh God, yes! Who is it, what have you got?'

The contact picked out by Hartmans was listed as a Gary Peters. 'In English I think you say, a nasty bit of work? We believe that he has worked within Andeslev's team for some time, as an enforcer, collecting debts, threatening to get what they want. There has never been enough to act on, because victims have been too afraid. But he's of real interest to us. And he's here, in London. At this address in Wandsworth. ' He mispronounced Wandsworth, but neither Fleur nor Mick gave a flying toss.

The Interpol agent, professional as required, was nonetheless also human. 'He'll be armed. No-one else should be hurt by this man or his associates.'

AJ, who had watched the entire exchange was caught between fascination at the high order of events he was currently being given access to and an appalled self-awareness that he was enjoying himself, however dreadful the core problem.

Fleur kicked into action. 'Mick, I'm going to get an armed response team sorted – you go and find Don and I'll meet you down in the car park as soon as I can. If you get a minute, tell Kurt what we're up to, but don't waste time. And you and Don, get your vests and helmets.'

They left the room, audibly followed by Hartman's wishes for their success.

Fleur short-circuited the procedure for securing the services of an ART, an Armed Response Team. She rang upstairs to Claire, Reith's secretary and explained her issue and its importance. It could take many minutes, even an hour, to mobilise an ART and she didn't want that. Claire saw the point and rang off, only to call back within five minutes, saying,

'It's sorted. Direct command of the CC. Here's your code to give the department.'

Fleur rang through to the Unit and relayed her request, making the tactical decision to give a brief summary of the back story. One of their own was always going to be a motivator.

Within ten minutes she was in the car park, clutching her vest and helmet. She, Brent and Cervantes bundled into an unmarked car and set off, already in communication with the activated ART and assessing each other's progress towards the target address. Fleur judged that she would reach the area first, which pleased her. She wanted a quick look before the whole thing got serious.

It was a quiet road of pleasant looking terraces and semis. As she pulled the car into an empty space further down the road from the one they sought, she checked the map app on her 'phone. Less than 20 minutes' drive to Mick and Maze's home; perhaps all the practical justification that had been needed for selecting this man for the dirty work. Talking to the ART leader on her radio she advised that they park at the end of the terrace containing their target, in the cross road that cut through the rows of early twentieth century housing. It would limit their exposure.

The three officers sat in the car and looked along the road. A pretty street, obviously well maintained by most of its residents. Some properties seemed to be flats now, but from the tidiness of the front gardens and the neat wooden shelters and bunkers obscuring rubbish bins, all three guessed that these were owner-occupied. Don tapped Fleur on the shoulder and for some reason, whispered. 'Gov – over there,'

Slightly behind their car and on the opposite side of the road was a silver Audi A5. Impossible to see the number plate from here, but chances were...

Further conversation on the radio ascertained that the ART were in place, with officers ready to approach the building from the front and rear. The unit leader expressed his clear advice that Cooper and her colleagues remain well back until their task had been completed. Not stupid, Fleur agreed, although she and her two colleagues did get out of the car and struggle into their vests and helmets. This was one of the things that caused hilarity in police dramas for them. Often the actors were seen wearing the vest, but not the helmets. To allow 'acting' to be visible, the officers always supposed, but the deadly chances of a head shot would prevent any officer with the full complement of marbles from doing anything so hare-brained.

It didn't take long. The armed team took out the front door with one experienced wham of the big red door knocker and yelled their warning. From their vantage point, Fleur's team could hear some sort of disruption at the back, but within three minutes the heavily armed and protected officers were escorting four people, three men and a women, from the building and into the four police vehicles that had shadowed the ART on its journey, waiting out of sight of the target property.

Cooper's team all noted the same thing. The three men were startling in their self control. Hard faces, buzz cuts, some impressive physiques. The woman was a different story. She was shivering in thin clothing and the female officer escorting her into the car sourced a blanket from the trunk to wrap around herself. The woman seemed grateful, tearful.

Fleur left Don and Mick by their car and headed to intercept the ART leader. He smiled warmly at her. He'd led on her firearms refresher the previous year and they'd discovered a similar sense of humour.

'All done ma'am. No real issues, they didn't see us coming and although there's plenty of fire power in there, no one had anything to hand when we arrived. Two of them tried to leg it out the back, but we sorted that.' He nodded towards the woman in the police car now drawing away from the kerb. 'She's interesting though. Found her locked in the back bedroom upstairs. Terrified. We've arrested her for form's sake as much as anything. I think she's going to need protection from the rest of them. She speaks excellent English, but I've a feeling she's not British. I've radioed in for Forensics and one of my lot's going to hang on here and hand over chain of custody when they arrive. I've told them it's maximum priority, life at risk level. They're en route.' He looked down at her, at least six six in his heavy kit and thick-soled boots.

'Guessing you want at that lot?' Tilting his head at the departing marked cars. 'Also guessing you won't get much, but maybe enough. Fingers crossed.' He headed back to his team and Fleur gestured to Brent and

Cervantes to join her. Pulling nitrile gloves from her pocket and pulling them on, she was pleased to see the two men do the same as they joined her.

'We can't touch anything, but I want to at least look. There might be clues, keys, leases. God knows, but I'm praying.' Tight lipped, the little group moved towards the house. From the outside it could be seen that the smart blinds were closed and the front door, unlike its neighbours, had no glass panel. Stepping over the threshold, the hallway bore no fruit for them, no table for keys, just an empty row of coat pegs. A man's umbrella on the floor. They moved first into the room at the front. Equipped with sofas, coffee table and TV, there was no sign of this being a home. Two coffee cups sat on the table and the TV was showing a late afternoon quiz programme. No pictures or ornaments. This felt like a good quality rental property.

The next room took up the rest of the ground floor. What had presumably been a quite large dining room had been knocked through into the kitchen to provide a light, airy space, although much of the light was blocked by window blinds, again closed. This room showed more signs of habitation, a couple of books, some papers on the right-hand counter. Careful to keep any disturbance to the minimum, Fleur flicked through the papers. Bills, all relating to this house. She turned to the row of built-in drawers at one end of the longest run of units. Cutlery, then cling film, foil. Then table mats, tea towels. In the bottom drawer the sort of detritus that collected in every house, leaflets, string, sticky tape. No obvious keys or clues to where they'd taken Reith and Leo. She didn't want to root down to the bottom of the rubbish. No point. This wasn't where they'd have kept that sort of stuff, it would have been needed at hand. She had a decision to make.

'Don – stay here. When Forensics get here, tell them what we're up against. Tell them that we're probably looking for another property, somewhere. Even if you have to sit on the front doorstep – don't leave!'

Cervantes, equally daunted and pleased to have what might be a key task, nodded and bid farewell to Cooper and Brent.

FIFTY SIX

Reith and Leo, uncomfortable on the hard floor but at least warm enough, dozed through the later part of the afternoon. Reith wanted to see if between them they could reach the window above them. He reckoned that their combined heights would do it, and he thought that it was probably high enough for Leo to wriggle through. What he couldn't tell in the limited lighting and from this distance was whether it would be possible to open it. And he was itching to understand what might happen next, back in the middle of Leo's work.

The next time Leo stirred, he voiced his thoughts.

'Can I ask a question?' He didn't wait for a response. 'I know you'd got stuff planned for first thing this morning, ahead of the American markets. Would they be able to action that, without you there, Kurt and Ajay?'

She understood him immediately. 'God, yes. In fact, *I* couldn't action the next bit – you need police or court authority. But you mean, would they understand what to do? Definitely, because of the bus thing.'

As so often in conversation with Leonie Merton, he was intrigued. 'What bus?'

'Well, you know, the one that you might get run over by. It's a good management principle. No-one is indispensable and everyone can be hit by a bus. So the list I left for Ajay and Kurt isn't detailed but I'm absolutely confident that they'd have been able to do it.' An unexpected glum rider. 'If they thought about it, that is.'

Reith didn't hesitate. 'At least one of them will, if not all. But you do need to be aware that it'll have been a shit decision for them, for Fleur in particular. They don't know where we are, or what these bastards want. They'll assume that your lack of activity might be a bargaining chip. So deciding to do it anyway means that a priority to stop them had to be noted and taken. Even if that makes it more dangerous for us.'

She thought for a while. 'I don't see that there's a choice. I'd really rather not die here, and I don't know if I'll cave if they torture us or something, but in principle stopping them is the only right thing. But the longer we're here without anything, no visitors, no food, no noise, nothing, the more I hope you're right that this was about holding me up, not permanently stopping us. And I'm guessing that anyone below full psychopath rating would prefer to avoid the shit storm that I assume would ensue if they bumped off a police superintendent.' She felt Reith nod in the near dark.

'Are you up for trying to reach the window, having a look, feeling along it to see if it's possible to get out? I know I can't stand on your shoulders, but I'm sure we could do it the other way around.'

Leo, as ever, was game. 'Of course, but let me just run on the spot for a minute or two, I need to loosen up. Stiff after all this loafing about.' He listened to her warm chuckle with both gratitude that her world view was so upbeat but also with an as yet sublimated fury towards those who had done this to her, to them. His watch said 18:39. Hunger and thirst were very much their enemies now. His professional judgement was that they'd just been left to rot. No-one had returned, absolutely no activity within or near their prison building.

Leo stopped her bouncing and sad, 'Shoes off, I think, but should I take one up with me, in case I can actually smash the window with a heel?'

'Good idea. Can you tuck it inside your blouse or something, so that it doesn't get in your way. He could feel her wriggling as she complied.

'Done. Tucked in the back of my knickers. If you can give me a piggy back, I think I can crawl onto your shoulders, if you lean against the wall for balance.''

The first part the manoeuvre was soon accomplished and even in the parlous current circumstances, Reith was immensely amused by Leo's commentary as she attempted to get atop his broad shoulders. He thought back to when he'd interviewed Harry Wilson from her company, the previous year, after the restaurant bombing. He remembered her then boss, now her co-director, saying that he'd been surprised by the fluency of Leo's cussing after she was blown off her feet and quite seriously injured by the blast. He now had no room to doubt that statement and grinned to himself as Leo castigated him for having such short hair.

'How in the name of all that's screwed up do you expect me to do this without something to hang on to. Honestly, you'd think you'd want to look different from the idiot criminals with their ugly crew cuts. '

She continued in this vein for another couple of minutes, until she was balanced with a foot either side of his head.

'Right, I'm directly in front of the window. I can't see it very well, but the surface feels a bit bobbly. I'm going to try whacking it with my shoe, but I've a feeling that it's that sodding awful, totally unwanted, useless feckin' wired glass.'

More wriggling as she retrieved her shoe, followed by several hefty thumps on the window, juxtaposed with yet more imprecations against the 'idiot who thought you needed security glass halfway up to heaven.'

She leant down towards him slightly and handed him the shoe. 'Can you just drop that nearby, so we don't have to crawl about looking for it in a minute? I just want to see what I can feel around the outside of the frame.'

He could feel her leaning in each direction as she explored the casement.

'Right. Bad news, it's not an opener. But good news – there are six screws in what feels like round loops. One in each corner and then one in the middle of each long side. I'd guess that they're all that's holding the glass frame in place. And more on the positives – I think they're flat head screws, not Phillips, or one of those fandangled star thingyme wotsits. Let me get back down and we can see if we've got anything at all that we can use.'

Leo slid herself down so that she was astride his shoulders and then asked him to bend forward to let her down. With the minimum of language this time she was soon on the ground and reunited with her shoes. They retreated to their makeshift camp and pulled Leo's handbag towards them,

'I know you said they'd taken everything useful, but let's have a think. We need something small, flat and strong that'll turn the screws.'

There was silence as he mentally assessed his attire. No metal buttons. He felt for his belt buckle but the pin was round and pointed, it wouldn't grip in the screws' slots. He was aware that Leo was doing the same. She laughed again.

'I've got a wired bra, but it feels like a round wire, not one of the flatter ones, so that's no bleedin' help.' The last three words were delivered in a creditable East End accent.

Reith said, 'I've got a metal watch strap, made up of small sections. I think the linking ones might be flat enough to turn a screw, especially if I leave a few of the bigger sections attached, to give you something to grip. But I can't think how to break it apart without damaging the very pieces we need."

Leo sighed. 'It's such a pity they took my little tool set. That would have done it.'

Reith couldn't stop himself snapping back. 'Your little what?'

'Tool kit', she replied calmly. 'It's like a little credit card shape and you pull it out. It's got two tiny screwdrivers, tweezers, scissors. All very small, but it'd work on a watch.' She mused a little more. 'Shame, because very often I've got the bigger set with me, but it's in my briefcase back at your station.'

Bemused, he said. 'What bigger set?'

She giggled and said, 'You'd love it. It's a hammer and pliers set, painted all over with flowers. The handle of the hammer keeps unscrewing, giving you smaller and smaller screwdrivers. I get a lot of stick for it at work, but I can't tell you how many men come to borrow it. But I only had the little one with me, in the umbrella pocket. To be honest, I'm surprised they even noticed it, but life's a bugger some days.'

Reith was suddenly hopeful. 'Um, what's an umbrella pocket? I didn't find an umbrella in your bag.'

She answered him in a surprised tone. 'Oh, I don't keep an umbrella in it – they're too bulky and they stick up into the main section of the bag. I keep that little tool kit, some first aid stuff and a sewing kit, you know, like the ones you get from a hotel.' Then she realised what he might be saying and hoisted her bag towards her.

'It's here, a zip right at the base of the bag. Oh for the love of Mike, Milly and Mandy, it's all here. They didn't notice it. And my bloody pencil torch! My sodding, bloody, wonderful bloody pencil torch!'

They quickly debated their to-do list. Getting a tool that would stand a chance with the window screws was their priority and there was nothing in the little tool kit that looked strong enough, though Leo pocketed the folding scissors and the tweezers, just in case. Since neither had any idea how long the torch would last it was agreed that dismantling the watch strap was step one. If necessary, Leo thought that she could attack the window screws by feel.

Reith was proven right. His watch strap was quickly separated into smaller pieces. The lip of the end piece, which slid under its partner and then clicked into place was certainly both slim and strong enough to try on a screw. With two pieces still attached on the opposite side to the makeshift blade there was a handle of sorts. It would be fiddly, but it might, just might work.

Leo repeated her earlier gymnastics and resumed her position in front of the window. She perched the torch, still shining brightly for the moment, on the narrow ledge and began with the bottom righthand screw. Reith listened to another bout of her progress analysis, less ripe this time. He figured that when she was actively engaged in a positive pursuit, her cussing wasn't needed. He grinned to himself. If and when they got out of here, he owed this entrancing woman the best meal of her life. No easy thing, he realised, as he remembered that her best friend owned a Michelin-starred restaurant.

Above him Leo was crowing with delight. 'It's out, it's out. Who's a clever girl then? Right, number two.' She worked on. Halfway through the second one she explained to Reith that she was going to turn off the torch.

'I can feel what I'm doing now and I'm going to need to be able to see outside, if I can get the window out'. The light disappeared and she continued with her task.

FIFTY SEVEN

Back at the station Cooper was met by the Assistant Chief Constable. It was a measure of their recognition of the desperate state of affairs that he hadn't sent for her, but had descended from on high to get a situation report. She quickly updated him, letting him know that Forensics had been alerted to the need to urgently seek in the Wandsworth house anything at all that might lead to Reith's location. More pressing was the need to interview the arrestees. She shared her rationale with her senior officer.

'I'm thinking that it'll take a lot of time if we're going to get anything out of the three men. They haven't asked for solicitors yet, but they're saying no comment to everything. And I don't doubt they know the system and all their rights. I want to start with the woman. The ART lead thought she'd been some sort of prisoner. If that's right, she may be able to give us something.'

He saw the force of the logic and she departed with his blessing. She rounded up Brent and they had the woman brought to the Sexual Violence interview suite. That might or might not be one of the things she'd endured, but it was a pleasant, non-threatening environment and might help her relax.

The woman had given her name as Roxanne Khan. When Cooper and Brent met her face to face in the interview room, both stopped thinking of her as a woman and reclassified her as a girl. She shared initial information easily enough. Her father was Turkish and her mother had been British. They'd met twenty years before when Roxanne's mother had been on holiday in Turkey. They'd married, and nineteen years ago had Roxanne. After this, it became a bit harder to extract anything cogent, as she became progressively more upset. Roxanne's mother had died the previous summer and her father, Muslim but a loving and not strict father had agreed that Roxy could come to the UK after Christmas, to see her grandparents. There'd never been any animosity between the families and there'd been plenty of family trips in both directions over the years. But this was Roxy's first solo trip. She thought now that she'd made her first mistake with the trip to the airport. She'd booked a taxi, because she didn't want her dad to be upset at the airport. She'd dressed in more Western clothes than usual, because her grandparents and a cousin were going to meet her at

Heathrow. Both officers got the impression that she liked this cousin and had wanted to impress him.

On the plane she'd been seated across the aisle from one of the men that they'd arrested at the same time as her. She said they'd had some pleasant conversation during the flight, thought he was her dad's age, didn't think anything of it. When they arrived at Heathrow, there was no sign of her grandparents, and when she looked for her 'phone, it was nowhere to be found. Her travelling companion had offered her a lift to Hounslow, to her grandparents. She knew now how stupid she'd been, but she accepted gratefully. Later, she realised he must have taken her 'phone and contacted her grandparents and deterred them from coming to the airport. It would appear that she'd been in the house in Wandsworth for around a week.

At this point it became very difficult to decipher what Roxy was saying. Fleur looked at Mick in consternation. Roxy needed help but they didn't have the time. Brent turned and stopped the machine recording the interview.

'Look ma'am', he said, his concern making him assume more formality than usual, 'I don't think Roxy needs to be under caution.' Fleur nodded. Brent carried on, 'She needs help, but so do we and I think the Super and Leo's needs have to take precedence. So, bear with me, I'll be back in a minute.' He left the room, pulling his 'phone from his pocket as he went.

Within five minutes he was back, obviously still connected to a call. He sat opposite Roxy and pointed the face of the mobile towards her. From her position, Fleur could see Maze, seated in her office chair. Clearly used to video-conferencing, Maze's camera captured her from the waist up, not too closely, so that Roxy got the full effect of Maze's impressive people skills.

Brent introduced the girl to his wife. 'Roxy, I'd like you to meet Maisie. I've asked her to talk to you for a few minutes. Is that all right?' Maisie's warm, approachable face smiled gently at the girl and she nodded, sobbing more quietly now.

Maisie began by summarising what she'd been told. As she did so she managed to convey the strongest impression of how impressed she was by Roxy's bravery and her ability to understand what had happened and why. The girl visibly calmed and began listening more carefully to the psychologist.

'Right Roxy. I'm going to make you a promise and then I'm going to ask you a favour. Is that OK with you? I wouldn't be able to do that with everyone, but I think you're a fabulous exception. What do you think?'

Roxy nodded. Clearly still upset but beginning to step outside of herself.

'OK. So first, my promise. While we're talking, the police are going to find your grandparents and get them here.

We're going to explain what's happened and they're not going to be angry with you. And after that, I'm coming over to you, to make sure that you get some help, coming to terms with all of this, so that it can just be a bad memory and nothing more. All right?' Roxy hiccupped her agreement.

'So, my favour. We really, really need your help. This man, Gary, and the others ones we've arrested. They've taken someone else too – two people in fact. We know they're in big danger. Not the sort of danger that you've been in, but maybe something much worse. We need to find them. Are you understanding what I'm saying?'

Miserable, frightened and ashamed as she was, Roxy demonstrated a little of the spirit that Maze hoped was usually there.

'Yes, yes, I understand. But I don't know about any other people being kept at the house. I might not have heard them, maybe?'

Maze was quick to reassure her. 'No, we don't think they were at the same place as you. We think they took them somewhere else. All I want you to do is to think really hard. Have you heard them talking in the last few days, anything at all that might help us?'

Roxy looked perturbed. I don't think so. For the last week they've let me come downstairs and watch TV with them. The rest of the time I was locked in the bedroom, unless

Gary came up.' She gulped. 'Two days ago he said he was going to share me and that I had to get to know the others. There are four of them, usually.'

Cooper and Brent both noted that they were a man down in their arrests. Maze continued.

'When you were watching TV with them, what did they talk about?'

'All sorts. I think, I think I was a bit surprised. Only one of them really liked sport. Mostly they liked quiz programmes and documentaries.' The nineteen year old peeped out. 'It was really boring.' Maze waited, letting her think.

'They were out a lot yesterday afternoon and evening. Gary didn't come up to my room at all last night, and I think I heard them all coming in about midnight. I can hear the chimes from a clock, outside somewhere.' More silence. 'This morning they all seemed to be in a good mood, you know. Like my dad is if his football team's won a match. Oh, one of them, I think he's called Josh, asked Gary if he was going across to the old market, and Gary sort of looked at him and Josh shut up. Is that the sort of thing you mean?'

Maze beamed at her and Roxy quietly clearly warmed in the glow. 'It absolutely is – oh well done! Now look, I'm going to come across to the station to meet you, if that's OK, and Mick and Fleur are going to get on with finding your grandparents. But not your cousin, yet, do you think?'

Roxy leaped gratefully on that, 'Oh no, not yet.'

'Right' said Maze. 'Mick's going to go and get someone to sit with you – Daisy, I hope, and while you're just sitting together quietly, waiting for your grandparents, I want you to do me another favour. I want you to think very hard about all of the bits of conversation you've heard, anything you've seen downstairs. I don't want you to think about upstairs yet – I'll help you with that, if you'd like?'

Brent left the room and returned within minutes, accompanied by Daisy. He'd briefed her on the way down and Daisy, a star in the interview process, took Roxy under her wing.

Fleur and Mick reconvened in the corridor. They agreed that the grandparents needed to be found, and wondered what Gary Peters had communicated to Roxy's grandparents. They assumed he'd done it by text and it must have been convincing, because when she'd been logged in at the Custody Suite no Missing Person alert had come up.

FIFTY EIGHT

Dear Diary

I passed all of the A levels. Three A's and a B! I haven't said anything at home; they don't really know when the results were due. Mrs Lewis let me use her office to email the university I want to go to. I haven't ever said anything to her about how much her help means to me. I have to think of a way to show her. In her spare room, where she put the suitcase for me, I've noticed there are some boxes now, with things like saucepans and duvet covers and stuff.

FIFTY NINE

Across town Cervantes felt that he'd ground most of his teeth to stumps. Doing nothing was an anathema to him. He paced the small front garden and bellowed 'Anything yet?' in the front door so frequently that the Forensics term were now ignoring him.

He looked up, across the road and then thought of something, immediately calling himself all of the names under the sun, idiot, numbskull and twonk featuring high in the list. He rang the Custody Suite back at the nick and quickly got the answer he needed.

He returned to the front door and bellowed again. 'Help, I need your help! Quick, quick!'

A disgruntled, Tyvek suited investigator appeared, ready to do battle. Cervantes launched his plea before anything could be said.

'I know, I know, I'm a pain. But you all know we need to find my boss, and quick. And I know that the silver Audi A4 over there belongs to one of our suspects. And now I know that he didn't have the car keys on him at the nick. So they should still be in there...'

The investigator was about to say something but then wheeled away. Cervantes saw him enter the kitchen and then disappeared from view for a couple of minutes. He reappeared in the hallway and turned into the sitting room. Within seconds he was back, holding some car keys.

'Down the side of a sofa.' Cervantes held out his hand and the man recoiled.

'Don't be daft. You can't touch the car. But I can. I'm thinking you want to see if there's any satnav history?'

The grateful Cervantes speeded ahead of his newly recruited mate, dancing impatiently by the driver's door of the car. It was speedily accomplished. Three addresses showed up in the onboard computer. Both professionals spared a moment to thank their lucky stars for the sometimes breathtaking stupidity of mankind.

Back at the station, Cooper and Brent were wrestling with what to do with the very limited clue of 'old market'. Cervantes call sent them scurrying to Google maps.

SIXTY

Reith waited patiently. Leo wasn't heavy, but she was getting more so by the minute, though he didn't mind. Actually doing something was a tonic for both of them. Above him he could hear her muttering imprecations under her breath, as one or more of the screws had the temerity to resist her assaults. Eventually she said, calmly. 'It's done. I can pull the window free, but I don't quite know what to do with it. If I drop it outside, might it alert the wrong people? Or the right people? What do you think?''

Reith stared at the dark wall just in front of his face.

'Is it too difficult to hold the window *and* the torch, see what's outside?'

Without her answering him he felt her weight shift again and he became aware of fresh air as she lowered the window out of the recess. 'It's heavy. I'm just going to lean it across the sill for the minute.' The torch was snapped on and she began to describe what she could see. 'Well, the torch isn't powerful over a distance, but I think we're not on the ground floor. Hang on a minute, I'm going to drop my tweezers out of the window, see if I can hear how far they fall.' He kept still and silent and he too heard the tinkle of the tiny object hitting solid ground.

'Yep, first floor I think, so too high to jump. The tweezers landed on concrete. From what I can see we're in a building on the edge of a derelict something or other. Wooden palings around the outside. Lots of old litter across the ground. What looks like old tables – no, like old stalls, like a street market. Does that mean anything to you?'

'No, but tell me about the street light. Can you see what's beyond that?' There was a pause as she squinted into the darkness.

'Well, it's not houses, I don't think. It's lower than this building, maybe only one story. Flat roof. Does that help?'

'Sadly not. Come down and let's have another think'.

'Well, OK, but what about the glass?'

'Can you prop it up so that it's reasonably secure? I don't want to waste it. If we do hear noise from outside it's our only real signal opportunity.'

Leo did as requested then shimmied back down to his level.

'Right. I don't care if this is going too fast. I need a bloody cuddle.' She huddled in under his chin; he pulled some of the blankets around their shoulders and they stood together, awaiting who knows what.

SIXTY ONE

Dear Diary

Everything is packed at Mrs Lewis' house. I moved some clothes out, but mostly it looks like nothing's missing, because I've grown out of some things, I'm too tall for them now. It turns out the saucepans and things were for me. Mrs Lewis said it wasn't a problem, that it was her son's stuff from when he was at university, and that she hoped I didn't mind second-hand.

Mrs Lewis teaches English Literature, and I know one of her all-time favourites is the poet T.S. Eliot. I've spent ages looking through second-hand bookshops, in town and online and I've found a copy of The Cocktail Party. It only cost me three pounds, but I know it's worth a lot more, because online it sells for hundreds. It was in a junk shop, where I know they do house clearances, so I guess they didn't know it was valuable. I had to think about it, because I wasn't sure that it was right not to tell them. I still don't really, but I *so* wanted to give it to Mrs Lewis.

SIXTY TWO

The whole team was now hunched over OS maps, over Google maps screens and using linked satellite data to scour the three areas found in the Audi's satnav system. Like many upmarket cars, it recorded recent journeys, whether or not they'd been entered as guided destinations. The difficulty was with the size of each of the three locations. They thought they were looking for an old market, but what kind? Indoor? An old street market? In that case the external signs would probably be long gone.

It was AJ who spotted it, at the northern end of Wandsworth. There looked to be a derelict site that from the aerial view still had some sort of external tables or stalls. Tucked in under a higher building that looked, from above, like some kind of warehouse, it would have been easy to miss if they hadn't been granted a clue as to district.

There was a brief and, in hindsight, comedic scuffle as they all tried to leave at the same time. Fleur gathered up the reins and assigned tasks.

'Mick, Don, with me. Kurt, sort the logistics. Ambulance, Forensics on standby. AJ, get back to Franz and keep working on the known contacts – we're missing a local one. Daisy and Maze are with Roxanne. I'll let Control know where we're going and ask for a uniform team equipped for entry. Does anyone see any reason to expect armed resistance?'

No one had an answer for that, so Cooper ran upstairs to Claire and briefed her, then asked her to get into the Assistant Chief Constable and ask for his orders as to the weapons situation. Briskly washing her hands of that decision she headed downstairs to the rear car park, re-joining Brent and Cervantes as they careered through the ground floor doors, meeting her as she leapt off the bottom step of the stairs. 'Uniform are on their way. I've asked them to go in dark and quiet until we get there. I want to do a recce, see if there any signs of life. We know we've got one man missing. He might be there. So vests, helmets please.'

There was silence in the car as they hurtled through the darkness, Brent forcibly and vividly reminded of his terror the previous summer when they'd taken a similar ride, going to the aid of his wife.

They and the two uniformed cars arrived almost simultaneously. The three detectives walked the length of the block, then around it, trying to assess access points and potential occupation. There was a door in the long side of the block, on the opposite side to the open air area.

Climbing onto a small Electricity Board junction cupboard she shone her powerful torch over the fence that protected the now disused outside market space. Two doors here, but she couldn't see that they'd been accessed recently. The fencing was old but secure, not apparently breached at any point. She shone her torch up the side of the building. A couple of big, filthy windows at one end, and just a small window at the other. She looked more closely. There seemed to be a problem with this window. She focused the beam more tightly. The window didn't seem to fit.

Inside, Reith saw the flickering light over the top of Leo's head. He shouted loudly, making her jump in surprise. Turning to see what had set him off she quickly joined in, yelling for all that she was worth.

Outside, Fleur and Mick thought they'd could hear something, but the ever-present rumble of London traffic made it impossible to be sure.

In their prison, Leo and Reith both recognised the potential problem and repositioned themselves under the window. Leo swarmed up Reith's form, no cussing or commentary needed. She waited for a second, hoping that the moving light would come back towards her. When it did, she thrust the glass frame forwards and away with all her might. She shouted, she waved her arms, begging to be noticed.

Fleur's heart leapt at the sound and Brent ran, fast, to the uniformed officers and then as a group round to the entry on the other side of the building. Fleur stayed where she was, flashing her light on and off at the window where she could now see someone waving.

Despite their protestations, Reith and Leo were consigned to the ambulance for a health check. Fleur was explicit.

'I've told the CC and the ACC that you'll be in the station tomorrow at 8 am. They were keen not to see you until next week. I said I knew there was no way you'd agree to that, but that I'd be most grateful if they'd give me the authority to ban you both until the morning.'

Bone tired, they nodded. Both knew the urgency of the tasks they needed to resume, but each of them knew they'd reached a breaking point. It was only when they saw each other under the ambulance lights that Reith realised that Leo had one hell of a bruise across her right cheek. He touched it. 'Why didn't you say? It must hurt.'

She laughed. 'Since we weren't sure we were going to ever get out of there, it didn't seem important. And you don't look too good yourself Mr Reith.'

They both laughed and held hands all the way to the hospital, a journey that was enlightened by Leo's graphic description of the hot, perfumed bath she intended to take, the large glass of Chablis that was now going to be a mandatory prescription and the extensive Chinese takeaway that she was already mentally ordering.

'My place. You coming?' He nodded. There was nowhere else he wanted to be. Tomorrow would have to be soon enough for business as usual.

SIXTY THREE

It was well before 7am when Reith and Leo re-entered the station. He'd spent the night at Leo's house. She showed him to a guest room and to the nearby bathroom, heading off to plunder some of the clothing that her brother kept in the house for his occasional visits to the capital. She then ran a deep, perfumed bath in the en-suite and enjoyed its warmth, trying to relax out the strain that she could feel in her neck and shoulders. Her outward calm always came at a cost. She hated drama queen behaviour, saw no point in it, but she felt the same fears as any sane being, and this often gave her stonking headaches.

Happily sporting a ridiculous onesie in the guise of a squirrel, she banged on the guest bedroom door, summarising the takeaway order she had in mind. Steve, weary to the bone and ravenous enough to eat one, would have approved anything.

By the time he came downstairs in a set of light fleece pyjamas that were broad enough but too short, and a towelling bathrobe with similar characteristics, there were two large glasses of Chablis sitting on the kitchen counter.

Tired as he was, he was alert enough to take in the pleasant surroundings. He'd known that Leo lived in this part of Chelsea and had been impressed by the attractive exterior of her three storey house. The hallway opened on the right to a large sitting room, then continued through to a spacious and airy kitchen diner. When she'd taken him upstairs, he was aware that she'd later climbed the next stairs to the top floor. He guessed her bedroom was up there.

In the kitchen she handed him a glass of the wine, while she busied herself with sorting plates and cutlery for their Chinese meal.

'Any other time, I'd get the Chinese bowls and chopsticks out, show off my skill, but I'm too ruddy hungry to eat one piece of bamboo shoot at a time!'

He laughed. 'Frankly, one of those baby food pusher things would do me at the moment. Fleur and the gang will tell you – I need regular feeding or I get grumpy.'

While they awaited the much-needed Chinese they sat in the beautiful sitting room, all creams, pale blues and touches of old gold, sipping their wine and beginning to turn their terrifying ordeal into the stuff of anecdotes. That way lay sanity. They both absolutely understood the gravity of what had been done to them. Without the slender tool kit, there had been nothing that could have aided their escape. They did now know that Cooper and the team had been narrowing down their search, but without any sign of occupation he knew full well that breaching the building would have been in contravention of regulations. As they talked, Steve reflected that he couldn't remember the last time he'd laughed as much as he did with Leonie Merton. Even in their imprisonment she'd prised real guffaws from him. He felt himself relaxing, inch by slow inch.

When the meal arrived, they repaired to the kitchen, eating at a small table for two that sat by a side window. Leo reached past him and flicked a switch. Outside a small walled garden came into view, with prettily arranged groups of flower pots, a covered barbecue at one end, a tarpaulin-covered mound that he guessed was a set of tables and chairs and three similarly covered bench shapes at the opposite end of the space. His experience told him that this garden faced south east and he guessed it would be a colourful, delightful retreat in warmer weather.

They made short work of the meal, even the prawn crackers all being dispatched. Both now too tired to think, they agreed that sleep was needed. Leo had walked him to the door of the same guest room where he'd changed. They hugged, smiled at each other, just a little shyly, for a couple of moments and then went separately to bed. Leo, if not Reith, absolutely understood that she could have pushed their relationship forward on this night, but she wanted to stick to what they'd agreed the night before, even if that conversation now felt like a different time, a different country. She'd set her alarm and banged on his bedroom door at just gone six.

'Coffee in ten. Clean socks and pants in your bathroom, courtesy of my brother. Disposable razor in there too, courtesy of my legs!' She laughed, and he heard her steps going down the stairs.

At the station, Leo was straight into her online work, now checking everything done in her absence on the previous day. Whatever their shared motivations from the preceding day, it was clear that they'd explicitly understood and implemented her required actions. Leo printed out the details of the identified accounts and all of the information that had been needed to both interrogate and freeze them. She thought they'd been in time, but she wanted everything double checked in minutes, because the American markets would be opening up.

Clutching the precious papers, she headed up the stairs to find Reith. Early as it was, she found Claire in her lair, just outside his office. From their conversations the previous day, Leo had learned how much he rated this woman, and Leo could see why. Tidy as a pin, she was here way before any reasonably expected time, obviously determined to help her boss. Leo thanked her quietly and gave her an unexpected hug.

'Steve said you would have been here all the time yesterday, until we were found. He wouldn't even get in the ambulance until Fleur promised to let you know straight away.'

Claire's eyes were moist, but she brushed the remarks away. And she'd never forget that this woman had taken the trouble to talk to her, properly talk to her.

Leo explained her urgent problem and Claire sent her on into the office.

'The Assistant Chief's in there, but from what Mr Reith said just now, you need action.'

In the office Leo wasted no time bringing Steve Reith and his line manager up to speed. She said,

'I've got copies of everything we need to justify the American intervention and investigation of the four accounts we've identified and temporarily frozen.'

Blocking their access to the money was only one step; apprehending them was the biggie.

'Thank the Lord they're in the US, because the financial agreements are still in place; if it was Europe, Brexit would have stymied that. I can't be absolutely certain but I don't think that this end of things knows that we've finished our little field trip. If we're lucky, we might be able to stop any more money being moved. But we need Interpol and their financial unit, and my mate from your Fraud Department.'

Even as he reached for the 'phone, Reith enjoyed a wry inward smile. Field trip!

Reith busied himself with the 'phone, while the Assistant Chief Constable expended some of his considerable charm on the attractive woman he was meeting for the first time. Reith, watching them as he waited for answers, was amused by her polite but obviously detached response to the man that he knew Fleur nicknamed 'Old Oily.' He hadn't noticed on their journey in, but Leo had magically hidden her impressive facial bruise. So definitely not a drama queen.

Within the hour all the action Leo had instigated was underway, and out of her hands. How successful they were was now a case of waiting to see. She headed back downstairs and into the detectives' area, aiming for the office in which she'd been working. She was startled to receive a smattering of applause from the room, many of whom she didn't know. For them, her appearance was confirmation of her commitment, acceptance that, for now, she was one of them. Cervantes was at her side in a bound and without compunction pulled her into a bear hug.

'Bloody hell! Bloody hell.' He repeated, three or four times. She hugged him back, just as whole-heartedly and then waved wordlessly at the door behind him, leading through to the sergeants' area and to the glassed-in offices. He released her and grinned easily, his natural diffidence washed away by relief.

Leo then retreated to the office next door to Fleur's and was delighted to see both Groehling and AJ already logged in and working through a task list that AJ had created the previous day. She listened to his rationale, approved it with vigour, added two additional chores to it and then the three of them bent to the one key task that they could secure. They were now hell-bent on identifying all of the players below the end users in the money laundering pyramid. Leo reckoned, from experience, that there were around eight distinct levels and that this particular bunch would give them around forty individuals. The room was silent apart from the tapping of keyboards and the occasional slurping of coffee.

SIXTY FOUR

Just before ten, Fleur heard a tapping on the window between her and the next door office. Pulling up the blind she saw Groehling beckoning her. Whisking through to the other side of the glass, she was eager to hear if any progress had been made.

Leo smiled at her, tired but triumphant. 'This stage is done. We're all confident that this,' she held up a sheet, 'this is a full list of everyone that joins your mucky little property people to the Andeslev layer at the very top.'

Fleur took the list and glanced at it, although at the moment nothing on it jumped out at her. Leo continued.

'Unless you want me to continue, I stop here. I'm not cheap, I know. But there is another layer that I could help with, because I think some of my resources will tuck in nicely with yours.'

Fleur raised an enquiring eyebrow, and Leo continued.

'The thing is, I know that you wanted the money launderers, but that neither you nor Steve thought that would lead you directly through to the murderer, or murderers. Is that still the case?'

Fleur nodded. 'Yes, that's still where my thinking, our thinking, is. The murderers seem much more likely to have come from the other side of the equation, from the victims of the property stuff, perhaps from the hijacking of insurance policies, under-pricing of properties or something like that.' She looked at Kurt Groehling. 'That's been particularly bothering you, hasn't it Kurt? The enormous complexity of that?'

Groehling nodded. 'Frightening me witless Gov, because it's a forest of possibilities.' He hesitated. 'I'd be more than grateful to work with Leo on this. I've already seen some of the access she has but, even better, she knows people, and I think that we're going to need industry help narrowing the funnel.'

He was referring to the commonly understood principal of putting raw data in at the top and adding increasingly fine filters until the relevant information fell out of the bottom. Effective but slow, unless really pertinent filters were identified early. And it always relied on accessing the data in the first place, which was where Groehling thought Leo's industry connections might be invaluable.

Fleur nodded. She understood their predicament, but she also had an eye to the budget.

'Let me go upstairs. I think we need to do it, but I need underwriting on the expenditure. Keep your fingers crossed.'

Groehling, Murtha and Leo sat down again and began to discuss, possibly hypothetically but certainly hopefully, the levels of filtering they thought they'd need. Each felt a range of different emotions. Leo, the sheer pleasure of working with a bright, motivated team and the accompanying banter. Much of her work brought her into contact with too many dry and dour souls with no natural light or humour. Kurt, a self-aware and open minded man was delighted to be learning new techniques and approaches, noting them all in his notebook, in his abysmal and ridiculously small handwriting. AJ, working at the very edges of his capacity in this area was grateful for the chance, nervous of looking like a prat and desperate not to let anyone down.

Upstairs Fleur Cooper had made an executive decision. She didn't think the waters were muddied at all, but she would always think strategically and she wanted to support Steve Reith, after the previous day's terrors even more than usual. So, rather than going to him for a budget decision, she spoke to Claire and explained both her request and why she thought it was best to take it to the Assistant or Chief Constable. Claire didn't need much explanation. Aside from all of her professionalism she'd become very fond of her boss. She knew he'd be her last one before she retired, and she had a hat that she very much wanted to wear on a special day…she wasn't having the chances of that scuppered. She'd thought that had been pie in the sky, wishful thinking, until the previous year, so she was taking no chances.

'Let me get you into the ACC. He's here and there's no one in with him. Mr Reith is in a meeting, so I can truthfully say that you need a decision as soon as possible.'

Within a couple of minutes Fleur was seated in 'Old Oily's' office and gratefully accepting a cup of decent coffee. She outlined her perceived need for more of Leo's services. She saw no necessity to add anything else.

All credit to her listener, he saw the point.

'Well, it's excellent that we're going to get so many in the financial chain – that's big bucks in the credit column for the Met.' She knew what he meant, even if it hurt her teeth. 'But, he continued 'the murders are just as important. It's a lot of money.' He pulled open a spreadsheet on his desk top computer and tapped around in it for a few seconds. 'Yes, I thought so. We're very heavily underspent in the data budget. I can't transfer it to another budget heading, so it'll be lost at the end of March. So this sort of thing fits very nicely into that account, thank you very much. I'm going to assign you ten days of Ms Merton's time. After that, I think I'd have to call it quits.'

Fleur, who had hoped for five but would have settled for three was delighted, but hid this well, thanked her superior officer with grace and warmth, and departed.

SIXTY FIVE

Dear Diary

My last entry before I leave. I resigned from both my jobs last night. I know I was meant to give notice, but I couldn't risk him finding out. I've made my bed and hidden a letter under the pillow. I don't think they'll even start to look for anything until this evening, and I'll be gone by then. I'm going to Bath. I've got sponsorship, which means in college holidays I report as a cadet for basic training. So the costs are covered. I'll get some bar work too, to be on the safe side.

Mrs Lewis loved her present. She cried and wished me a happy future. I won't lose touch with her. She's driving me to Bath. She must be an amazing mum.

SIXTY SIX

Fleur beat a happy path back to the Chief Inspector's office and shared the glad tidings.

'Leo – can you map out an action plan? I'm guessing that you can't personally investigate everything. There must be things the broader team can do, but it's best if that's all identified by you, so that we're looking in the same direction. Would 4 o'clock suit you, if I call a meeting of the people I think you need? A couple of our more skilled admin folk, part of the data analysis team, as well as you two?' She included Groehling and Murthi in her glance.

Leo, relieved at the potential support, nodded.

'I'll start mapping now.' She paused. 'Um, I don't want to be selfish, but what do you all do about lunch? I brought some with me on the first couple of days, but not this morning. And I definitely work better if I'm not hungry!'

One of the few nicks still with its own canteen, Fleur was able to say 'I'll come and get you in about thirty minutes and take you down. The food's not bad actually, and there's always plenty of it.'

The day passed more slowly than the previous ones on this case. At tea time, Leo met with her new team and laid out her targets and ambitions. Well chosen by Fleur Cooper, this little cohort knew its way round the web, deep and dark. Deep being the bad stuff, where depravity and illegality sat in multi-layered horrors. Dark, where sites and blogs and messages lay inactive after being abandoned, but could still provide breadcrumbs to follow.

Brent, Daisy Jones and Cervantes continued their interviewing of the victims and their families, each looking for any grain of information, any hint that might help Leo's team. The more people they spoke with, the less convinced were they that a solution would be found through this pursuit. As Cervantes said to Brent, when they met in the car park just before 8pm that night,

'Apart from Mrs Szabo, there isn't anyone mourning this lot. I know that might seem like a motive, but virtually everybody's got an alibi for the murder of their nearest and not so dearest, and most of them are covered for the other ones as well. So that makes Mrs Brent's Strangers on a Train scenario impossible too.' He looked concerned.

'Mick, do cases like this go unsolved?'

Mick Brent nodded glumly. 'Yep. Much more than you'd realise. And the big worry for this one is that the field of potential suspects is enormous. If you think that each of the people that Leo has identified, up the money chain, could have a motive on the financial issues alone, that's bad enough. But if you look at the main thing, where I think it's really hiding, then it's a bloody nightmare. There are hundreds of transactions that might have triggered this, scores of insurance policies that might have been hijacked.'

Reith had already reached the same conclusion. In discussion with Cooper, he'd said.

'Right. It's time to be practical. Even with what Leo is doing, the chances that we'll find our murderer, murderers are slim. But I don't want to pull the plug on what she's doing because I think we need to see this now, at least in part, as a prevention exercise. So, for example, if we look at the annuities and insurance policies, we don't want anyone caught in that, down the line. So I've got to do some work upstairs, with the High Heid Yins. I think I can sell this on the basis of the great PR we can get from success on that front.

'So far the papers haven't picked up anything. I suppose it's because all of the deaths look like health incidents, but that surely can't last. Some of the families might talk. If they do and it gets out, I'll get nowhere upstairs, but at least I can start there.'

Departing on his errand, he asked Cooper to sort a full team meeting for 8am the following morning.

Still dark outside, in the meeting room early on the next day the case Leadership Team took the full group through the actions, events and results so far. Reith pulled no punches.

'This is our worst nightmare. It's not a hit and run, it's not a domestic, there's no clear line through to suspects. The only way we're going to get anything is by following the trail that Ms Merton and her gang are laying out for us. I know it's our least favourite work, but at the very minimum we need to identify potential victims – the ones who won't have any financial protection when their husband or wife or parents die. We know about one – Harriet Brand. She saw the policy alteration in time and got it sorted. If she wasn't so ill, maybe she'd have made more of a fuss and it would be out in the newspapers – that might alert people?' He raised an eyebrow at the group in front of him, interested in opinions.

Leo spoke first. 'It might, but I also think it'll make the insurance companies slam the doors on us, because of the poor publicity. I already know that most of our real victims – the ones being ripped off – have insurance policies across a number of companies. Any one of them ending up in the media will shut them all up. I know you can get warrants and the like, but I think I've got contacts where we can get it done nice and quietly.'

The room seemed to offer support for this view, through its very silence. Everyone in the meeting had suffered the frustration of being blocked from information they wanted, having to wait for the official machinery to operate, only to find that what they'd needed had slid away in the days of delay.

Reith picked up the threads. 'Right, so it's a very strong focus on this aspect. Leo and team – how quickly can you identify potential victims in the insurance stuff?'

Leo again. 'It's done, we finished it last night. I just need your permission to start talking to the insurance companies. And ideally, a senior officer to come with me. These are good, mutually trusting contacts and I want them to know that I'm neither scare-mongering nor trying to drop them in the brown stuff.'

Reith was still in a strange place emotionally. The long night and day of incarceration had shifted his world view a little and whilst he'd worked his socks off yesterday, as ever, this disjunction left him a little more cantankerous than usual. He knew his schedule for the day; as ever, meetings and more meetings and all of them 'small p' politics. He didn't fancy them one bit, and just for today he thought he'd put them where the sun don't shine.

'I'll do it.'

Fleur and Brent grinned inwardly. Good, more time together for Steve and Leo. They'd have been surprised to discover that it was only after he'd said it that Reith realised that this was the upside of his decision, time in Leo's company. Had he considered that in advance, he might well have backed off and assigned Fleur.

The team dispersed, each to their tasks. Leo busied herself with the 'phone and then went to find Steve Reith. She found him talking with Claire, rearranging his meetings for the coming days.

'Our first meeting is in Oxford. The other four are all back here in the Smoke, so I thought maybe we could do the furthest one first, then move backwards. Is that OK with you?'

Reith was more than agreeable. 'So I'm thinking, train? It'll take ages to drive out of London on a work day, and we can get across to Paddington in twenty minutes on the Tube. It's only about an hour to Oxford. I presume it's in one of the business areas outside town, so we can get a taxi.'

It was agreed and Claire swiftly booked tickets, making the executive decision to send them First Class. This Reith usually declined, but Claire thought that the upper class might provide more discretion for case discussion.

By eleven thirty, the two erstwhile colleagues were seated in the office of Neill Friderson. A long term friend of Leo's from college, they spent a little time catching up and discussing mutual friends. Now the Vice President responsible for Europe within his company, Neil was the highest authority she could access and she deemed this to be necessary to her cause.

Once the formalities were dispatched, Leo asked Steve Reith to give an overview of the case, stopping short of the insurance implications. Fascinated but puzzled as to his involvement, Neill Friderson nonetheless listened without interruption.

Leo picked up the story. 'I know. Why are we here? Well, I think everyone would like this kept absolutely quiet. We don't want the papers mucking in, because the police don't want the murderers alerted. And I'm damn sure you don't want this across the front pages.'

He kept a straight face, experienced professional that he was, but raised an eyebrow.

Leo slowly outlined what had been uncovered by Harriet Brand in relation to her life cover. Friderson was a little paler after hearing this history. Not only would this be execrable PR but it would also keep his many agents occupied for months, disproving the many fraudulent, hopeful or deluded claims that would subsequently come their way, not to mention the valid ones. He spoke.

'I'm going to keep this in the room for the minute.' Picking up the 'phone he asked whoever he connected with to 'Come up here, as fast as possible and with minimum fuss. Bring your laptop.'

By apparently mutual agreement, the three of them picked up their earlier social chat while they waited. Leo had barely finished teasing Neill about a Cambridge lad being based in Oxford before there was a quiet tap on the door, which opened to reveal a man in his mid to late fifties.

Friderson introduced them to each other. 'This is Andy Heversecht. He's our overall Head of Compliance. Andy, this is Superintendent Steven Reith from the Metropolitan Police, and this is Leo Merton, from Wilson Merton.'

Heversecht was a tiny man, barely reaching five feet, by Reith's reckoning. He had a high forehead and a bright, alert set to his face and head. From his wedding ring and the generous quantity of laughter lines around his mouth, Leo's take on him was that he was probably a much-loved dad.

Friderson outlined the quest, Reith chipping in once to elucidate. Heversecht nodded in quiet comprehension, some concern on his face.

Leo handed him a list of just over two hundred names.

'These are the policy holders who relate to you. Ideally, we'd like to see if all of these people are the actual beneficiaries in each of the policies.

Heversecht's gaze flickered down the pages. He glanced at his boss then took himself off to a small work table in the corner of the room.

'If I may, I'll just pull up a few of these, see if there's anything...' He bent to his task. The other three watched him in silence, each only too aware of the potential. For Reith and Leo, no results meant another dead end in an already fruitless search for the killer. Friderson was already damage-limiting, mentally assessing how to handle this practically, what to do with the main Board, how to square it with the shareholders. Each camp wanted a diametrically opposed outcome.

It wasn't long before Heversecht looked up, his expression grim.

'I've checked ten. Four of them seem to list a beneficiary or beneficiaries that are as you'd expect – same name. That'll need deeper checking 'though. But three cite Calum Grant, two Neville Humberstone, and the fourth a Kendell Bell. '

Friderson sighed audibly. Reith and Leo rejoiced inwardly, as a courtesy to their host. He spoke.

'Right. I'm not going to prat about asking for warrants etc. Andy and I will work through this list and send you the details as soon as possible.' He caught the merest flicker of consternation across Reith's face.

'Don't worry – I mean in the next few hours. The only thing I ask in return is that you keep this as quiet as possible on the street. I'm going to have to do some spin doctoring both internally and externally and if I can get ahead on that while it's still confidential, I'd be immensely grateful.'

Leo looked at Reith, hoping. He nodded.

Relieved, Friderson continued. 'I'm going to try to make some positives from this, so later on maybe I could ask for an officer to come and talk with the Board, maybe be a bit kind about us being helpful, heading off a media shit storm and so on?'

Again, Reith nodded. 'But I'd like to ask in return if you can help with one more step?' Neill Friderson again raised an eyebrow.

'We have more companies to see, today if at all possible. Leo wanted to start here because she describes you as one of the good guys. I know she has excellent contacts in some of these companies, but not all. Can you help?'

Leo handed over her list of planned visits, pointing out to her old college mate the two where help would be much appreciated. Friderson smiled slightly.

'Yes, I'm on good terms with both of the CEO's. What do you want me to do?'

Reith glanced at Leo as he spoke. 'It would be helpful if you could ring them, as soon as possible. Explain that we're on our way, suggest strongly that they fit us in as a matter of urgency. But please don't tell them why – I don't expect everyone to have your immediate clarity of vision or principle. But if there's any way you feel able to stress Leo's credentials and professionalism, that might help us a fair bit. In return, when we speak to the potential victims, we'll take a very low key approach. Something along the lines of a precautionary check, nothing to worry about etcetera, don't expect anything to come of it and so on. Does that suit? '

Leo took a moment to thank Andy Heversecht as they left the room. She, far more than Reith, understood that his work in Compliance would take him down a very nasty rabbit hole on this one. He'd be fighting a two-way battle, looking backwards to identify how this had happened, and forwards to build barriers to prevent it happening again. It would be the role of Friderson and other senior staff to restore the subverted policies to the right shape, and to attempt to limit any harm to the company.

On the train back in to London, Leo and Steve Reith talked in muted tones, careful not to use any names or descriptions that would permit any keen eavesdropper to ascertain their topic. But both were quietly happier than they'd been for the past two days. Perhaps their killer was somewhere in one of the lists they hoped to have soon. Perhaps not, but it felt like progress for now.

By the time they were in the queue for sandwiches at the Marks and Spencer in Paddington Station, Reith had received an email from Andy Heversecht. He showed it silently to Leo, who puffed out her cheeks in relief. He drew her attention to a final comment in the email, and said,

'I hadn't thought of that. He's right, we also need to ask about cancelled policies. He's got one, revoked by the policy holder, no reason given.'

Their afternoon followed much the same pattern as their morning. Despite Reith's natural distrust of big business, Leo's good name and the preparation done by Neill Friderson meant that all but one took the same line as he had. The exception was swiftly dealt with by Leo.

Leo Merton regarded the last senior executive on their list with a stern gaze, more serious than Reith ever thought he'd seen her. The Chief Exec was a tall, raw-boned woman in her late fifties. Privately, Leo thought that the money she'd obviously spent on her clothes was a total waste. She'd be forever destined to make her apparel look like something stolen from a charity shop; somehow, they just didn't sit right on her. She'd been combative from the first minute and quickly began introducing all the legal niceties she'd listed on her desk pad. It was obvious that she'd already taken legal advice from in-house counsel before she even had any details. Leo leaned forward.

'Mr Reith will tell you that your attitude is absolutely within your rights. But me, I'll tell you something else. Everyone else, everyone, all of your opposite numbers in other companies, have taken the reverse approach. Mr Reith and I will do our level best to keep *their* names out of the news, away from the front pages. Because this is that sort of deal. Mean, nasty, money grasping insurance companies supporting fraud against the newly bereaved, widows, children. A wet dream for a reporter.' She stopped, and locked a steely eye with the woman in front of her.

'I know two very reputable reporters.'

Reith quaked inwardly, at least as much because he was momentarily taken aback by this new facet of Leo's character as by the potential explosion they might be about to witness. It didn't happen. They were treated to a wintry smile, an admin assistant was summoned and they were sent on their way.

'Jessica, please take Superintendent Reith and Ms Merton to Mr Hall, in Compliance.' To her departing visitors she merely said.

'I'll ring ahead. He'll give you all the help you can possibly need. I therefore assume we will not be contacted by your so-called friends Ms Merton.'

The door closed quietly behind them.

Later, outside, as they made their way back to the station, Reith looked at her, raising a quizzical eyebrow.

'What? Oh, I know, but it's one of the things I can't stand, people not wanting to help people. And I didn't think you'd be allowed to be as bolshy as me.'

He smiled. Even locked up together she hadn't been this stroppy, though he had been aware that she'd been furious with the situation. The more he discovered about her, the more he wanted to explore.

Back at the nick, the team were crowded around the desk in Fleur's room, undertaking an end of day wash up. Reith, looking at the clock hands heading towards eight o clock said .

'Does anyone fancy a Chinese?' Everyone nodded gratefully and started pulling wallets from pockets. Reith shook his head. 'I'll sort it.'

By the time eight thirty had been reached they were all seated round a large work table in the largest meeting room, a random assortment of plates and cutlery before them.

Reith summed up their day's successes and passed copies of the lists they'd received so far; only one company hadn't yet sent over their findings, but as they'd promised it for first thing the next day no alarm bells were needed.

Without being aware of it, they all breathed a sigh of relief. A thread to pull on.

SIXTY SEVEN

The next morning, over a week since the first killing, the core team reconvened so that Fleur could assign tasks. The need to get out and interview the identified victims of the insurance frauds was now paramount. Mick Brent had grouped them according to time of day and potential location, to minimise travel. Fleur approved the logic and efficiency of this and then allocated a group each to Brent, Cervantes, Daisy Jones and Murtha.

'Go and find a uniform to go with you. You might be talking to a murderer, so I don't want to be an alarmist, but try to keep a physical distance. I don't think our murderer is a spur of the moment merchant, but I'm quite fond of you. Go, get on with it.' She flapped her arms at them and the small group left the room.

Kurt Groehling and Leo Merton looked at the Inspector with interest, waiting.

'Right, well we're all hoping that what they're off to do stirs up some leads, but I'm not convinced yet. Leo, what other avenues have you been looking out, any ways in which other people have been impacted by what Bell and his mates were doing? I don't mean the money laundering side, I mean real people, not seasoned fraudsters and crims.'

Leo nodded.. 'I've made a start on that. As far as I can see, there are two possibilities. To be frank, I wouldn't normally look at this end of things, because in my experience the average money launderer doesn't waste too much time on the profit angle. They need to get dirty money in, clean money out, so losing money in the transaction is generally seen as an on-cost, a business cost if you like, for the process. But this little group seem to have done a couple of things. They've certainly set up an almost contractual arrangement with the chain above them. You can measure that by the fixed sums that appear in their bank accounts after both purchases and sales. That bit's generally expected, though this is maybe a little tidier than I'm used to seeing. But, with the stuff around the insurance policies in mind, I started to think about how I'd do it, if I was looking to make the maximum personal profit.

'So my first focus was the potential undervaluing of a property going onto the market. I've had a quick look at half a dozen of the purchases made by Ken Bell, just to see if there's any discrepancy between the price paid and the average price in that post code. I'm no expert, but I think there are some quite obvious ones, just in that little sample. But that sort of shenanigan is only possible if you've got an estate agent on side, so that needs looking at too. Or, possibly, there's a crooked surveyor in the mix. If they 'identified' an imaginary structural problem I'm thinking that it would be quite easy to persuade the seller to lower the price to get out from under. So we need to do a couple of things on that, obviously.'

Groehling was scribbling away. 'Yep, identify the estate agents and surveyors used and map the pricing differentials for the area for properties of a similar kind. I think it's interesting that there are absolutely no commercial property purchases in this at all. That seems to bear out the idea that they were playing fast and loose with prices in the domestic market. Individuals would be easier to sucker in.'

Leo agreed. 'In the commercial market, company property is part of the company's assets. If any of that was suddenly and heavily reduced in value it'd show up in the end of year accounts and questions would be asked, very loudly indeed.' She continued,

'The other possibility is that they had something going on in the mortgage and loans area. All of their own purchases were with cash. Now that's fairly clear, because obviously they needed to move the grubby money. After that, they seem to have been making money on the side with the inflated price when they sold something on. That's less likely to have been played about with, especially if the purchaser was taking out a mortgage on the property, because the mortgage society would use their own accredited surveyors, so that'd be a lot harder to influence. But what if our nasty little bunch also dabbled in introducing financial advisors to broker mortgage deals? A bit more convoluted this one, but poor practice, let alone fraudulent intent, from a mortgage advisor can lead to a purchaser paying fees that just aren't necessary. If someone was borrowing at the top of their credit rating, or beyond, they might not argue the toss. They'd probably accept inflated fees as the price of their situation.'

Groehling chipped in. 'Right. So we also need to explore the funding sources for the purchases.'

Again, Leo concurred. 'Mm. See, we wouldn't ever look at that side of the transaction, because the point is that it needs to be clean money. If they did do this, well, the money would still be clean, but the ethics stink. Perhaps someone broke their own back on the repayments or fees.'

Next steps agreed, the group headed off to their individual tasks. Leo gathered four of the admin team she'd worked with on the previous day and got them started on the necessary research into estate agents involved in the identified purchases. Groehling mirrored this, but with a focus on the surveyor possibility.

Fleur needed to step back into the mountain of admin tasks that threatened her desk and email inbox. It didn't take long to lose the plot with the consent, persistent barrage of procedural requests, data collection and all of the duties required in the management of so large a team. She started with the updating of her personal work log. At some point, or at least so they all hoped, a prosecution would require the careful mapping of all activity that had led to the identification of the murderer. Or murderers. This was odd. In most cases of death in suspicious circumstances it was clear whether it was a group, such as organised crime or a street gang or an individual, someone with a personal motive. But the indications here were unclear.

Brent was enjoying himself. Out of the station and talking to people was one of his favourite scenarios. Before they'd left the nick they'd agreed with Fleur what would be said as regards the life policies. The insurance companies didn't want a major stench and Reith's proposal to them all on the previous day had been accepted with little argument.

The uniformed officer he was working with he recalled slightly, but couldn't bring the circumstances to mind. A young chap called Simon Colbin. It soon transpired that Colbin remembered their previous meeting very clearly. He'd been one of the first officers on the scene of their restaurant bombing the previous summer and had been stuck outside on crowd control. Reith, picking up the young officer's frustration when he himself had arrived on the scene, asked Brent to let the youthful policeman take a very careful look at the scene, later in the day. Brent had done so and Colbin had never forgotten. Reith and Brent now seemed to have assumed oracle status – Colbin was clearly a fan.

As they travelled to their first address, Brent outlined what they needed to do. He stressed,

'It needs to be very low key. We don't want any alarm bells ringing.' Colbin wasn't convinced.

'Well, yes Sarge. I get that the insurance people don't want to look like they've been caught napping. But maybe it's better if it does get out in the news, because then everyone would check and that would be best, wouldn't it?'

Brent, usually a kind man and certainly always one who appreciated enthusiasm and intelligence backed up by some basic principles, responded to the point.

'On one level, I have to agree with you. But there are a couple of things that'll cause us a major problem if that happened. First, will it alert our murderer? We simply don't know. Second, it'll certainly cause the insurance companies a major headache because, as you say, everyone will want to check. You can imagine the nightmare that would cause. Routine procedures will take much longer to go through, all sorts of policy cover will be delayed, from cars to business to mortgages and life. So then everyone is paying a price. But most importantly, at least after the murderer issue, is that the insurance companies are already scrubbing through every policy now. So things will be put right, but quietly. Most people won't even realise what's gone on. They'll just get a letter through the post saying that as part of a periodic check, can they please confirm in writing the beneficiaries of their policy. I'm no fan of big business, but in this case, the companies didn't do anything wrong, unless you wanted to blame them for a loophole?'

Colbin, reflecting on the points made, said.

'OK. Yes, I can see where you're coming from. I suppose it's about efficiency? And if we start blaming the insurance people for not seeing the possible crime. And if we do that, we'd have to start blaming rape victims for what they wear, and burglary victims for having nice ornaments in the window.'

Since there were plenty of police officers who did blame those very victims, Brent was heartened by Colbin's more open view.

Their first visit was to an upmarket boutique, just off Oxford Street. It was the owner they were seeking and the incredibly skinny and immensely snooty shop assistant reported that he was to be found in the offices above his shop's premises. She rang him on her mobile and then asked the officers to wait, saying that he'd be down in a minute.

As the two colleagues awaited his descent from above they browsed the merchandise, Colbin initially thinking that he might bring his girlfriend here, to choose a present. Having identified a handbag in pale blue denim that he thought she'd like, he was thunderstruck to see the price was almost two thousand pounds. He showed it silently to Brent, who'd been having a similar epiphany with a scarf. As they were to agree later, the bag sported no leather, the scarf no silk. So it was solely about the labels.

The boutique owner appeared from the back of the store, curious to see why the police wanted to talk him. Used to periodic visits from beat officers he was a little taken aback to be hosting a detective, and a sergeant at that. Brent asked,

'Is there anywhere we can go for a private chat?' The owner considered.

'Well, there's not really room upstairs. The office only has one chair and the rest of the floor is storage. The top floor's a flat, but it's let out. There's a coffee shop two doors down. They'll be quiet at this time of the morning. Will that do?'

They repaired to the café and ordered a hot drink each, Colbin, having spotted the prices on the chalk board, prayed that someone else was paying.

Settled in the back corner, far from anyone else, Brent began.

'It relates to your life insurance policy.' He named the company Reith and Leo had first visited.

'They've found some discrepancies in a couple of policies, and one of them is yours. Now, at this stage, it's not a criminal investigation as such. It might just be clerical errors.'

The boutique owner looked alarmed. 'Excuse me! I'd never be involved in anything dodgy!'

Colbin, having seen the prices in the shop, withheld judgment on that one. Brent was quick to respond.

'Oh no, sir. It's nothing you've done. It's just, can I check who's the beneficiary for your life cover, if anything happens to you?'

'My wife, and then my kids, in trust if they're still minors. So what's happened?'

Provided with a carefully edited version of events, he narrowed his eyes as he considered what he'd heard.

'Right. Well, have you considered that it might actually *be* a crime. Because I arranged my cover through a chap called Neville Humberstone, and I have to tell you I didn't warm to him one bit. I set up the policy when we bought our current house. The estate agent recommended him, but I didn't rate him at all. Slimy little git in fact. But I assumed it was all good, national, reputable company and all that.'

Brent gave a very good impression of considering a new possibility.

'Thank you for that. Well, of course it's why we're involved, just in case, you know. The company will be in touch in the next couple of days, to put it straight. No harm done, eh?' he said firmly.

Their day, and that of their colleagues pursuing the same trail, took pretty much identical shape. Back at the station at the end of the day, each nursing a hot drink, they all reported to the core team.

Brent summed it up. 'Nothing. No sudden starts of overacted amazement, no shiftiness, nowt. Still, we've got the other half of our list to cover tomorrow.' His enthusiasm for the assignment had waned. No-one enjoys zero results.

The others all related similar experiences. Daisy had met the person that they already knew had cancelled her policy.

'Justine something, it's in my notes. No alarm bells or anything that made her do it. She just said her boss had found a better deal, so she took out a new policy and stopped the old one.'

Brent looked around at his colleagues, most of them good friends.

'Does anyone fancy a meal at ours tonight? We can rustle something up, perhaps do what the Super likes to do, sum it all up, look for new approaches?'

Fleur was tired but keen, eager for anything to break the deadlock.

'I'll go and see if the Super and Leo can do it, as well as Kurt and Ajay. What time do you think, Mick?'

She found Leo, Ajay and Kurt most amenable to being fed, Ajay being very much of the Cervantes mind, delighted to be included. After that she climbed the stairs to Reith's floor, finding Claire packing up for the day.

'He's in Fleur, and no-one's with him, go on in.'

Fleur Cooper tapped lightly on the door and headed in, finding Reith heavily marking a thick document, scowling as he did so. She smiled.

'I've come to take you away from all this, if you want?'

He grinned in appreciation. 'For the love of Mike, please do. And who is Mike, anyway...?'

Fleur ignored him. 'Brent says supper's at his house at eight tonight, if you want. Everyone else can go.'

Reith looked pleased, but then frowned a little. 'It's a good idea, but..' he paused and she cut in.

'I know. Leo and the last time we were there. I'm suggesting that I'll be taxi driver tonight, with you, me, Leo and Cervantes in the car. I'll pick you all up from your homes and then drop you off afterwards, Leo first, so she feels the safety in numbers. Does that work?'

Grateful, he agreed.

SIXTY EIGHT

It was a quieter group than usual that convened in the Brent's beautiful, comfortable kitchen. Maisie, forewarned, had pulled some fish from the freezer. With some ham left over from a gammon roast, some tinned crab and plenty of potatoes she'd made an enormous pot of fish chowder. Brent had been sent to the supermarket on his way home and brought with him four different kinds of bread and half a dozen cheeses, ranging from the frankly stinking to the more delicate.

They settled in to their usual places, shuffling around, all subconsciously ignoring Simon Fletcher's absence.

As they tucked in to the delicious soup, Reith started them on their usual round up, but this time with a difference.

'Look, we know that we're well on with the money laundering angle. Twenty four arrests so far and the others on the way. The Yard's very, very pleased with that, and I'm not knocking it because it's good work. But it's not where we started and I'm not comfortable that we don't seem to have anyone at all in our crosshairs. No one, nothing. Normally we have a sense of shape, of roughly where we need to look. I'm not getting that at all.' He sighed. 'I'm not explaining what I mean very well.'

Cervantes offered a perspective. 'I did A level Chemistry.' Hoots of derision from his colleagues, which just made him grin.

'I know, but I sort of get what the Super is saying. Did you know that when they first drew up the periodic table, Mendeleev, I think, he left gaps in it? He knew there must be other elements that belonged, but they didn't know what they were yet. They knew because they categorised the elements in groups, and then in each group according to their characteristics. There's an exponential pattern, and there are predictable relationships between known elements that suggested other ones, so they could predict what they didn't know.' He looked towards Reith. 'That's what you mean, isn't it Sir?'

The group, fascinated by the bit of science previously only known by Leo and Fleur, shared glances. Yes, that made sense and it was what they were feeling.

In their now customary fashion they worked their way around the room, each highlighting things that needed to be done. As always, Steve Reith ended the process with Maze Brent.

'Go on Maze. What have we missed? Open our eyes.'

She threw her napkin at him, laughing. 'You're an evil man Steve. You know more than I do about all of it.' She reflected.

'I will say one thing. And it's an absence for me too. There's no sense of team, of coordinated action here. It's quiet, efficient. Like a mission you watch in a spy movie. They had their targets, they dealt with their targets, they finished. From a psychological point of view there's no pointers to narcissism, to any of the O'Pathys.' She referred to her in-joke with Brent over people's willingness to use descriptors like sociopathy and psychopathy when they really didn't know what they meant.

'No. I think this is one, single, highly intelligent person. Motivated, certainly, but I think that might be as much a case of wanting to prevent more people getting caught up in this as it is a matter of revenge. There are no unnecessary flourishes, no drama. Just a job done.'

It was while Brent was slicing into a deep baking dish of sticky toffee pudding that Fleur took a call from the station. She listened carefully and then said,

'Send it round here, straight away.' She gave the Brent's address. 'Motorcycle it if possible, reduce the traffic delays.'

She disconnected the call and looked at Reith.

'That was the front desk at the nick. A courier just delivered a plain envelope. When they opened it they found another envelope. They've scanned it and it looks like a USB stick. They haven't opened it because the internal envelope says 'Strictly for the attention of Superintendent Reith only. Matters pertaining to an ongoing enquiry related to seven deaths.'

Maze was the first to speak. 'It's them. Quiet, no fuss. And unless you've got a leak, only you know it's seven.'

Cooper and Reith were not so quick to be convinced. Reith would always want proof or at least better clues before he accepted something. Cooper was feeling something else. As they ate their puddings, for the first time not really noticing the calibre of food they'd been given, she realised it was irritation. Of course, the communication might have nothing to do with anything. It could be some sort of perverted blackmail. But if Maze was right, then it was a totally out of their control, bloody external factor, and that offended all of her copper's instincts. The arrival of the answer to their problems, but with none of their efforts having delivered it. It was annoying in a book or a film and it was downright infuriating here and now.

SIXTY NINE

It was twenty minutes before the doorbell rang. Brent had already set up a laptop on the kitchen counter and Reith, returning from the door, opened the envelope. Just a USB, no letter or note.

Brent said 'I've come off line, so if there's any ridiculous bug or virus on here, it can't spread.'

Groehling took charge of the USB and inserted it, then clicked on the folder that opened. Just one file.

'Bear with me a minute.' He searched the folder properties, looking at disk space. 'Yes, just one audio file.' He set the laptop's speakers to maximum and opened the MP3 file.

A warm, cultured voice filled the room, although most listeners detected a London note in some of the turns of phrase.

'Please listen to the end of this before you do anything else. It would be a waste of valuable time and I promise you I don't want that for you.

I've contacted you because it occurred to me, probably later than it should, that my most serious crime might be wasting police time. You won't be expecting to hear any of what I'm about to say. I know that you'd have been unlikely to identify me because there aren't any real links to me and why. It's feelings and history, not direct connections from life today. In fiction, I think they'd call me a deus ex machina, something not expected. But there, life is exactly like that in my experience. So, just to be clear I'll explain as fully as I can.

My name's Matthew Kirk. I live just outside Farnham and at the moment I'm the founder and owner of Kirk Foods. You might not recognise the name, because we own-brand for the better supermarkets, but I guarantee you've eaten one of my ready meals.

I killed Lauren Greenwood, Edward Horbridge, Calum Grant, Kendell Bell, Gordon Szabo, Irfan Patel and Neville Humberstone. There aren't any others, in case you were wondering about that. I've sent you this because it's been on my conscience, you spending time looking for me, when the real case is what these people did, or at least all bar one of them. There are others behind them, up the dirty chain. Your job now. I've got as far as I could. You need someone skilled in that arena. I'm guessing you've got people like that, or at least access to them. Sad to say, got some information too late on one of them and made a dreadful error. I might pay for that in another court, who's to say?

I want you to know why I did all of this. I say I killed them, which is true, but I won't call it murder. That always implies the victim has some level of innocence and I don't believe that for this hand-picked bunch. Far from it. To understand, I need to take you way back to the 70's, when I was just a lad starting out.

Hilda was my neighbour, at least eventually. I can't really even begin to describe her. Nowadays, maybe I'd call her a warrior? Back then she was the linchpin in our street. She was such a force, kind and strong and noticing, if you know what I mean by that? Anyway, I'd managed to get a job on Billingsgate, good work, and the possibility of an apprenticeship. I was still living at home then, with my mum. I can't say that I was a happy lad, but then my mother wasn't a happy woman. I think she'd never forgiven my dad for dying, resented it all, you know? That was all right but every now and then I'd get a new uncle. Sometimes they were OK, but more often than not they just wanted regular income, and the widow's pension from my real dad's railway job was good. They were, back then in the 70's, all state support and good conditions. But this latest bloke, he was a nightmare. Big man, handy with his fists. I hadn't grown into myself then and I was an easy target. It started to get difficult at work, explaining all the bruises. One afternoon – we started early, finished early - I sat in the park by St Dunstan's, thinking about what I was going to do.

Hilda sat down next to me. I didn't know then, didn't find out until later, that she'd got off the tube because she wasn't feeling well, got too hot in the carriage. She never did enjoy a fuss about herself. I don't know how she did it, but I found myself telling her all about it, the bullying, my job, being afraid. And that was that; she knew a neighbour had a bedsit going and she sorted it. I never *looked* back, collected my belongings then never *went* back. Used to send a card and present to my mum every birthday and Christmas, and I included a post box address so she could get in touch. Never heard anything. It used to hurt, but by then Hilda had pulled me into her world.

I loved Hilda, her whole mad family, her husband, her two sons and daughter, the aunts and uncles and cousins. There was always something going on. And music, and dancing. Oh, she did love to dance. If we were out, then the gold or silver shoes came out, ready for the dance floor. And sing, there was always a song in their house when anyone was cooking or cleaning or just sitting in the kitchen. It was like a real-life musical, someone would come in whistling something, or there'd be a tune on the radio and it would start a whole day of different songs, different people picking up the thread. Not performances, like, just happiness as they got on with the stuff in hand. It made me so happy, joyous I suppose you'd say, for the first time in my life. Hilda taught me to laugh, proper laugh. She had a real smoker's voice, deep, and when she laughed it was a glorious sound. She taught me the real benefits of a cuppa and a natter; she always had time for that. When I got accepted on to the apprenticeship, she was so proud – took me for pie and peas and insisted it was her treat. It felt warm, for the first time ever, knowing someone really cared, knowing I could go and ask anything, anything at all. A dish of jellied eels on the way home from a night out, a whole group of us, young and old, memories that I'll take with me forever.

Hilda taught me a lot. She had opinions, did Hilda. A very clear sense of right and wrong. Not necessarily what you coppers might think, but proper morality, you know. She didn't let people take the Mick, she hated bullies and she wouldn't stand for any nonsense from the local kids. But she was patient and kind too, always understood about genuine mistakes, laughed along with you, you know? And she was terrified of mice. I saw her pick up huge spiders to take them outside, but she'd have moved house if you told her she needed to live with a mouse. It's only in recent months I've realised that the man I became started there, learning from Hilda, picking up her world view.

So many memories, but not really a huge amount of time. Things I never told her. Like I was a bit in love with her daughter, but she never noticed me in that way, and I think I'd never have dared. She was beautiful and funny and kind and mad, and set fair to be her mum in later years. I was a bit afraid of her too, but then I was of Hilda. You'd have been daft not to be. I never told Hilda that I hated eels either, didn't ever seem to be the right thing to say.

I stayed in that bedsit right through my apprenticeship, but at the end of that I got taken up by one of the big supermarkets. They were just beginning to become what we have now, with all sorts of national training and I saw a job for a trainee butchery manager and I got it. Never seemed to bother them that I knew about fish, not meat. Part of that was spending two years being moved from region to region. The supermarket sorted all of that, the accommodation and that. By the end I'd been moved on to the store manager training programme. And I did that too, got a Deputy Manager job, then a small store, then a large one. But by then I'd started to think a bit bigger and a bit different. I thought that there was a market for more ready-made foods, so I started to look at that.

I still saw Hilda whenever I was in the South. But it started to become obvious that she wasn't well. I knew she was going back and forth to the doctor's but they were bloody useless. By the end we knew it was ovarian cancer. Over the years I've heard that called the silent killer, and I know it's never got any better. Poor Hilda went through absolute hell. It was just wrong.

One of the last times I saw her I told her about my idea, about ready food. She was her usual self. Said it was a good idea because there were more and more people watching the TV instead of their friends and family and that no doubt they'd be glad to forget anything useful in the kitchen too.

But while I was there she also told me something else. Their landlord was squeezing them by seriously increasing their rent. The word was he needed everyone out so he could sell it to a property developer who wanted to gentrify it – that's when that whole thing started. It really stressed her out and it made me really angry. I even looked into it a bit, see if there was anything I could do. The developer was a man called Bell. He looked about twelve, even to me, but it was obvious he was a mean, nasty man. Really fancied himself. But Hilda and her lot got lucky. This Bell chap had looked into the planning permissions he'd need and there was no way he was going to get them, not then, back in the days of a very Labour London. So he backed off.

But I never forgot. Didn't forget Hilda and didn't forget him and how he'd made her feel when she didn't need anything else on her plate. Don't get me wrong, I didn't write his name down in a little book of revenge or anything, but I didn't forget it either. I'll come back to that.

The ready meal thing worked, well, you already know that. I started with a rented unit and just me, then a couple of women helping out, and it went from there. Funny, because I spent a lot of time reading the menus outside restaurants, looking for ideas. Couldn't afford to eat inside though. Spaghetti Bolognese was a new thing then, we'd only just heard about chilli con carne and no-one made curry at home unless it came out of a packet. But it all coincided with foreign holidays getting popular, people being a bit more adventurous with what they'd try. So here we are, a multi-billion industry and me with a multi-million slice of that.

So now you're asking yourselves what made me, with all that behind me, do this? Well, I'll start with this. I'm proud of what I've done, with one exception. I didn't realise that Gordon Szabo was an unwitting front, picked out to present a decent façade. I truly regret that. But the rest, no. I did my homework. Apart from Mr Szabo, there's not a decent soul in my little bundle of execution, and no-one is regretting their loss now.

As to what made me do it? Three things, maybe.

The first was my PA. To start with I didn't think anything of it, never directly connected it with any of this, but it made me think, because she got diagnosed with ovarian cancer, and that took me right back to Hilda. They got Justine's diagnosis early, Stage 2 apparently, and it should all be fine. Usually, like Hilda, they don't pick it up until Stage 3 or 4. But Justine will be good, they think. But while she was going through the first part of it, she asked my advice on finances and property. She bought her own house in Basingstoke a few years back. She's bringing up her teenage nephew. I think his mother's a bit of a coke-head, and Justine stepped in years back to give him a more stable environment. When Justine didn't know what the outcome was going to be for her, medically, she wanted to be sure that Jake, her nephew, would be all right. He should be off to university next year and she didn't want any of that to be in danger.

So she handed me over a file of her mortgage info, some savings accounts, the shares she has in Kirk Foods and a couple of insurance policies, one of which she'd taken out when she bought her house. Most of it shook out just fine, but she didn't have any of the policy updates they send you every now and then, and I thought I'd better just check that no terms and conditions had changed that might affect her. She's an organised soul, and the account login details were in the file, so I went online and checked them out. One was absolutely fine. The other one was absolutely not. I couldn't see any terms and conditions changes that would cause any issues, but for both policies I thought it wise to check current addresses, name and date of birth for Jake and so on. But Jake wasn't the beneficiary. On the paper copy in Justine's file, he was, but not in the real McCoy that I'd logged into. That was Kendall Bell.

And you can guess, that took me right back to Hilda and what that Bell man had done in her last few months.

I didn't show the whole thing to Justine, I didn't want her to worry, so I just said it wasn't as strong cover as she'd want. I helped her cancel that policy and got a good friend of mine to set her up with a new one, cast iron, no matter when she pops off or why.

Maybe that on its own wouldn't have been enough. Then I started with a cough. Of course I ignored it for a while, but eventually I got seen and I don't have forever left. OK for a while, but not for long.

And that's it really. Not having long, thinking about Hilda and then people like Kendall Bell. Or Bellend, as I like to think of him. Not polite but most appropriate. I expect you know all that by now.

Other things too. Losing my wife early, Christine. God knows why I say that. I didn't bloody lose her, she died. No-one's fault. Brain aneurysm. Here and then gone in two minutes. But no kids, and I'd no heart for starting again. In many ways, she was like Hilda, just not so East End. Not replaceable anyway. The business will go on, I suppose it's a legacy of sorts. The Board are buying me out – that'll be finished by the time you listen to this. Money in the bank. What's left when I'm gone will go to some charities. Ovarian cancer being one. Big Issue and Shelter. I always think it could so easily be any of us, out on the streets. I'm not one of those fat cats that think 'get off your arse and get a job'. It's never that easy. Just one missed rent payment, one vicious 'uncle' or whatever, and there you are, under the arches. We've all got a breaking point.

And anger. Never realised I had so much inside. Working hard always kept it under control. People like Hilda and Christine kept it at bay. Never wanted to disappoint them and I don't think I did. But it made me think, right back to my mother's boyfriend. Though he wasn't a boy or a friend. But that's where a lot of the anger started, and just maybe my dad dying without warning. Not fair, you know? And when Justine got the cancer the anger was there again, no barriers. And when I found out more about what they've been doing, this lot, it lit a sort of flame I suppose. Gave me an outlet. It was an accident, finding out. Probably. Maybe some things are meant. I was going to a meeting at a hotel in Russell Square and I spotted this event about property development. And there he was, Bellend. I know a lot of people will think I'm wrong, taking it into my own hands, bit Old Testament. I did think about that for a while, but I talked myself round. Books and TV and films and the like, I've never enjoyed the ones without a proper ending. And for some reason, I wanted a proper ending to this, as much as I could.

So that all took me to thinking about Bell and what he'd done over the years and I thought I'd just have a quick look. Easy in my world to get the financials on people, so I did. And it didn't add up. You lot will know what I mean. Guessing you're already into that aspect of it, but there's a file in my study at home, marked for the attention of the senior investigating officer. Just in case I found out anything you haven't yet, something or other that might be useful. Once I'd started looking at Bell, it led on to the others. I actually went to one of their property presentations once, to see them in the flesh. That was fun, I put on heavy framed glasses and grew a moustache, parted my hair and used gel. I'm not famous, but anyone who follows the business news will know me. I realised no-one really notices other people. The presentation was well done, and it's partly why I thought Gordon Szabo must have been instrumental, because he was front and centre.

I needed to work out how to do it. I'm still outwardly healthy, but I couldn't manage an actual fight these days. I wanted it to be quick and quiet and I didn't want it to be too obvious that it was deliberate, at least not immediately, because I was worried that the others would start to hide themselves away. So they had to be done in quick succession, as it were. So a bit of research led me to drugs, and the rest you know. When you've got some money it really isn't hard to get whatever you want. But just in case, I've left you the details of where I got my supplies – be a good idea to shut that down, I think? I used the same needle system they use for adrenaline shots, like for allergic reactions. I reckoned it would be easy to knock someone quite hard and they probably wouldn't realise about the injection for a couple of seconds, by which time it would already be having an effect. You'll find a weighted tailor's dummy in a guest room at my house. I practised.

Then there's the joys of social media. Between what people post online and a bit of homework to get mobile numbers and whatnot, I could either work out where people were going to be or contact them by text or email to arrange to meet. You lot should shut down half the crime dramas they show these days – got a lot of my methods from there, like burner phones.

Lauren Greenwood was the first. She didn't always travel to work the same way, or from the same starting point, but she always had lunch in the same place, so I just barged into her. You need to look into all the property transactions she's had her hands on. From what I could see, there's two fields. She used clean, normal sales as a front for the rest, but I think the proportions were far from balanced. She has money leaking out of every orifice. I've left full details in the file. I expect you're ahead of me, but belt and braces as they say.

I knew Edward Horbridge was going to the AGM in Manchester and I just followed him up and back. I got on the same train going back to London as him, but then swapped into his carriage. It was lucky, having an empty seat next to him, but I could have done it anywhere on the journey. Just a case of waiting my moment. I listened to him on the way up, snapping at his wife on the mobile. He reminded me of that last boyfriend of my mother's. Different social background, but exactly the same class, you might say. I hope Mrs Horbridge has a long and happy life from here on.

With Calum Grant I arranged to meet at the garden centre. Sent him a text saying that I'd heard he could put me in touch with some nice property deals. Called myself Harry Allen for that – Hilda was Hilda Allen. I thought she'd enjoy coming along for the ride. This one I disliked more than the others, with the possible exception of Neville Humberstone. Seemed to me that there was a lot of sadism in our Mr Grant. From what I could see, he looked carefully for extra 'edges' to take advantage of people.

Ken Bell was easy enough – man was always drunk. Reminded me of that sleazy film maker, every time I saw him. To begin with, I thought he was the brains of the bunch, but in the end I didn't think so, because by the time I found him again he was just a disgusting degenerate. He certainly deserved his awful wife, but I'm not sure that was ever anything except a mutual insurance policy. I just followed him to the nearest pub after he came out of his offices in Soho. Some of his leisure pursuits are very worrying and there are two private clubs I've listed for you where I think they're using trafficked girls.

Gordon Szabo I'm so sorry about, but now there's nothing to be done. A casualty of my desperation to get it done without alerting the others. I'd had work done on all of their financials, but I totally missed that Mr Szabo's funds never came from or followed the same route as the others. I got him, as you know at the train station on his way home.

Irfan Patel was in the car park. I knew he was a newcomer, but I also knew other stuff about him. He has three daughters. One hasn't been allowed to leave the house since she finished school last summer. From her aunt's Facebook I know she's getting married next month to a man of 64. I'm guessing the same fate is up ahead for her sisters. I'm hoping you can do something about that, now you know.

Neville Humberstone was the last and he was a bit harder to track down. Serial philanderer that one, and I had to wait until he got home from his most recent conquest at the end of the weekend. I think he and Grant and the Greenwood woman were the nasty little brains behind all of this. I believe they have the much deeper connections that I think you'll need on the finance side. I can't get to those.

So, now you know it all. Will I be easy to find? I doubt it, and even if you do, a bigger judge may happen along sooner than you can arrange for an earthly one. Or I'll just be helping the daisies grow somewhere. I've covered my traces very well, although let's be honest, I'd never have come up on one of your lists anyway, because there's no immediate connection between me and anyone at all involved in this mess. You might pick up on Justine's policy, but I thought possibly not, because it's been cancelled. That's not a criticism, by the way. Just an ironic observation. As I said, this is just a courtesy to avoid wasting your time and public money. One of the charities I've left money for is the Police Pensioners' Housing

Association. And ditto for military veterans. It's the homes thing, of course.

I wish you well in your search for the real bastards. I'm not sure what would be an appropriate way to sign off this message, so I'll just end with this thought. Jodie Picoult, I think.

When you begin a journey of revenge, start by digging two graves. One for your enemy, one for yourself.

SEVENTY

The evening had ended abruptly. Everyone except Maze Brent headed back to the station, each to explore different aspects of Matthew Kirk's letter.

Fleur, not the only one to suffer the pangs of an anti-climax, quickly lost sight of that as she made telephone calls to launch the process of alerting all ports and airports as regards their fugitive, although she had also dispatched uniformed officers to his home and his business premises, alerting the local police force as to their imminent arrival and their undying gratitude should they be able to offer the appropriate assistance.

The rest of the team. Leo included, were awarded sections of the letter's information to interrogate. Leo's particular task was to see how far she could get with both business and personal financial records.

The midnight oiled burned. Maze Brent watched mindless television while she waited for her husband.

He arrived home just after five o'clock the next morning. He sank down next to her and pulled her into a hug.

'It's him. It's done.'

EPILOGUE

They did track down Matthew Kirk, in a hospice in Switzerland. The decision was easily made not to pursue prosecution, since it was obvious that the man had days rather than weeks. No-one from the team travelled from the UK, the budget not permitting. After his death a number of charities benefitted to significant levels from his bequests. One minor one was the funding for the installation and upkeep of a bench and nearby flower bed in St Dunstan's gardens. The inscription just said.

'Hilda Allen, my friend'

The bird flu turned out to be rather more, and the world slowed on its axis for nearly twenty four months after the two police cases were resolved, but it couldn't stop the law and its relentless pursuit of justice.

The unpicking of the finances for the families of the murder victims took a while to complete. Proceeds of crime aren't legal tender and a judgement had to be made as to the levels of forfeiture to be applied. Chloe Antoine kept her home, since that had been half-funded by her anyway. An estimation was made of Calum Grant's net worth outwith the property sales and, whilst not a multi-millionaire, Chloe would be comfortable even if she never worked again. That would never have suited her character and she swiftly divided the amount into a rainy day fund for the future, just in case, and then used the rest to set up college trust funds for Harriet's children. She thought, wryly, that this would have seriously angered Calum, and she was glad of that. Harriet survived long enough to know about the trust funds. She died, with her children and in-laws beside her, in a sunny room at the hospice near her children's new home in London. She left memory boxes for each of them, as well as letters for each of their birthdays.

Caro Horbridge underwent much the same rationalisation of her finances, keeping the house and her husband's substantial pension, as well as a lump sum that reflected his holdings before he commenced his life of crime. The months following her husband's death had been difficult in some ways, but life-affirming in others. Her neighbours pulled her into a Covid 'bubble' and continued her education in the real world, helping her with all manner of practicalities, but most of all teaching her how to laugh again.

Rose, her daughter, had contacted her as soon as she'd finished her interview with Cervantes. Rose, now a Head of Department in a London high school had never been that far away. The Covid outbreak gave them both a chance to catch up over the 'phone and Caro even learned to Zoom. She'd been delighted to learn that Rose was engaged and that they were saving for a deposit for their first home. Caro had considered this carefully, and following the first lockdown consulted a range of estate agents. The huge, hated house was worth a great deal of money and she happily put it up for sale. Further along the same road, out of sight of the marital home that had seen her browbeaten into submission for so many years, was a new terrace of pretty little townhouses, with gardens to the rear, ideal for the kitten she wanted to find. She signed for one of these and then gifted the rest of the proceeds of the old house to her daughter. They argued about this for some time, Rose being unwilling to accept anything that had been her father's. Caro had thought this through and simply said,

'It's not your father's. It's my earnings from all of those years of drudgery and misery and tears.'

Lizzie Szabo suffered no financial impact from the legal proceedings. Leo had proven without doubt that Gordon and Lizzie had run a legitimate and law-abiding business. On the personal front her life was much, much harder. She and Gordon had been friends as well as partners. Fleur made the decision to tell her the whole story. It didn't help in any practical way, and Lizzie would never be able to forgive what Matthew Kirk had done, but at least what had happened was now in an understandable context, bizarre as it might be. She changed the business model after the two final properties that she and Gordon had worked on together and moved into project managing similar projects for other investors. Her beautiful, bohemian colours and clothing gave way to quieter, more muted tones and outfits.

Ajay returned to the Transport Police with the grateful thanks of his temporary team and a glowing reference from Fleur Cooper. He and Don maintained contact and planned some activities once Covid loosened its grip.

Simon Fletcher was taken through a Disciplinary process which found that his working methods and attitudes to his colleagues and senior officers were inappropriate. This was highlighted by his behaviour during the hearings, when he insisted on reading out detailed diatribes as to the failings of the entire team, person by person. When told by the chair person, and his Police Federation representative, that this was unacceptable and not relevant to the matter in hand, he produced a similar and very personal list identifying the failings of all three panel members and his own rep. He was given a final written warning. Being Simon Fletcher, no-one was able to predict his next move and Fleur awaited this with some trepidation. He could resign, or even apply for early retirement, or ask for a transfer. Any of those would have delighted her, but she feared that he might stick to his guns and stay put. Maze had suggested that cognitive behavioural therapy could be very useful for Simon, but so far no-one could see how to manoeuvre that into an actual thing.

Daisy was formally transferred out of uniform and then promptly resigned. After years of trying unsuccessfully for a baby she was pregnant and she had every intention of never seeing the inside of a nick again. She enrolled on a course to qualify as a chiropodist, having learned that she'd earn more from that in a year than she could in the police force, even if she made it to sergeant.

Three new trainee detectives were selected to join the team and Cervantes was tasked with mentoring them, moving him from newbie status to old hand, to his obvious delight.

Reith and Leo moved slowly forward, Covid driving them to Zoom communications for a while, and many long and detailed telephone conversations. They formed the habit of meeting for late night walks, a couple of metres apart, roving through housing areas and guessing who might live in them, and window shopping. This was particular fun for them both, though Steve had resisted at first. She would halt them in front of a large store window, preferably homewares, or furniture. They each then had to say what they liked, loved or hated. After trying this on a few occasions she then moved them on to guessing what the other would think. They laughed a lot, learned a great deal and spent not a penny. Reith found himself able to tell Leo about his past much more easily through a telephone handset or walking side by side than face to face, and that shifted them to another level of mutual understanding. From their shared ordeal and from her behaviour in their previous case Reith had come to recognise that Leo didn't really do panic. She might be afraid, but drama wasn't in her nature and Reith began to see a future for them, maybe.

Peter Howard, Fleur's partner had taken the opportunity in the aftermath of Reith's and Leo's captivity to remind Fleur that life needed to be seized. She explained her concerns as to her background as opposed to his and he laughed loud and long.

'Yep, we've got money, but you need to know where it came from. Grandad was a scrap metal merchant, and my dad still is, though on a bigger scale. No-one in our house is an inch up themselves. I'm sorry if I've never explained that. Open up Fleur, let me in.'

Fleur told him she'd think about it for a few days.

At the end of the following week she rang him and said she'd like to meet in the park near to his offices. She offered to bring a picnic.

When he arrived she'd found a bench and had spread some plastic boxes and cold drinks across it, protecting her ownership. She made room for him, then poured him a drink. She said,

'You're right. I can be too insular and there's no-one I want to let in more than you. But look, this is going to be hard for me, but I do want you to understand why that is. She reached into her large handbag and produced a package wrapped in a scarf, opening it out to reveal an immensely battered soft toy, possibly once a teddy bear, though it would be hard to be certain. She looked up at Peter.

'Let me introduce you to Freddie. And I want to tell you about Buzzer, his old friend, and some other stuff.'

Printed in Great Britain
by Amazon